# THE HOUSEMAID IS WATCHING

FREIDA McFADDEN

The characters and events portrayed in this book are fictitious or are used fictitiously. Any similarity to real persons, living or dead, is purely coincidental and not intended by the author.



Published by Poisoned Pen Press, an imprint of Sourcebooks
1935 Brookdale RD, Naperville, IL 60563-2773
(630) 961-3900
sourcebooks.com

Cataloging-in-Publication Data is on file with the Library of Congress.

Printed and bound in the United States of America.
LSC 10 9 8 7 6 5 4 3 2 1

# ALSO BY FREIDA MCFADDEN

*The Intruder*
*Dear Debbie*
*The Tenant*
*The Crash*
*The Boyfriend*
*The Teacher*
*The Coworker*
*Ward D*
*Never Lie*
*The Inmate*
*The Housemaid*
*The Housemaid's Secret*
*The Housemaid Is Watching*
*Do You Remember?*
*Do Not Disturb*
*The Locked Door*
*Want to Know a Secret?*
*One by One*
*The Wife Upstairs*
*The Perfect Son*
*The Ex*
*The Surrogate Mother*
*Brain Damage*
*Dead Med*

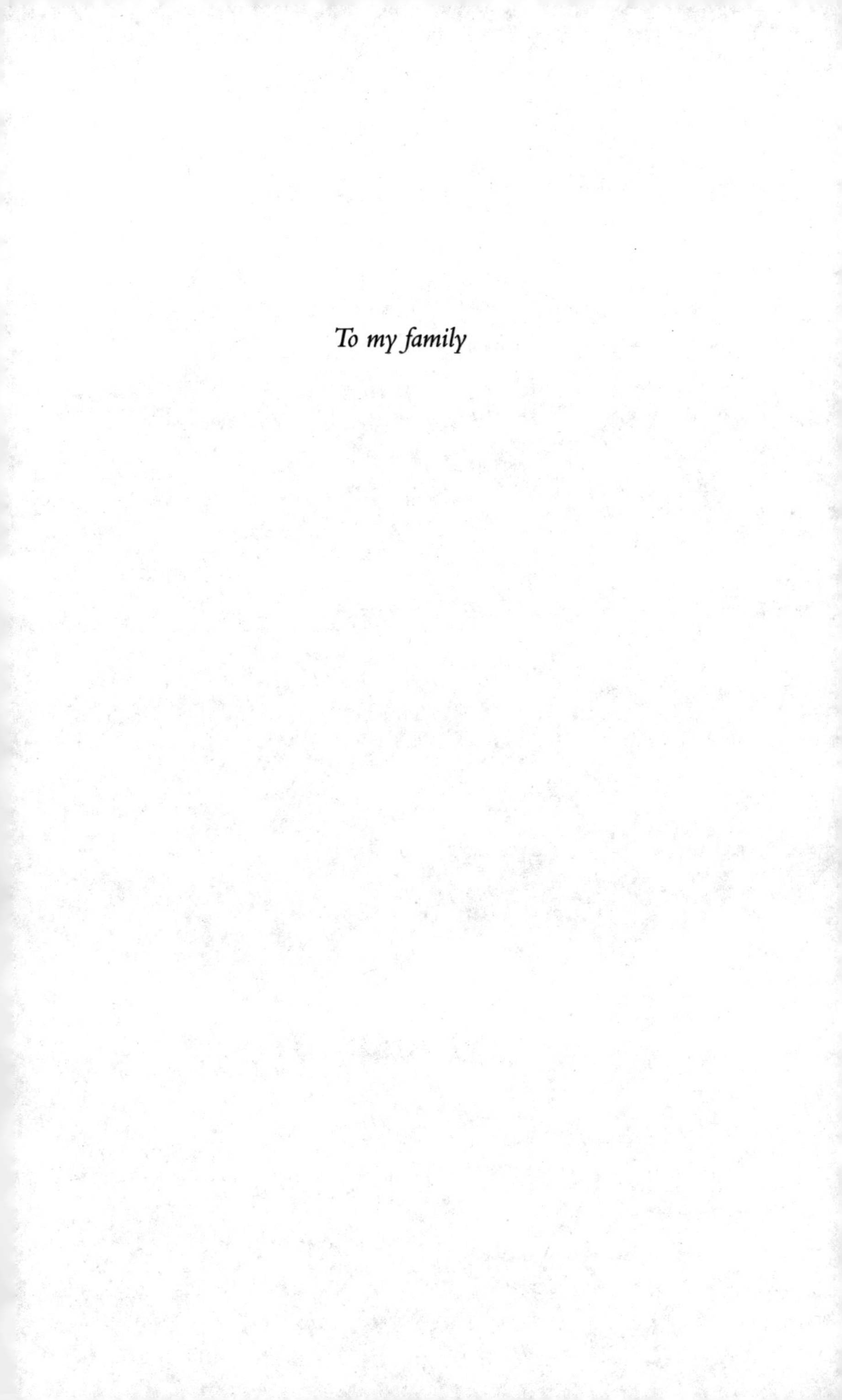

*To my family*

# AUTHOR'S NOTE

Even though my books are thrillers, a genre that traditionally has dark elements, I do my best to keep them as family friendly as I possibly can. You're not going to come across any graphic scenes of violence or S-E-X. (Mostly because I know my family members will be reading!)

However, people have emotional responses to different things, and some of my books delve into more controversial topics. So for this reason, I created a list of content warnings for all my thrillers, which can be found linked off the top of my website:

freidamcfadden.com

This is a resource that can be used by readers who need to protect their mental health as well as for adults whose kids are reading my books. Please also keep in mind that in a few cases, these content warnings are major spoilers for twists that take place in the book.

With that in mind, I hope you safely enjoy this journey into my imagination!

# PROLOGUE

There's blood everywhere.

I've never seen so much blood. It's soaking the cream-colored rug, seeping into the nearby floorboards, speckling the legs of the oak coffee table. Perfect oval droplets have made it all the way to the seat of the pale leather sofa, and large rivulets drip down the alabaster wall.

It's endless. If I look hard enough, will I find flecks of blood on the car in the garage? On the blades of grass in the lawn? In the supermarket across town?

Even worse, it's all over my hands.

What a mess. Despite the fact that I don't have much time, I am itching to clean it all up. When there's a stain, especially on the carpet, I was taught you're supposed to clean it quickly, before it sets. Once it dries, the stain will become permanent.

Unfortunately, no matter how hard I scrub, it won't do a thing for the dead body lying smack in the middle of the pool of blood.

I assess the situation. Okay, this is bad. My fingerprints in the house are expected, but the crimson caked into my fingernails and the grooves of my palms is less easy to explain. The darkening stain on the front of my shirt is not the kind of thing I can shrug off. I am in deep trouble.

*If* someone catches me.

I inspect my hands, weighing the pros and cons of washing off the blood versus getting the hell out of here right now. If I wash my hands, I will waste precious seconds in which I could be caught. If I leave immediately, I'll be walking out the door with blood all over my palms, smearing itself onto everything I touch.

And then the doorbell rings.

The chimes echo throughout the house as I freeze, afraid to even breathe. "Hello?" a familiar voice calls out.

*Please leave. Please.*

The house is silent. The person at the door will realize that nobody is home and decide to come back another time. They have to. If they don't, I am finished.

The doorbell rings again.

*Go away. Please go away.*

I'm not one for prayer, but at this point, I'm ready to get down on my knees. Well, I would if doing so wouldn't get blood all over my knees.

They must assume nobody is home. Nobody rings a doorbell more than twice. But just when I think there's a chance I might be safe, the doorknob rattles. And then it starts to turn.

Oh no. The door is unlocked. In about five seconds, the person knocking will be inside the house. She will walk into the living room. And then she will see…

*This.*

The decision has been made. I've got to run for it. There's no time to wash my hands. There's no time to worry about the bloody footprints I might be leaving behind. I've got to get out of here.

I only hope nobody discovers what I've done.

# PART I

# ONE

THREE MONTHS EARLIER

## MILLIE

I love this house.

I love everything about this house. I love the giant front lawn and the even more giant back lawn (even though both are edging toward brown). I love the fact that the living room is so big that *multiple pieces of furniture* fit inside rather than just one small sofa and a television set. I love the picture windows overlooking the neighborhood, which I recently read in a magazine is one of the best towns to raise a child.

And most of all, I love that it's mine. Number 14 Locust Street is all mine. Well, okay, thirty years of mortgage payments and it will be all mine. I can't stop thinking about how lucky I am as I run my fingers along the wall of our new living room, bringing my face closer to admire the brand-new floral wallpaper.

"Mom is kissing the house again!" a voice squeals from behind me.

I quickly back away from the wall, although it's not

like my nine-year-old son caught me with a secret lover. I have no shame about my love for this house. I want to shout about it from the rooftop. (We have an amazing rooftop. *I love this house.*)

"Shouldn't you be unpacking?" I say.

Nico's boxes and furniture have all been deposited in his bedroom, so he should be unpacking, but instead he is repeatedly throwing a baseball against the wall—my beautiful, floral wallpapered wall—and then catching it. We have lived in this house for less than five minutes, and he is already determined to destroy it. I can see it in his dark brown eyes.

It's not that I don't love my son more than the world. If it was one of those hypothetical situations where I had to choose between Nico's life and this house, of *course* I would choose Nico. No question.

But I'm just saying, if he does anything to harm this house, he is going to be grounded until he's old enough to shave.

"I'll unpack tomorrow," Nico says. His general life philosophy seems to be that everything will be done tomorrow.

"Or now?" I suggest.

Nico throws the ball in the air, and it just barely grazes the ceiling. If we had absolutely anything valuable in this house, I would be having a heart attack right now. "Later," he insists.

Meaning never.

I peer up the stairwell of the house. Yes, we have *stairs*! Honest-to-goodness stairs. Yes, they creak with every single step, and there's a chance if you hold on to the banister too tightly, it might fall off. But we have stairs, and they lead to an *entirely different floor of the house*.

You can tell I have lived in New York City far too long. I was hesitant to come back to Long Island after what happened last time I lived here, but that was nearly two decades ago—the distant past.

"Ada?" I call up the stairs. "Ada, can you come out here?"

A few moments later, my eleven-year-old daughter pops her head into the stairwell so that I can see her thick, wavy black hair and dark, dark eyes peeking out at me. Her eyes are the same color as Nico's, inherited from their father. Unlike her brother, Ada has undoubtedly been unpacking her belongings since we arrived. She's a straight-A student—the kind who does her homework without having to be told, a week before it's due.

"Ada," I say. "Are you almost done unpacking?"

"Just about." No surprise there.

"Do you think you could help Nico unpack his boxes?"

Ada nods without hesitation. "Sure. Come on, Nico."

Nico immediately recognizes this as an opportunity for his sister to do most of the work. "Okay!" he agrees happily.

Nico finally stops terrorizing me with the baseball and sprints up the steps two at a time to join Ada in his room. I start to tell her not to do all the work for him, but that's a lost cause. At this point, I've got about sixty boxes of my own to unpack. As long as it gets done, I'll be happy.

We were extremely lucky to get this house. We lost

half a dozen bidding wars in neighborhoods that weren't even as nice as this one. I didn't think we had a snowball's chance in hell of landing this quaint former farmhouse in a town with such highly rated public schools. I almost cried with joy when our real estate agent called me to let me know that the house was ours. At 10 percent less than asking!

The universe must have decided we deserved some good luck.

I peek out through the front window at the moving truck parked on the street outside the house. We live in a little cul-de-sac with two other houses, and across the way, I can see the silhouette of a person at the window. My new neighbor, I suppose. I hope they're friendly.

A banging sound comes from within the truck, and I wrench open the front door to see what's going on. I jog outside just in time to see my husband emerging from the truck with one of his friends who has agreed to help with the move. I wanted to hire a moving company, but he insisted he could do it himself with his friends helping. And I have to admit, we need to save every penny if we want to make our mortgage payments. Even at 10 percent below asking, our dream house wasn't cheap.

My husband is holding up one half of our living room sofa, his T-shirt plastered to his torso with sweat. I cringe because he's in his forties and the last thing he needs is to throw out his back. I expressed this concern to him when we were planning the move, and he acted like it was the silliest thing he's ever heard, even though I throw out my back every other week. And it's not from lifting a sofa. It's from, like, *sneezing*.

"Will you please be careful, Enzo?" I say.

He looks up at me, and when he grins, I melt. Is that normal? Do other women who are married to somebody for over eleven years still get wobbly in the knees over them sometimes?

No? Just me?

I mean, it's not like it's *every minute*. But boy, he still gets me. It doesn't hurt that he seems to get inexplicably sexier every year. (And I just get a year older.)

"I am careful," he insists. "Besides, this couch? Is light! Weighs almost nothing."

That warrants an eye roll from the guy holding the other end of the couch. But admittedly, it's not exactly a heavy-duty couch. We got it from IKEA, which is a step up from the last couch, which we grabbed from the curb. Enzo used to have this theory that all the best furniture came from the curb outside our apartment.

We've grown up a little since then. I hope.

As Enzo and his friend bring the sofa into our beautiful new house, I raise my eyes again to look at the house across the way. Number 13 Locust Street. There's still someone staring at me from the window. The house is dark inside, so I can't see much, but that silhouette is still at the window.

Somebody is watching us.

But there's nothing ominous about that. The people in that house are our new neighbors, and I'm sure they are curious about who we are. Whenever I used to see a moving truck outside our building, I always watched through the window to see who was moving in, and Enzo would laugh and tell me to stop watching and go introduce myself.

That's the difference between him and me.

Well, it's not the *only* difference.

In an effort to change my ways and be more friendly like my husband, I lift a hand to wave at the silhouette. May as well meet my new neighbor at 13 Locust.

Except the person at the window doesn't wave back. Instead, the shutters suddenly snap closed and the silhouette disappears.

Welcome to the neighborhood.

# TWO

Enzo is carrying the last of the boxes into the house while I'm standing out on our sparse lawn, avoiding unpacking while fantasizing about how the lawn will look after my husband rejuvenates it. Enzo is a wizard when it comes to lawns—that's sort of how we first met. This one almost looks like a lost cause with its brown patches and crumbly soil, but I know that a year from now, we will have the nicest lawn in the cul-de-sac.

I am lost in my fantasies when the door of the house directly next to ours—12 Locust Street—swings open. A woman with a butterscotch-colored layered bob emerges from the house wearing a fitted white blouse and red skirt with spiky high heels that look like they could be used to gouge out somebody's eye. (Why does my mind always go there?)

Unlike the neighbor across the way, she seems friendly. She raises her hand in an enthusiastic greeting and crosses the short path of cobbled pavement separating our houses.

"Hello!" she gushes. "It is *so* good to finally meet our new neighbors! I'm Suzette Lowell."

As I reach out and take her manicured hand in mine, I'm rewarded with an impressively painful handshake for a woman. "Millie Accardi," I say.

"*Lovely* to meet you, Millie," she says. "You're going to absolutely adore living here."

"I already do," I say honestly. "This house is amazing."

"Oh, it really is." Suzette bobs her head. "It was lying empty for a while because, you know, such a small house is a hard sell. But I just knew the right family would come along."

Small? Is she *insulting* our beloved house? "Well, I love it."

"Oh yes. It's so cozy, isn't it? And…" Her gaze rakes over our front steps, which have slightly crumbled, although Enzo swears he'll fix them. It's one of a long list of repairs we'll need to make. "Rustic. *So* rustic."

Okay, she's definitely insulting the house.

But I don't care. I still love the house. It doesn't matter to me what some snooty neighbor thinks.

"So do you work, Millie?" Suzette asks, her blue-green eyes zeroing in on my face.

"I'm a social worker," I say with a touch of pride. Even though I have been doing it for many years now, I still feel proud of my career. Yes, it can be exhausting, soul wrenching, and the pay is nothing to get excited about. But I still love it. "How about you?"

"I'm a real estate agent," she says with an equal amount of pride. Ah, that explains the way she was insulting our house in real estate speak. "The market is jumping right now."

Well, that's true. It occurs to me now that Suzette was not involved in the sale of this house. If she's a real estate agent, how come her neighbors didn't want her to sell their house?

Enzo emerges from the truck, carrying more boxes, his T-shirt still clinging to his chest and his black hair damp. I remember filling one of those boxes with books and being worried that I had made it too heavy. And now he's carrying not only that box, but he's put another one on top of it. My back aches just watching him.

Suzette is watching him too. She follows his progress from the moving truck to our front door, a smile spreading across her lips. "Your moving guy is *really* hot," she comments.

"Actually," I say, "that's my husband."

Her jaw drops open. Looks like she thinks more of him than she does of the house. "Seriously?"

"Uh-huh." Enzo has deposited the boxes in the living room, and he is coming out of the house for more. How does he have the energy? Before he reaches the truck, I wave him over. "Enzo, come meet our new neighbor, Suzette."

Suzette quickly tugs at her blouse and tucks a strand of butterscotch hair behind her ear. If she could, I'm pretty sure she would have given herself a quick once-over in a compact mirror and refreshed her lipstick. But there's no time for that.

"Hello!" she gushes with an outstretched hand. "It's so nice to meet you! Enzo, is it?"

He takes her hand and flashes her a broad smile that

makes the lines around his eyes crinkle. "Yes, I am Enzo. And you are Suzette?"

She giggles and nods eagerly. Her reaction is a bit over the top, but to be fair, he is turning up the charm. My husband has lived in this country for twenty years, and when we talk at the dinner table, his accent is relatively mild. But when he's trying to be charming, he turns up his accent so that he sounds like he's right off the boat. Or as he would say, "right off boat."

"You are absolutely going to love it here," Suzette assures us. "It's such a quiet little cul-de-sac."

"We already love it," I say.

"And your house is so cute," she says, finding yet another creative way to point out that our house is substantially smaller than hers. "It will be perfect for you and your kids, especially with another little one on the way."

When she says that, she looks pointedly at my abdomen, which definitely does *not* contain any little ones on the way. There have not been any little ones in there for nine years.

The worst part is that Enzo swivels his head to look at me, and for a second, there's a glimmer of excitement on his face, even though *he knows very well* that I had my tubes tied during my emergency C-section with Nico. I look down at my belly, and I notice that my shirt does bulge in an unfortunate way. I'm dying a little bit inside.

"I'm not pregnant," I say, for both the benefit of Suzette and apparently also my husband.

Suzette clasps a hand over her red lipstick. "Oh dear, I am *so* sorry! I just assumed…"

"It's okay," I say, cutting her off before she makes

it worse. Honestly, I love my body. When I was in my twenties, I was a stick figure, but now I finally have some womanly curves to show off, and I daresay my husband seems to enjoy them as well.

That said, I'm throwing away this shirt.

"We have two children." Enzo flings an arm around my shoulders, oblivious to Suzette's insult. "Our son, Nico, and our daughter, Ada."

Enzo couldn't be more proud of our two children. He's a great father, and he would have wanted another five of them if I hadn't nearly died giving birth to our son. We would have loved to adopt or do foster care, but with my background, it was out of the question.

"Do you have children, Suzette?" I ask.

She shakes her head, a horrified look on her face. "Absolutely not. I'm not the maternal type. It's just me and my husband, Jonathan. We are happily child-free."

Excellent—she has a husband of her own. She can stay away from mine.

"But there is a little boy in the house across from yours," she says. "He's in third grade."

"Nico is in third grade too," Enzo says eagerly. "Maybe we can introduce them?"

When we moved, we had to pull the kids out of school right in the middle of the year. Trust me—the last thing you want to do is yank two grade-school-age kids out of their classes in the middle of March. I was racked with guilt, but we couldn't afford to pay the mortgage and the rent until the end of the school year, so we didn't have a choice.

Nico, who is outgoing like his father, didn't seem bothered by it. For Nico, a whole room full of new kids to impress with his antics would be a fun adventure. Ada took the news calmly, but later I found her crying in her room at the thought of leaving her two best friends behind. I'm hoping by the fall, they will both be settled in and the trauma of moving in the middle of the school year will be a distant memory.

"You can try to introduce yourself to them." Suzette shrugs. "But the woman who lives there, Janice, is not very friendly. She hardly ever comes out of the house except to bring her son to the bus stop. I mostly just see her in the window, staring out at the street. *Such* a busybody."

"Oh," I say, wondering how Janice can apparently never leave her house yet also be so nosy.

I look across the way at 13 Locust. The windows all look dark, despite the fact that it's the middle of the day and the people who live there seem to be home.

"I hope you're getting some good blinds for your windows," she tells me. "Because she has a great view."

Enzo and I simultaneously rotate our heads in the direction of our brand-new house, the realization suddenly dawning on us that not one of the windows in the entire house has blinds or curtains. How did we not realize that? Nobody told us we needed to buy blinds! Every home we ever lived in before now came with them already installed!

"I will buy blinds," Enzo murmurs in my ear.

"Thank you."

Suzette looks amused by our cluelessness. "Your real estate agent didn't remind you to buy blinds?"

"Guess not," I mumble.

I suppose the implication is that Suzette would have

reminded us if she had been our real estate agent. But it's a bit late for that. For now, we are blind-less.

"I can recommend an excellent company that will install blinds for you," she says. "They did our house last year. They put in these beautiful honeycomb blinds on the first and second floor and then these adorable shutters in the attic."

I can't even imagine what such a thing would cost. Far more than we have to spend, that's for sure.

"No, thank you," Enzo says. "I can do."

She winks at him. "Yes, I'll bet you can."

Seriously? I am getting a little sick of this woman hitting on my husband right in front of me. It's not like other women don't do the same, but for God's sake, we're neighbors. Can't she be a little more subtle? Part of me is tempted to say something, but I'd rather not make an enemy five minutes after moving here.

"Also," she says, "I wanted to invite your family over for dinner. The two of you, of course, and…the children can come too." She doesn't look excited about the idea of our kids entering her home. And she doesn't even know about Nico's propensity to break something expensive within five minutes of entering any room.

"Sure, that will be wonderful," Enzo says.

"Fabulous!" She beams up at him. "How about tomorrow night? I'm sure your kitchen won't be up and running by then, so this will take the stress off."

Enzo looks at me with raised eyebrows. He has boundless energy for social events, but I'm the introverted one, so I appreciate that he defers to me before accepting. Truthfully, I loathe the idea of spending an evening with this woman. She seems a bit *extra*. But if we're going to be living here, aren't we obligated to be friends with the neighbors? Isn't that what normal suburban families *do*? And maybe she won't be so bad once I get to know her.

"Sure," I say. "That will be really nice. We hardly know anyone in Long Island."

Suzette throws her head back and laughs, revealing a row of pearly white teeth. "Oh, Millie…"

I glance over at Enzo, who shrugs. Neither of us seem to know what's so funny. "What?"

"You don't know how you sound," she giggles. "Nobody says '*in* Long Island.'"

"They…they don't?"

"No!" She shakes her head like I'm just too much. "It's '*on* Long Island.' You're not *in* an island—that sounds so ignorant. You're *on* an island."

Enzo is scratching at his dark hair. He has zero gray hair on his head, by the way. If not for my bottles of Clairol, I would be pretty much gray and have been ever since Nico was born. All Enzo's got is a few gray strands in his beard when he grows it out. But when I pointed that out to him, he dug around on his scalp until he found a single gray hair to show off to me, as if that made it any better.

"So I don't understand," I say. "Does that mean people should say they live *on* Hawaii? Or *on* Staten Island?"

The smile drops off her face. "Well, Staten Island is an entirely different case."

I try to catch Enzo's eye, but he just seems amused by the whole thing. "Well, we are happy to be here *on* Long Island, Suzette. And we look forward to having dinner with you tomorrow night."

"I can't wait," she says.

I have to force my own smile. "Should I bring anything?"

"Oh." She taps her index finger against her chin. "Why don't you bring dessert?"

Great. Now I have to figure out what on earth I'm going to bring for dessert that will live up to Suzette's standards. I'm thinking a box of Oreos won't cut it. "Sounds good!"

As Suzette walks down the path back to her own much larger house, her heels clicking on the pavement with each step, I feel a twinge of something in the pit of my stomach. I was so excited when we bought this house. We've been crammed into tiny apartments for so long, and I finally have my dream house.

But now, for the first time, I wonder if I have made a terrible mistake moving here.

# THREE

Tonight, the four of us are having dinner at our kitchen table. Do you know what a kitchen table is? That's a table that *fits inside our kitchen.* Yes, our kitchen now has room in it for a whole table. Our last kitchen barely had room in it for a person.

We ordered Chinese food from a restaurant that had sent us a menu in the mail. I'm not very picky about food, and neither is Enzo. The only thing he won't eat is Italian food. He says that no restaurant does it right, and it's always a disappointment. But he'll eat delivery pizza. Because that's not actually Italian food, in his assessment.

Ada is easygoing in the same way, but Nico is super picky about food. That's why, while the rest of us are chowing down on lo mein noodles and beef with broccoli, I have prepared a plate of white rice for my son, seasoned with a pat of butter and lots of salt. I'm pretty sure buttered rice is flowing through his veins right now.

"Our first dinner in the new house," I announce proudly. "We are finally christening our kitchen table."

"Why do you keep saying that, Mom?" Nico says. "Why do you keep saying we're christening everything?"

To be fair, I'm not sure he's ever heard me use the word "christen" before, and I have used it at least five times in the last several hours. When we were sitting on the couch earlier, I said we were christening the living room. Then when he went out in the backyard with his baseball, I said he was christening our yard. And at some point, I might have mentioned that I would be christening the toilet.

"Your mom is just excited about the house." Enzo reaches for my hand across the kitchen table. "And she is right. Is a very beautiful house."

"It's *kind of* nice," Nico concedes. "But I wish it were painted red. And had arches on it that were yellow."

Okay, I'm pretty sure my son is telling me he wants to live at McDonald's.

I don't care. We bought this house for the two of them. Back in the Bronx, we were cramped into a tiny apartment, and men were starting to leer at Ada while she walked home. Now we are in an amazing school district, and they will have room to play in the backyard and wander around the neighborhood without worrying about being mugged. Even if they don't appreciate it, this is the best thing we could have done for them.

"Mom?" Ada pushes some noodles around her plate, and I realize she's hardly eaten anything. "Are we starting school tomorrow?"

Her dark eyebrows are scrunched together. Both of my kids look so much like their father, to the point where it seems they are both clones of him, and I was merely the incubator who birthed them. Ada is beautiful, with long jet-black hair and brown eyes that take up half her face. Enzo says she looks just like his sister, Antonia. Right now, she is coming to that transition between child and adult, and someday soon, she will be a woman who will turn heads. When that happens, I'm fairly sure Enzo is going to have to walk around with a baseball bat all the time. He won't admit it, but he is very protective of her.

"Do you feel ready to start school?" I ask her.

"Yes," she says, even as she's shaking her head no.

"It's the end of their spring break," I point out. "So nobody will have seen each other for about a week. They probably won't even remember each other."

Ada does not look even the tiniest bit amused, but Nico giggles.

"I can drive you tomorrow," Enzo offers. "We could take my truck."

Her eyes light up because she loves riding in her father's truck. "Can I sit in the front seat?"

Enzo looks at me with raised eyebrows. He loves to indulge them, but I appreciate that he won't do it without checking with me.

"Actually, honey," I say, "you're still a little too small for the front seat. But soon."

"I want to take the bus tomorrow!" Nico declares. We were too close to the elementary school last year to get the school bus. So now he has elevated "taking the bus" into an experience on par with visiting a chocolate factory filled with Oompa Loompas. It's all he can seem to think about. "Please, Mom?"

"Sure," I say. "And, Ada, if you want to go with your dad..."

"No," she says firmly, "I'll go on the bus with Nico."

Whatever else you can say about my daughter, she is incredibly protective of her little brother. I heard that toddlers can be very jealous when you bring a new baby into the house, but Ada was immediately enamored with Nico. She abandoned all her dolls and took care of him instead. I have some achingly adorable photos of Ada cradling Nico on her lap, feeding him his bottle.

"Also..." Nico scoops more white rice into his mouth, only about 80 percent of which manages to get through his lips. The rest is speckling his lap and the floor below him. "Can I have a pet, Mom? Please?"

"Um," I say.

"You said when I was older and more *responsible*, I could have a pet," Nico reminds me.

Well, he *is* older. As for the responsible part...

"A dog?" Ada asks hopefully.

"We still have to get the yard fenced in before we consider a dog," I tell them. Plus I'd like to be on more stable financial ground before we add another member to our family.

"How about a turtle then?" Ada suggests.

I shudder. "No, please not a turtle. I *hate* turtles."

"I don't want a dog *or* a turtle," Nico says. "I want a praying mantis."

I nearly choke on a broccoli floret. "A *what*?"

"Is actually a good pet," Enzo chimes in. "Very easy to take care of."

Oh my God, Enzo *knows* that Nico wants to bring

this horrible thing into our house? "No. We are not getting a praying mantis."

"But why not, Mom?" Nico presses me. "They are super cool. I'll keep it in my room, and you don't ever have to see it. Unless you want to see it."

He flashes me that endearing smile of his. Right now, he has this adorable round face and a gap in his teeth. But you can just tell that in another six or seven years, he's going to be breaking hearts like his father used to before we were together.

"I don't care if I see it," I say. "I'll know it's there."

"We will keep it contained," Enzo tells me, flashing his own version of that same smile. Damn my husband for being so handsome.

"What do you feed it?" I ask.

"Flies," Nico says.

"No." I shake my head. "No. We are not doing this."

"Don't worry," Nico says. "They're *flightless* flies."

"They are *walks*," Enzo jokes.

"It won't even cost you anything," Nico adds. "We're going to grow the flies ourselves."

"No. No, no, no."

Enzo reaches under the table and gives my knee a squeeze. "Millie, we pulled the kids out of school and made them move here. If Nico wants a praying mantis…"

Bullshit. *He* wants the praying mantis too. It's just the type of thing that Enzo would think is cool.

I look over at Ada for help, but she's too absorbed in making little piles of noodles on her plate. She is spelling out her name in noodles. She doesn't generally play with her food, so she must be really anxious.

"If I were to say yes," I say, "where would we purchase a praying mantis?"

Enzo and Nico high-five each other, which would be adorable if I wasn't so terrified of this insect they are bringing into the house.

"We can buy a praying mantis egg," Nico explains. God, how long have they been discussing this? It seems like they have a very firm plan in mind. "And then it hatches and there are hundreds of them."

"Hundreds..."

"But is okay," Enzo says quickly. "They all eat each other, so then usually there's only one or two left."

"And then we can christen them," Nico adds. "Okay, Mom?"

I imagine how horrified Suzette Lowell would be to discover there is a praying mantis as well as a colony of flightless flies in her perfect cul-de-sac, which is the only thing amusing about this situation. Okay, fine, I guess I'm going to let this happen. But I swear to God, if there are flies all over my beautiful new home, Nico is going to have to move out.

# FOUR

If I unpack one more box, I am going to throw up.

I have unpacked five billion boxes today. That's a conservative estimate. And now I am standing in the master bathroom, staring down at a cardboard box on which I wrote "BATHROOM" in permanent magic marker, and I just don't have the will to open it. Even though it has crucial bathroom stuff inside it. Maybe I can brush my teeth with my finger tonight.

The sound of footsteps grows louder outside the door, and a second later, Enzo pops his head into the bathroom. He smiles when he sees me standing there with my BATHROOM box.

"What are you doing?" he asks.

My shoulders sag. "Unpacking."

"You unpack all night," he points out. "Enough. We do it tomorrow."

"But we *need* this stuff. It's for the bathroom."

Enzo looks like he's going to try to talk me out of it,

but then he thinks better of it. Instead, he reaches into the pocket of his worn blue jeans and pulls out the pocketknife he always carries around. His father gave him that knife when he was a boy, and it is engraved with his initials: EA. The knife is nearly forty years old, but he keeps it razor-sharp, so it cuts easily through the tape holding the box of bathroom supplies together.

Together, we unload the bathroom supplies. When I first met this man who made me weak at the knees, I never imagined a future in which we would be standing together in a bathroom, picking through bars of soap and sticky shampoo bottles. But strangely enough, Enzo has happily taken to domestic life.

We had been living together for less than a year when, in spite of diligent birth control use, I missed my period. I was terrified of telling him, but he was over the moon excited. *Now we get to be a family!* he said. His parents and sister were all dead, and I never realized how important it was to him to start a family of his own. We got married a month later.

And now, over a decade later, I am living the sort of domestic suburban life that I never dreamed of for myself. Not with Enzo—not with *anyone*. A lot of people would call it boring, but I love it. All I ever wanted was a normal, quiet sort of existence. It just took me longer than most people to get it.

Enzo removes his razors from the box, and now it's finally empty. We are finished. Okay, we have another five billion boxes left in the house, but at least one more has been emptied so now it's five billion minus one. I expect we will finish unpacking sometime in the next three or four decades.

"Okay," Enzo says. "Now we are done for the day."

"Yes," I agree.

He glances over his shoulder at the queen-size bed with a fresh sheet spread across it, then he looks back at me with a grin on his face.

"What?" I tease him. "Do you want to christen the bed?"

"No," he says, "I want to *defile* it."

I let out a laugh, which gets cut off when he grabs me and heaves me up into his arms, carrying me across the threshold to our bed in our beautiful new master bedroom. I would tell him to be careful about his back, but considering he lifted boxes that weigh twice as much as I do (I hope), I'm assuming he knows what he's doing. He doesn't stop until we reach the bed and he deposits me onto the sheets.

Enzo rips off his T-shirt and climbs on top of me, kissing my neck, but as much as I want to be into this, my eyes get drawn to the two picture windows right next to our bed. Why didn't we get blinds? What kind of idiot moves into a house without making sure the windows are covered?

From my position on the bed, I have a great view of the house across the way. The windows are dark, yet I detect a flash of movement in one of the upstairs rooms. At least I think I do.

Enzo notices I've gone stiff and pulls away. "What is wrong?"

"The windows," I murmur. "You can see everything."

He raises his head, peering through our own window to 13 Locust Street. "The lights are out. They are asleep."

When I peer out the window this time, I don't see

any signs of movement. But I saw it before. Just a second ago. I'm sure of it. "I don't think they are."

He winks at me. "So we give them show."

I stare at him.

"Fine," he grumbles. "How about we turn out the lights?"

"Fine."

Enzo crawls off me so that he can flick off the light switch, plunging the room into darkness.

I squirm on the sheets, unable to wrench my gaze away from the bare window. "Do you ever wonder about why we got this house so cheap?"

"Cheap?" Enzo bursts out. "We had to use all our savings to pay the deposit! And the mortgage is—"

"We got it below asking though," I point out. "*Nothing* was selling for below asking."

"Is fixer-upper."

"So were all the others." I prop myself up in bed. "And we weren't able to win the auction on any of them."

Enzo flashes me an exasperated look. "We get you your dream house, and now you have problem with dream house? We got lucky! Why is that so hard to believe?"

Because let's face it—I am never lucky.

"Millie…" Enzo says in that husky voice that he knows I find impossible to resist. "Let us enjoy our first night in our dream house. Yes?"

He climbs back into the bed beside me, and at this point, I'm helpless to resist his charms. But I manage to take one last look out the window, and even though it's all the way across the street, I swear I can make out a pair of eyes on my body.

Watching us.

# FIVE

Today, the kids are starting at their new school.

Ada puts on the dress that I picked out for her first day. It's sleeveless and pale pink, and if my son wore it, it would be smeared with dirt and grease probably before he even got out the front door, but she loves it and will almost certainly manage to keep it clean. As for Nico, I'm just happy he managed to put on some clean clothes that didn't have any holes in them.

I was advised that the school bus stops in front of 13 Locust Street, so I herd the kids out the door, past Suzette's house at 12 Locust, over to the house of the neighbor that I've been convinced has been staring at us through our shutterless windows since yesterday. Sure enough, there's a woman and a child waiting at the bus stop, but they're not what I expected.

First of all, the woman is older than I expected. I'm not the youngest mother among the parents of my kids' friends, but this woman looks old enough to be *my* mother. She is bone thin with wiry gray hair and spindly fingers that almost look like claws. And even though Suzette told me her son is Nico's age, the little boy at her side appears at least two years younger. He's just as emaciated as his mother, and even though it's a warm spring day, he's wearing a thick wool turtleneck sweater that looks extremely itchy and uncomfortable.

Of course, maybe she's not his mother. Maybe she's his grandmother. She certainly looks old enough to be his grandmother. But I would never ask. I'm no Suzette. That's one of those things you don't say to a person when you first meet them, along the same lines as, "Are you pregnant?" (Stupid lumpy shirt.)

As I approach them, the woman narrows her eyes at me through her horn-rimmed spectacles. I can't help but notice the silver chain attached to her glasses, which is something I had always associated with elderly people, although one of Ada's friends back in the Bronx wore one, so maybe they're cool again.

"Hello!" I say cheerfully, determined to befriend this woman. After all, I would love to make some friends in Long Island. Oops, I mean *on* Long Island.

The woman shoots me a half-hearted smile that is more like a grimace. "Hello," she says in the most expressionless tone I have ever heard.

"My name is Millie," I say.

She stares at me, a hollow look in her eyes. This is when most people would tell me their name, but she apparently didn't get the memo.

"And these are Nico and Ada," I add.

Finally, she places a hand on the little boy's shoulder. "This is Spencer," she says. "I'm Janice."

The boy suddenly shifts, revealing what looks like a hook on the bottom of his backpack, which has an attachment coming off it that the woman is holding on to. Oh my God—it's a leash. The poor child is on a leash!

"Nice to meet you," I say. Or should I say *good dog*? "I hear Spencer is in…third grade?"

It seems impossible as I'm saying it. The little boy is nearly a head shorter than Nico, who is average height for his age. But the boy, Spencer, nods his head. "Yes," he confirms.

"Cool!" Nico's eyes light up. "I have Mrs. Cleary as my teacher. Who do you got?"

"Who do you *have*," Janice corrects him.

Nico peers up at her, blinking his dark brown eyes. "I said I have Mrs. Cleary," he says in a slow voice, like he thinks she's stupid. I stifle a laugh.

Before Janice can clarify that she was attempting to correct his grammar, Spencer bursts out with, "Me too! I have Mrs. Cleary too!"

The boys start chatting together excitedly, which makes me happy. Nico is so outgoing, he's able to befriend even the shiest kids. I envy his skill.

I flash Janice a conspiratorial smile. "Well, it looks like Nico has made his first friend here."

"Yes," Janice says with considerably less enthusiasm.

"Maybe they can have a playdate sometime?"

"Maybe." She frowns as the lines crisscrossing her face grow more pronounced. "Has your son had all his vaccinations?"

All public schools require a full set of vaccinations, and I'm sure she knows this. But fine—I'll humor her. "Yes."

"Including influenza?"

It's not even flu season, but whatever. "Yes."

"You can't be too careful, you know," she says. "Spencer is very fragile."

Admittedly, the boy does look a bit fragile, with his nearly translucent skin and tiny body, swimming in that giant woolen sweater. But some color has come into his cheeks now that he is chatting with Nico.

"It would be nice to get to know each other since I'm new here," I say. "My husband and I are having dinner with Suzette and Jonathan tonight."

"Oh." Her lips curl in distaste. "I would watch yourself around that woman." She gives me a knowing look. "And I would especially watch that handsome husband of yours."

I don't like what she's implying. Yes, Suzette is very attractive, and yes, she was a bit over-the-top flirtatious. But I trust my husband—he's not going to cheat on me with the next-door neighbor. I'm also not thrilled that Janice has taken it upon herself to comment on this.

"Suzette seems…nice," I say politely, even though I'm not sure I believe it.

"Well, she's not."

I don't know what to say to that, but fortunately, at that moment, the school bus arrives, and Janice detaches her child from his leash. (But I'm sure he has a microchip with GPS implanted in his brain or something.) Nico barely acknowledges my slightly tearful goodbye, because he's so involved with his new friend. He does allow me to plant a kiss on his forehead, which he has the good grace not to wipe away until he's climbing the steps to the bus. Ada, on the other hand, gives me a big hug and clings to me long enough that I wish I were taking her directly to the school.

"You're going to make a ton of friends," I murmur in her ear. "Just be yourself."

Ada gives me a skeptical look. Ugh, I can't believe I said that. Telling someone to be themselves is like the worst advice ever. I've always *hated* it when people said that to me. But I don't have any better wisdom than that. If I did, I'd have more friends.

I wish Enzo were here. He would know exactly what to say to get her to smile. But he had a landscaping job he left for early this morning, so it's just me.

"I'll be waiting at home this afternoon!" I call after them. I am taking a half day today to make sure I'll be there when they arrive, although in the future, they will likely beat me home by thirty minutes to an hour.

The doors to the bus slam shut and it drives away, carrying my two children away with it. I get that twinge of anxiety that I always feel when I'm separated from my children. Will that ever go away? It was so much easier when they were growing inside me. Well, except for the life-threatening preeclampsia I got in my third trimester with Nico, which was what prompted my decision to get my tubes tied.

It is only after the bus has disappeared from the cul-de-sac that I notice Janice is staring at me, a horrified expression on her face.

"Is something wrong?" I ask as politely as possible.

"Millie," she says. "You're not honestly expecting them to walk home all by themselves, are you?"

"Well, yes." I point to my house, barely a stone's throw away. "We live *right there.*"

"So what?" she shoots back. "We live right there." She points to her house, which is literally right behind us. "And you don't see me leaving Spencer alone for even a second. If a predator is after your child, they could snatch him just like that."

Then she snaps her fingers right in my face to demonstrate the immediacy of the threat.

"It's a pretty safe town though," I say tentatively, not wanting to outright tell this woman that she's ridiculous for keeping her grade-school-aged son on a leash.

"False security," she sneers. "Do you know that an eight-year-old boy vanished right off the street three years ago?"

"*Here?*"

"No, a few towns away."

"Where?"

"I said, *a few towns away*." She gives me a look. "His mother let go of his hand for *one second,* and he was snatched away. Vanished without a trace."

"Really?"

"Yes. They did everything they could to find him. Called in the police, FBI, CIA, National Guard, and a psychic. Even the *psychic* couldn't find him, Millie."

I don't know the details of this alleged abduction, but I certainly never heard of anything like that on the news. And it didn't even happen around here. To Janice, "a few towns away" might very well mean California. I'm not sure it would help to share the statistic that almost all child abductions are committed by family members. Janice seems to have her mind made up. Spencer will probably remain on a leash until he's thirty.

"Well, they're going to have to go home themselves

eventually," I say. "My husband and I both work, and we can't pick them up every day."

She looks at me in amazement. "You work?"

"Um, yes."

She clucks her tongue at me. "When my husband passed, he left me enough money so that I wouldn't have to work anymore."

"Um, that's nice."

"It's so terribly sad," she goes on, "that your children don't get to have a mother at home. They will never know the love they deserve from a mother who won't leave their side."

My mouth falls open. "My kids know I love them."

"But think about how much you're missing!" she cries. "Doesn't that make you sad?"

The words "at least my kid isn't on a leash" are at the tip of my tongue, but by some absolute miracle, I manage to keep my mouth shut. My children know that I love them. Also, I love my job, and I do good things for people at the hospital. And even if I didn't, we need every penny of both of our incomes right now while Enzo is rebuilding his business out here.

"We make it work" is all I say.

"Well, I'm sure you do your best with the little time you have with them."

Somehow, I don't think Janice and I will be great friends. I was so excited to move here, but it's starting to seem like I've chosen the least friendly cul-de-sac in town. One neighbor is hitting on my husband, and the other is judging my dedication as a mother.

Once again, I wonder if moving here has been a terrible mistake.

# SIX

School was a success today.

When the kids get off the bus, they are bursting with stories about their first days of school. Nico has already befriended every child in the third-grade class, and he successfully made milk squirt out of his nose during lunch. (This is a skill he's been cultivating for months.) Ada is less enthusiastic than her brother but assures me she's made some new friends. Switching schools midway through the year is a hard thing to do, and I'm so proud of both of them.

"And Little League tryouts are at the end of the week," Nico says. "When is Dad getting home? He promised he would practice with me."

I check my watch. Suzette told us to show up at her house at six, which is less than an hour from now. Knowing Enzo, he's going to cut it as close as possible. "Soon. I hope."

"When?" he presses me.

"*Soon*." He doesn't look satisfied with this answer, so I add, "I have a great idea. Why don't you go hit the ball around yourself in the backyard?"

His eyes light up. "I love having a backyard, Mom."

Me too.

Nico goes off to practice on his own in the backyard, which is a luxury we didn't have back in the city. I go upstairs to the bedroom and apply a fresh layer of concealer to cover the circles under my eyes that seem like they're always there these days. I start to put on some mascara but manage to get a glob of it in my eye and then have to wash it all off because I'm tearing so badly. I apply a layer of something called nude lipstick, which is apparently lipstick that makes it look like you're not wearing lipstick at all. I can't imagine why they would make such a product, although a better question is why did I buy it?

We haven't purchased a full-length mirror yet, so I am doing acrobatics to check my appearance in the small vanity mirror over the sink. It involves some amount of contortion, but I finally decide that I look fine enough. Anyway, I have to figure out the dessert situation, because that is my contribution to the evening.

On the way home from work, I stopped off at the supermarket and bought an apple pie. Now, don't get me wrong—I love apple pie in all forms. But when I get downstairs to the kitchen and pull it out of the grocery bag, it looks like exactly what it is: a cheap pie from a local supermarket.

I can only imagine what sort of commentary I'm going to get from Suzette on this pie. She probably goes to some fancy French patisserie for all her desserts.

I pull the pie out of the plastic wrap but leave it inside the metal tin. Then I grab a fork from the silverware drawer. With artistic precision, I rough up the edges of the pie and poke the center a few times. The pie looks decidedly less assembly-line perfect now. Could I pass it off as home baked? Maybe.

As I'm scrutinizing the pie, the front door hinges squeal as the door swings open. Enzo is home. Thank God, since we don't have much time left. I rush out to the front door to meet him, but immediately, my face falls. My husband is literally covered head to toe in dirt. And we have to be at the Lowells' in…

Fifteen minutes. Great.

"Millie!" His face lights up when he sees me, but then I notice he's looking at the pie. "Apple pie…my favorite American dessert!"

"I made it," I say, testing the waters.

"Really? It looks like from supermarket."

Damn. I guess I didn't make it rustic enough.

He comes over to give me a kiss, but I back away, holding up a hand to ward him off. "You're filthy!"

"I was digging a hole," he says, like it would be silly to think he was doing anything else. "I'll shower after I do the baseball with Nico. He wants to practice."

"*Enzo.*" I glare at him. "Suzette invited us for dinner! We need to be there in fifteen minutes. Remember?"

He looks at me blankly. I am amazed by his ability to forget any sort of social engagement, although he seems to be very good at keeping track of his work obligations.

"Oh," he says. "Was it in the family calendar?"

Enzo always tells me to put things in the family

calendar on our phones, but as far as I can tell, he does not check that—ever. "*Yes*, it was."

"Oh." He scratches his neck with his dirt-encrusted hand. "I guess…I shower now then."

Honestly, sometimes it's like having a third child. Actually, he is more like the second child, because Ada is much more like an adult.

I turn back to the pie. On a whim, I throw it into the oven. Maybe if it's hot, I can pass it off as my own. Somehow, I feel this desperate need to impress Suzette Lowell. I've worked for a lot of women like Suzette back in the days when I was cleaning houses, but I've never been in a position to be anything more than the servant of a woman like her.

I don't like Suzette, but if we can be friends with the Lowells, it's a step up. It means I have finally achieved the normal life I always dreamed of. The life I'd do anything to get.

# SEVEN

Twenty minutes later, we are standing at the front door of 12 Locust Street.

It took a little longer than expected. Even though Enzo took a quick shower, he then came downstairs in wrinkled jeans and a T-shirt, because of course he did. So I had to send him back upstairs to change into something a little more respectable. Now he's wearing the button-up black dress shirt I bought him six months ago when I realized he had absolutely no dress shirts, and as expected, it perfectly complements his dark eyes and hair, and he looks achingly handsome. Also as expected, he looks very uncomfortable and like there's a chance he might rip it off at some point during the evening. (Suzette would *die*.)

The apple pie is now warm, which helps it look more homemade. It's also very hot to hold. It's currently scalding my hands, and I can't wait to put it down.

Nico is tugging at his own short-sleeved dress shirt,

which has an even higher chance of being ripped off due to discomfort tonight than his father's. "Do we have to go to a boring dinner?"

"Yes," I say.

"But I want to play baseball with Dad."

"We won't be there long."

"What are they making for dinner?"

"I don't know."

"Can I watch TV while we're there?"

I turn my head to glare at my son. "No, you can*not*."

I look over at Enzo for support, although he looks like he's trying not to laugh. He probably wishes he could watch TV too.

After a minute of my hands being scorched by the supermarket pie, an unfamiliar woman pulls open the front door. She is about sixty years old and built like a linebacker, with graying hair pulled back into a tight bun. She has the most perfect posture I've ever seen—like if you put a book on her head and checked on it two days later, it would still be there. She's got on a flowered dress with a white apron over it. She stares at me with dull gray eyes that bore right into me.

"Um, hello…" I say uncertainly. I check the house number on the door, as if I might have somehow gone to the wrong house next door. "I'm Millie. We're here for…"

"Millie!"

Behind the woman who greeted us, a voice floats out from within the depths of the house. A second later, Suzette descends the stairs, looking simultaneously slightly breathless and yet without a single hair out of place. She's wearing a green dress that makes me realize her eyes are actually more green than blue, and whatever miraculous bra she's wearing pushes her boobs practically up to her chin. Her butterscotch-colored hair is shiny, like she was just whisked out of the salon, and her skin almost seems like it's glowing. She looks gorgeous.

I look over at Enzo to see if he's noticing how she looks, but he's busy fiddling with a button on his shirt. He *really* hates that shirt. Hopefully he can keep it on till we get home.

"Millie and Enzo!" she cries, clasping her hands together with more delight than anyone could possibly have over the neighbors coming to visit. "I'm *so* glad you could make it. And so fashionably late."

Sheesh, we're only five minutes late.

"Hi, Suzette," I say.

"I see you've already met Martha." Suzette's eyes twinkle as she puts a hand on the older woman's shoulder. "She helps out here two days a week. Jonathan and I are just *so* busy, and Martha is a lifesaver."

"Yes," I murmur.

I have been many families' Martha in the past. But I was never able to play the part as well as this woman clearly does. She looks like a maid right from out of the fifties. All she needs is a little feather duster and one of those vacuums with the comically large engines.

Yet there's something unnerving about her. Possibly because she's still staring at me like she can't rip her eyes away. I'm used to women staring at Enzo, but she's not interested in him or my children. Her gaze is laser-beam focused on my face.

What is so interesting? Do I have spinach in my teeth? Is there a celebrity I resemble and she wants an autograph?

"Could Martha get you anything to drink?" Suzette asks me and Enzo, although she's looking at him. "Water? A glass of wine? I believe we also have some lovely pomegranate juice."

We both shake our heads. "No, thank you," I say.

"Are you sure?" she says. "It's no trouble for Martha."

I look over at the older woman, who is still standing there rigidly, waiting for the word to dash back in the kitchen and fetch us a beverage. "It's no trouble," she chimes in, her voice low and gravelly, like she's not used to using it.

"We're fine," I assure her, hoping she'll leave. She doesn't.

Suzette finally notices Nico and Ada, who are patiently huddled in the doorway. "And these must be your two beautiful children. How completely precious."

"Thank you," I say. It always struck me as odd that when you compliment someone's children, the parent says "thank you," like they are the owner of the child. Yet here I am, saying thank you.

Suzette turns her attention back to Enzo. "They both look *exactly* like you."

"Not exactly," Enzo says, which is a bald-faced lie. "Ada has Millie's mouth and lips."

"Hmm, I don't see it," Suzette says.

She doesn't see it because it's not true. Neither of them look anything like me. And while we're at it, neither of the kids shares my personality. Nico is a lot like Enzo, and I don't know where on earth my intelligent, reserved daughter came from.

"By the way," Suzette says. "I just found out some *fantastic* news. Another family that Martha works for has just moved away. I'll bet she would be happy to clean for you too."

"Oh." Enzo and I exchange looks. *Of course* I love the idea of someone besides me cleaning my house, but we can't afford it. "That's so nice of you, really, but I don't think..."

"I'm free Thursday mornings," Martha tells me.

"Would Thursday mornings work for you?" Suzette asks me.

How do I explain to this woman whose house is twice the size of ours that we can't afford a cleaning woman? And even if we could afford one, there's something about Martha that makes me incredibly uncomfortable. "Um, the time is okay, but..."

Before I can come up with an excuse that doesn't involve me admitting that we don't want Martha's services, Suzette's eyes drop to the pie in my hands. She lets out a tinkling laugh. "Oh no, Millie, did you *drop that* on the way over?"

Ugh, I guess I made it *too* rustic.

Thankfully, I at least manage to put down the pie on the coffee table in their living room while Martha disappears to the kitchen. The living room is much larger than ours. Every part of their house is twice as large as ours or possibly three times. The outside is just as old as ours—the house was built in the late 1800s and not much has been altered—but unlike ours, the inside of their house has been fully renovated. Enzo has promised to renovate our house the same way, but I suspect it will take the better part of the next decade.

"The house is gorgeous," I comment. "And you have so much space."

Suzette rests her hand on a large piece of furniture that I guess you would call an armoire. I wonder if we could get an armoire for our house. (Who am I kidding? We're lucky we can afford chairs and tables.) "All three of these houses used to be farmhouses originally," she says. "This house was the main house where the owners lived. And 13 Locust was the servant quarters."

"And what about our house?" I ask.

"I believe that was the shelter for the animals."

*What?*

"Cool!" Nico says. "I bet my room was the pigs' room!"

Okay, she has *got* to be messing with us. I mean, if it were a house for animals, it wouldn't have stairs, right? Or maybe the stairs were put in later. I *have* noticed sort of a smell that…

"Jonathan!" Suzette cries.

Suzette's blue-green eyes are on the twisting stairwell leading to the second floor of their house, where a man is descending to the first floor. He's wearing a white dress shirt paired with a navy-blue tie, and unlike my husband, he seems very comfortable dressing up. Also unlike my husband, his looks are otherwise completely unassuming. His facial features are blandly pleasing, his light brown hair is neatly trimmed, and he's clean-shaven. He's only a couple of inches taller than I am, with a slight build. He seems like the sort of man who could disappear into any crowd.

"Hello," he says with an easy smile. "You must be Millie and Enzo." He turns to address the kids. "And company."

After Suzette's pretentiousness, Jonathan feels like a

breath of fresh air. "Yes, I'm Millie," I say. "You must be Jonathan."

"That's right." He reaches out to take my hand, and unlike Suzette's death grip, his palm is smooth and he doesn't make any attempt to break even one of the bones in my hand. "So good to finally meet you."

Jonathan shakes Enzo's hand next, and if he is at all threatened by my husband—some insecure men are—he certainly doesn't show it.

I instinctively like Jonathan. I can't say why, but it's just a vibe I get. I've worked in a lot of households in my lifetime, and I've gotten pretty damned good at reading people.

Especially reading couples.

You can tell a lot from body language. There are certain gestures I've seen husbands make that suggest they are exerting their power in the relationship. For example, a kiss on the forehead rather than on the lips. A hand on the small of the back while they walk. It's subtle but I've come to notice it. However, Jonathan isn't doing any of that with Suzette. There's nothing to make me think that they are anything more than what they seem—a happily married couple.

"So how are you enjoying the new house?" he asks us.

"I love it," I blurt out, having forgotten my shame about my house possibly having previously served as a shed for barn animals. "I know it's small, but—"

"Small?" Jonathan laughs. "I think it's a perfect size. I would have grabbed that house if it were available. This one is so ostentatious, especially for just the two of us."

Score another point for Jonathan.

"So you have no children?" Enzo asks them.

Before Jonathan can answer, Suzette blurts out, "Oh *no*. We're not *children* type of people. They're so loud and messy and constantly need attention—no offense. People who want to make that sacrifice are absolute saints." She laughs as she says the words, as if it's hilarious that anyone would want to give up their life to be a parent. "But it's just not for us. We are absolutely in agreement about that. Right, Jonathan?"

"Right, yes," he says amicably. "Suzette and I have always agreed on that."

"It's not for everyone," I say.

Although I couldn't help but notice that while Suzette was gushing about how wonderful it is to be child-free, Jonathan had a morose look on his face. It makes me wonder if they really are "absolutely in agreement" on the issue of parenthood. I wouldn't judge anyone for not wanting to be a parent, but it's sad when one person in a couple has to give up their dream to suit the other.

"I was telling Millie that I love how cozy and quaint their house is," Suzette says. "I agree, this house is just so sprawling and extravagant. Honestly, we just don't know what to do with all this space. Especially our massive backyard."

At the mention of the word "backyard," Enzo perks up. "I have a landscaping business if you are looking for help with your yard."

Suzette arches an eyebrow. "Do you?"

He nods eagerly. "I have clients in the Bronx, but I am now trying to move out here. Such a big drive to the city."

"The Long Island Expressway is murder," Suzette agrees.

Yes, especially the way Enzo drives. Every time he merges onto 495, I'm certain he will die a fiery death. He had a very decent business back in the Bronx, but he's making an effort to get more clients out on the island so he doesn't have to keep making that long drive every day. The goal is to transition his business to the surrounding neighborhoods within the next few years. And there are enough wealthy families around here that there's good potential for the business to grow and expand.

"I am excellent at landscaping," Enzo adds. "Whatever you want me to do with your yard, I do it."

"Anything?" Suzette asks in a voice dripping with suggestion.

"All landscape services, yes."

She rests a hand on his biceps. "I just might take you up on that."

And then? She just *leaves her hand there*. On my husband's arm muscles. For way, way too long. I mean, there's got to be a limit to how long you're allowed to keep your hand on the muscles of a man who is not your husband, right?

But it's harmless. Her own husband is *right there* after all. And Jonathan doesn't seem the slightest bit upset over it. He probably knows that Suzette is a flirt and he's learned to ignore it.

I tell myself I have nothing to worry about.

And I almost convince myself too.

# EIGHT

I've never experienced quite such an elaborate dinner.

Okay, for starters, we have place cards with our names on them. Place cards! And I can't help but notice the place cards have assigned Suzette to sit on one side of the table with Enzo, and me on the other side with Jonathan. Moreover, our kids aren't even at the same table! There's easily enough room for two more people at this massive mahogany wood table, but instead, another smaller table has been set up across the entire room. We practically need binoculars to see them.

"I assumed the children would want their privacy," Suzette says.

In my experience, children never want privacy. *Ever.* It's only recently that going to the bathroom has ceased to be a family experience. Not only that, but the children's table is far too small. It looks like it would be better suited for the living room of a dollhouse. I can see from the expression on the kids' faces that they are not pleased.

"That's a table for babies," Nico grumbles. "I don't want to sit there!"

"*Fai silenzio*," Enzo hisses.

Our children, of course, both speak perfect Italian because he spoke it to them all the time when they were little so they'd grow up bilingual. He says they both have terrible American accents, but they sound pretty good to me. In any case, the warning quiets them down, and they reluctantly take their seats at the comically tiny table. I sort of want to snap a picture of them at that little table with their identical miserable faces, but I suspect that will enrage them.

Enzo looks just as perplexed by the place setting in front of him. He plops down in the chair assigned to him and picks up one of the forks that have been laid out. "Why is there three forks?" he wants to know.

"Well," Suzette explains patiently, "one is a dinner fork of course, then there's the salad fork, and then you have a spaghetti fork."

"How is a spaghetti fork different from a dinner fork?" I ask.

"Oh, Millie," she laughs. And she doesn't answer, even though I thought it was a very good question.

"So how are you liking the neighborhood so far?" Jonathan asks us as he settles into his own high-backed wooden chair and carefully lays a napkin on his lap.

I squirm in my own chair. The chairs look painfully expensive, constructed from solid wood, but they are surprisingly uncomfortable. "We love it."

Suzette leans her chin on her fist. "Have you met *Janice*?"

"I have."

"She's a trip, isn't she?" she cackles. "That woman is afraid of her own shadow. And she's so nosy! Isn't she, Jonathan?"

Jonathan takes a sip from his water glass and smiles vaguely at his wife but doesn't say anything. I appreciate that he doesn't immediately jump to bad-mouth his neighbor, even if it might be deserved. Suzette, on the other hand…

"She did have her son on a *leash*," I recall. "It was coming off his backpack."

Suzette giggles. "She's hilariously overprotective. She thinks there are gremlins waiting to snatch her child at every corner."

"She was paranoid about some boy a few towns over that she was saying was kidnapped."

"Right." She bobs her head. "It was a custody battle between the parents, and the father drove him over the border to Canada. They got him back. It was in the news at the time, but she acts like the boogeyman is out there! And that's not even the worst thing about living next door to her. You should hear some of the crap she's pulled."

I wince. "What else?"

"So we had the grill going in the backyard once," she says, "and we were hardly even cooking anything. Only some crayfish and a filet. We only had a few guests over, right, Jonathan?"

"I don't really remember, dear," he says.

"Anyway," she continues, "right in the middle of our little barbecue, the police show up! Janice called the police and told them we had started a fire in the backyard! Can you imagine?"

"You have a grill in the backyard?" Enzo asks with interest.

"You should get one," Jonathan says.

"Or try ours out," Suzette offers. "You're welcome to come over and give it a whirl if you want."

"Could I?" he asks excitedly.

It's funny because when I first met Enzo, nearly two decades ago now, he seemed so much more exciting than any man I have ever met. He was practically *dashing*. Now I realize the cold, hard truth: this man's biggest fantasy in life is grilling burgers in the backyard. Or that's what you would think as he quizzes Suzette about the ins and outs of grilling. I would be able to get more on board if, while Suzette is talking to him, she didn't feel the need to touch his arm *the whole time*.

Like, you can talk to somebody without touching their arm. It's possible.

Thankfully, the conversation about grills is interrupted when Martha emerges from the kitchen, carrying plates of salad for the four of us. I don't know what's in it, but it smells like raspberries and there are little lumps of cheese in it.

"Thank you, Martha," I say when I notice Suzette didn't bother to thank her.

I wait for her to say "you're welcome," but instead she just stares at me again until I have to look away.

I can't eat with Martha's gaze on me, but as soon as she leaves the room, I dig into the salad. I'm not much of a salad person, but wow. I mean, *wow*. If all salad tasted this way, I might *be* a salad person. I had no idea it was possible for salad to be this delicious.

"Millie," Suzette giggles. "You're using your spaghetti fork to eat the salad!"

I *am*? I look around the table, and everybody is eating, apparently using a different fork than I am, even though the truth is they all look identical to me. And Enzo, who definitely does not have more fork knowledge than I do, points to the fork farthest from my plate. How did he know that?

Wow, this is weirdly embarrassing. I swap out the forks as quickly as I can.

"So what do you do, Jonathan?" I ask to draw attention away from the fork debacle.

"Finance."

I offer a smile. "Sounds interesting."

He shrugs. "It pays the bills. It's certainly not as exciting as what Suzette does."

When he says that, he reaches across the table for her hand. She allows him to hold it for only a split second before pulling away. "I love being around people," she says. "Because of my job, I know everyone in this town. Actually…" Her eyes widen as a thought seems to occur to her. "I could be of help to you, Enzo."

Enzo frowns. "Me?"

"Yes!" She dabs her lips with her napkin, and I can't help but notice her lipstick is completely intact. I'm fairly sure mine rubbed off several lettuce leaves ago, but I guess that's okay since it was the exact same color as my lips. "You're looking for customers for your landscaping business, aren't you? Well, I know everyone in all the surrounding towns buying new houses. I can put your name in the welcome package."

His mouth falls open. "You would do that?"

"Of course, silly!" And then she touches his arm again. Again! Is she trying to go for some sort of world record? "We're neighbors, aren't we?"

"You do not know if I am any good."

Enzo is *really* good at what he does. Sure, some percentage of the women who hire him only do so because he's hot, but he *keeps* clients because his work is stellar, and he knows it. But he also feels strongly that he should prove himself.

"In that case," she says, "maybe you should give me a private demonstration."

I don't like where this is going.

"We desperately need work on our backyard," Suzette explains. "I would love to do some serious gardening back there, but I'm afraid I don't have a green thumb. If you could show me what you can do and give me a little instruction on top of that, I would be happy to recommend you to everyone I know."

Enzo looks over at me. He opens his mouth, almost certainly about to ask if I'm okay with this arrangement, but then Suzette says, "You know what I love about the two of you? You trust each other, unlike a lot of other couples. Enzo doesn't have to ask your permission, Millie, for any little silly thing."

And then he shuts his mouth.

"So what do you say?" she asks him. "Do we have a deal?"

I flash a desperate look at Jonathan, hoping he will intervene and say that he is not okay with this. But he is just sitting there, shoveling bites of that weirdly delicious salad into his mouth, not the slightest bit perturbed. Of course, why *should* he be upset? All Enzo would be doing is a little yard work next door. There's no reason to get jealous.

And let's face it, it's not like Suzette is the first woman to hit on my husband. She's not the first and she won't be the last.

Except there's something about Suzette's flirting that enrages me more than the usual bored housewife who sees my husband as eye candy. I can't quite put my finger on it.

"Sure," Enzo says. "I am happy to."

Martha comes back out of the kitchen, carrying more plates of food. I glance back at the children's table to see if they've made any progress on their salad—usually something eaten only under threat of punishment—and I'm shocked to discover that even Nico has nearly cleaned his plate. I'm also mildly jealous of the fact that the kids only seem to have been given one fork each.

Martha pulls away our salad plates and lays down a dish in front of me that looks like something Italian. Unfortunately, Suzette had no idea that Enzo is so picky about Italian food. Well, she's about to find out.

Enzo looks down at the plate, inhaling deeply. "Is this pasta alla Norma?"

Suzette bobs her head excitedly. "Yes! Our chef is Italian, and I guessed from your accent that you are Sicilian, so he thought you might enjoy this."

I hold my breath, waiting for Enzo to push it away or possibly take a few bites to be polite. But instead, he takes a mouthful of spaghetti, and his eyes almost start tearing up. "*Oddio*… It tastes just like how my *nonna* used to make it."

"I'm so glad you like it!" she gushes. "It does have a

wonderful mouthfeel, doesn't it? Of course, I'm sure it's not as good as it is when Millie makes it."

"Millie does not cook this dish," Enzo says.

Suzette's long eyelashes flutter. "No?"

Everyone at the table is now staring at me, like I am the worst person in the universe because I don't make my husband pasta à la Norway or whatever the hell it's called. In my defense, anytime I try to cook something Italian, he acts like I just tried to feed him poison. Who knew he would like this so much that it would make him *cry*?

I pick up my fork and spear what looks like a piece of eggplant. I shove it in my mouth, and…

Wow, that is pretty good. I'm not about to start crying over it, but this is some really good pasta.

"Oh, Millie," Suzette giggles. "You're using the *dessert* fork!"

By the end of this night, if I have not stabbed Suzette with one of these forks, it will only be because I'm not sure which one to use to do it.

# NINE

"You are mad," Enzo notes.

I don't know what his first clue was. Maybe the way I barely said a word as we walked home from the house next door, me carrying the apple pie because even after instructing me to bring dessert, Suzette had her chef go ahead and make some amazing chocolate soufflé. Maybe it was the way I slammed the refrigerator door as I shoved the uneaten pie inside. Or the way I stomped up the steps to our bedroom and shut the door behind me, only coming out to say good night to the kids.

"I will eat the apple pie," he says as he crawls into bed beside me. "I love the apple pie. I don't care if you dropped it on the floor."

"I didn't drop it on the floor."

"No?"

I groan. The fact that Enzo has no idea what I am upset about is making it hard to be mad. Also, he's not wearing a shirt, which makes it even harder to be mad.

"Do you really have to work in Suzette's backyard?" I say.

He leans back against the pillows and sighs. "Oh. This."

"Well? Is it really necessary?"

"Why does that bother you?"

"Because."

"Because is not an answer," he says, which is irritatingly something I say to the kids constantly.

"I just feel like Suzette has an agenda."

"Agenda?"

I fold my arms across my chest. "You know."

"I do not know."

"Oh my God." I flop over in bed. "Enzo, that woman was flirting with you shamelessly all night! She didn't let up for a second!"

He clutches his chest in mock horror. "A woman flirting with *me*? *Ma va'!* How can I possibly resist that?"

I roll my eyes. "Okay, okay..."

"We will probably run off together."

"*Okay.*"

He grins at me. "I am flattered you worry. But, Millie, you know I would never ever look at another woman."

"Oh really?"

"Really," he says. "I would be stupid to cheat."

"Would you?"

"Oh, yes." He flops on his side, propping his head up on his hand. "You are my wife. The mother of my children. I love you so much."

"Okay..."

"Also," he adds, "I know better than to double-cross you. I would like to keep breathing."

I snort. "Yeah, right."

"How can you say you're worried about Suzette?" he retorts. "Suzette...*she* is the one who needs to worry."

"Ha ha, very funny."

"I am not making a joke," he says, although his lips twitch. "I am scared of you, Millie Accardi."

I make a face at him. "Right. Like *you're* Mr. Nice Guy."

Truth be told, we have both done some pretty bad things. Unspeakable things, although I'd like to think they were all in the name of serving justice. But either way, if you made a tally, I would come out far ahead of my husband. I've done much worse things than he has. After all, he's never done anything so bad that they took away his freedom.

But of course, that's only the stuff I know about. I get the feeling that Enzo had a whole life back overseas that I don't know about. I once worked up the nerve to ask him if he ever killed anyone, and he laughed like I was making a joke, but he didn't say no. And then he quickly found a way to change the subject.

I only asked the one time. Because after that, I wasn't sure I wanted to know.

Enzo runs a finger slowly along my jawline. "Millie..." he whispers.

I glance over my shoulder, at the window where moonlight pours into our bedroom. "When are you going to put in those blinds?"

"Tomorrow. I *promise*."

I close my eyes, trying to enjoy the sensation of my husband's touch and then his lips on my neck. But with my eyes closed, I become aware of something else. A sound from somewhere else in the house.

My eyes fly open. "Do you hear that?" I ask him.

He lifts his head from my neck. "Hear what?"

"That sound. It sounds like…something scraping."

It's a very disturbing sound. It almost sounds like nails on a chalkboard. Again and again and again.

And it's coming from somewhere within the house.

He grins at me. "Maybe is man with hook for hand on roof?"

I smack the top of his head. "I'm serious! What *is* that?"

We both lie there for a moment, listening. And of course, that's when the sound stops.

"I do not hear it," Enzo says.

"Well, it stopped."

"Oh."

"But what *was* it?"

"Was probably the house settling."

"House *settling*?" I make a face at him. "That's not a thing. You just made that up right now."

"Yes, is a thing. And anyway, are you the big expert on houses? Houses make noises. It is a house noise. No big deal."

I'm not sure I agree, but at the same time, I can't very well argue now that the noise has stopped.

He raises his eyebrows. "So…may I *continue*?"

I'm not feeling super amorous after listening to that scraping sound coming from within the house, coupled with the completely exposed window. But Enzo is already kissing my neck again, and I have to say, it is extremely hard to ask him to stop.

# TEN

Thursday is my morning off.

The kids walk to the bus stop by themselves, like they have been doing since yesterday. I'm sure Janice is traumatized when the two of them show up all alone, but I'm not too worried about it. I do watch them from one of the windows in the front of the house (which now has blinds—thank you, Enzo), and I watch the bus collect them and carry them away to school.

They're fine. Motherhood is a state of constant low-grade worrying, but I refuse to be the type of woman who puts her child on a leash. At some point, you have to let go even if it drives you nuts.

Once they're gone, the house is so quiet. Ada generally keeps to herself, but Nico is always a whirlwind of activity. When he's not home, the house seems deathly still. It was quiet back when we were in a small apartment, but now that we are in a larger house (albeit *cozy*), it's so much more quiet. I think our house has echoes. *Echoes.*

I don't know what to do with myself. Maybe I'll make myself some breakfast and read a book.

I walk over to the kitchen and pull out a carton of eggs. As I get older, I've been trying to eat healthy, and I've heard eggs are pretty healthy if you don't fry them in oil or butter. (Which seems patently unfair, because that's what makes them taste the best.) So I've started the water boiling for my oil/butter-free egg when the doorbell rings.

I hurry over to the front door and fling it open without checking who is out there, because that's the sort of neighborhood I live in now. Back when we lived in the Bronx, I never opened the front door without checking who was waiting on the other side. If it was someone I didn't recognize, I demanded ID to be held up to the peephole. But this neighborhood is so safe. I don't have to worry about anything anymore.

But I am extremely surprised to see Martha—Suzette's cleaning woman—on the other side of the door, clothed in one of her flowered print dresses paired with a crisp white apron, a pair of rubber gloves in one hand and some sort of advanced mop in the other.

"Hello," I say, because I'm not sure what else to say.

Martha stares at me with that same penetrating gaze, her broad face a mask. "It is Thursday. I am here to clean."

What? I remember her mentioning that she was free on Thursdays, but I don't remember agreeing to let her come. In fact, I distinctly remember trying to come up with a nice way of telling her we weren't interested before I got distracted by Suzette insulting my pie. Would she just *show up* here without having confirmed the plans?

Did Suzette put her up to this?

"Um," I say. "I…I appreciate you coming and all, but as I was saying the other night, we really don't have…"

Martha does not budge. She's not getting the message.

"Look," I say, "we don't… I mean, I can clean the house myself. You don't need to—"

"Your husband told me to come," Martha interrupts me.

What? "He…he did?"

She nods almost imperceptibly. "He called me."

"Um," I say again. "Excuse me for one second."

Enzo has a late start today, so he's sleeping in this morning. But I sprint up the stairs, and when I see him lying on his side of the bed, I give his shoulder a shake. His eyelashes flutter, but he doesn't open his eyes. I shake him more violently this time, and he finally looks up at me sleepily.

"Millie?" he murmurs.

"Enzo," I say, "did you call that cleaning woman Suzette recommended?"

He sits up slowly in bed, rubbing his eyes. There have been mornings when I have seen him be instantly alert and leap out of bed, immediately at attention. But I haven't seen him do that in a long time. Maybe not even since the kids were born. These days, it's a five-minute process to get him coherent enough for a conversation.

"Yes," he finally says. "I called her."

"Why would you do that? We can't afford a cleaning woman! I can do it myself."

He yawns. "Is okay. Not that expensive."

"Enzo…"

He takes another few seconds to wake himself up

fully. He swings his legs over the side of the bed. "Millie, you are always cleaning for people. Ever since I know you. So this time, someone cleans for you."

I wring my hands together. "But—"

"No but," he says. "She will only come twice a month. Not that much money. Also, Nico is going to empty the trash now, and Ada will do the dishes. I talked to them."

I start to protest again, but actually, it *would* be nice not to have to clean for a change. He's right—it's something I have always done. I went right from cleaning other people's houses to cleaning up after my children. Not that Enzo doesn't ever help, but cleaning a house of four people is a big job.

"Not that much money," he says again. "You deserve this."

Maybe I do. Maybe I do deserve it. And anyway, his mind seems made up, so I'm not going to argue.

Except why does it have to be *Martha*?

I return to the living room, where Martha has efficiently located our cleaning supplies and put herself to work. Okay, she does have a bit of an issue with staring at me, but plenty of people are socially awkward, and she seems to be an incredibly competent cleaning woman. Most families I worked for had endless instructions on how they wanted everything done, but I vowed if I ever could afford that kind of help, I wouldn't be so obnoxious.

"Enzo says it's okay," I report back to her.

She gives me a crisp nod. The woman hardly ever talks. She reminds me a bit of those guards for the royal palace in England who can't talk or smile.

I attempt to make my egg in the kitchen, but it's hard to cook with Martha right next to me, efficiently scrubbing our countertop while also glancing up at me every few seconds. Even though our kitchen is much larger than the one we had back in the city, it's weird to be here while she is cleaning. It feels awkward, like I'm some sort of fancy, rich person who employs servants, which is funny considering…well, we can barely even afford this house, even at 10 percent below asking. This house that possibly used to be occupied by barn animals. (Although I don't actually believe that. I mean, I'm pretty sure.)

I awkwardly step aside so Martha can get her work done. "Excuse me," I mumble.

Most people I worked for used to leave the house when I was cleaning, and I appreciated that. Even if the employer was not actively telling me how to clean, which some of them did, I always felt like they were silently judging me when they were in the house. Or watching me to make sure I wasn't stealing anything. And even if they weren't doing either of those things, they were simply *in the way*.

Finally, I give up on the egg. I grab a banana instead, because it's the only breakfast I can think of that doesn't involve cooking. I carry my slightly brown banana out to the living room and plop down on the sofa with my phone in my other hand.

Maybe I can take Wednesday mornings off instead.

I sort through my emails, dealing with what I can. The kids have been at their new school for less than a week, and already, I've got dozens of emails from the school. The principal seems compelled to write to all the parents daily. That is a stark difference between this school and the previous public elementary school in the Bronx. We may not be paying tuition here, but the parents expect a lot. Daily emails, apparently.

I end up deleting almost all the emails from the school. I mean, how many messages can you read about the upcoming book fair or something called Lego Lunch?

The banana isn't terribly satisfying, but it does the job. I figure I'll go get some errands done outside the house while Martha is cleaning. Except when I get off the sofa and turn around, I almost jump out of my skin.

Martha is standing rigidly at the entrance to the kitchen.

She is so still. She almost looks like a robot standing there—or is "cyborg" the correct terminology? Either way, it startled me. I thought she was busy cleaning in the kitchen, but apparently she's been standing there and staring at me for God knows how long. And when I catch her doing it, she doesn't look away. She is unapologetically staring at me.

"Yes?" I say.

"I didn't want to bother you," she says.

"Um, it's fine. What do you need?"

She hesitates for a few seconds, as if carefully measuring her words. Finally, she blurts out, "Where is your oven cleaner?"

Is *that* why she was looking at me so intently? She was just confused about the location of the oven cleaner? Is that really all it was?

"It's in the cabinet right by the stove." Where else would it be?

Martha nods at my answer and returns to the kitchen. But I still feel a little uneasy. Even if Enzo wants us to have a cleaning woman, that doesn't mean it has to be Martha. I'd rather not have a cleaner who won't quit staring at me. But on the other hand, she's already working here. If we find someone else, I'll have to fire her. I have never fired anyone in my life, and I'm not looking forward to it.

Maybe this will be fine. After all, she knows where the oven cleaner is now, and according to Enzo, her rates are very reasonable. Suzette's house is spotless, so she's obviously good at what she does.

And like Enzo said, I deserve this.

# ELEVEN

Nico has a playdate today with Spencer, the boy who lives at 13 Locust.

This playdate was nearly impossible to arrange. We've been living here for two weeks, and this was the first opening. I had to provide Janice a copy of Nico's vaccination record—no joke. I'm surprised she didn't require blood and urine samples.

But it's worth it, because Nico is always bouncing off the walls on the weekends, and he doesn't have a bunch of friends nearby like he did at our old apartment. The playdate is at three o'clock on Sunday afternoon at Spencer's house, but starting at one, Nico asks me roughly every fifteen minutes if it's time for the playdate yet. It gets to the point where every time he says the word "Mom," I want to scream.

"Mom," he says at a quarter to three. "Can I bring Little Kiwi to Spencer's house?"

Enzo and Nico decided they didn't want to wait for a

praying mantis egg to hatch and all the mantises to eat each other, so instead they purchased a baby praying mantis that arrived last Monday. Nico named the praying mantis Little Kiwi in a weird homage to one of his favorite fruits.

"Not if you ever want to be invited back," I reply.

Nico thinks about this. "Can I bring my baseball and bat?"

Tryouts for Little League were a week ago on Friday, and Nico made the team, which is great because it'll be another way for him to make friends and burn off some of that pent-up energy. But as a result, he's been even more obsessed with baseball than he was before. Enzo has been tossing the ball around with him every night. It's very cute to watch, because Enzo narrates every move like an actual baseball game. *He comes up to the plate, he swings at the pitch… He gets a hit! He runs to first base, second base…*

"Okay," I agree, although I'm slightly worried that Nico is going to let the ball get out of control and break a window, at which point Janice will have a stroke. He has a good swing, but he is not quite as good at control.

Finally—*finally!*—it's three o'clock, so we can head over for the playdate. Ada is sprawled out on the sofa, reading a book, her glossy black hair splayed out behind her. Once again, I am struck by how beautiful my daughter is. I don't even think she realizes it. God help us all when she does.

"Ada," I say, "do you want to come with us?"

Ada looks at me like I've lost my ever-loving mind. "No, thank you."

"Do you have any friends that you want to have playdates with?" I ask her. "I'm happy to drive you."

She shakes her head. I hope she's making friends at school. She is not nearly as outgoing as Nico, but she has always had her little tight group of friends at school. It must be hard to start over in fifth grade, and Ada is not the type to complain. Maybe I'll suggest a girls' night out for the two of us, and I can probe a bit to see how things are going.

I consider inviting Enzo along, but then I realize I haven't seen him all afternoon. He must be working. He had a lot of clients back in the city, but he's trying to relocate all his business to the island, so he's been hustling a lot. He's incredibly concerned with our ability to make our mortgage payments. I appreciate what he's doing, but at the same time, I wish he were around more.

Anyway, it looks like it's just going to be me and Nico heading over there. So I grab my purse and we walk across the cul-de-sac to 13 Locust—the house that supposedly used to be for servants. As we pass Suzette's house on the way over, I can't help but notice a lot of noise coming from the backyard. What are they doing back there?

When Janice opens the door for us, her face falls, like in spite of the invitation, she had been hoping we might not show.

"Oh," she says. "Come in, I guess."

"Thanks," I say.

As we step onto the welcome mat inside her house, she points down at our feet. "Shoes off."

I slip out of my closed-toe sandals, and Nico kicks off his sneakers, which, to my horror, go flying down the hallway. I race over to retrieve them and place them gingerly in the shoe rack. We have barely left the house today, so I have no idea why his sneakers are caked in dirt. And when I look at his socks, they are equally dirty. How did that happen?

"Why are your socks so dirty?" I ask him.

"I was playing in the backyard, Mom."

"In your *socks*?"

Nico shrugs.

He ends up peeling off his socks, and underneath the socks, his feet are *also* dirty, but I guess less dirty than the shoes or the socks. I need to dip this kid in bleach tonight.

Spencer and Nico seem overjoyed to see each other, like long-lost friends, even though they were in school together literally two days ago. They race off to the backyard, as Janice shouts after Spencer, "Be careful!"

Janice is wringing her hands together, looking in the direction of the backyard. I don't know if I should offer to stay or if she even wants me here. What she really looks like she needs is a stiff drink. She finally turns to me, and I'm certain she's going to offer me some lemonade or cheese and crackers, but instead she says, "How often do you check Nico for lice?"

My mouth drops open. I want to be offended, but Nico has actually had lice three times. So has Ada, and that was much harder to deal with, because you can't exactly shave the head of an eight-year-old girl. That's the sort of thing she would have been describing in therapy years later.

But I definitely took a razor to my son's head. He wasn't thrilled about it at first, but when Enzo offered to shave his own head too, then it became fun.

"He doesn't have lice," I say.

She narrows her eyes at me. "But how do you *know*?"

I don't know what to say to that. "He's not scratching so…"

"Do you have a good lice comb?"

"Um, yes…"

"What brand?"

I don't know if I can take much more of this. I mean, I dislike lice as much as the next person, which is a lot. But it's not a favorite topic of conversation.

"Listen," I say, "I should get going…"

"Oh." Janice's face falls. "I thought maybe you could stay for a bit. I squeezed some fresh juice."

Her face fills with genuine disappointment. Even though she was so rude about my choice to be a working mother, if she does stay home all day, she might be very lonely. And I've never been great at making friends either. Maybe Janice and I got off on the wrong foot, and she'll be my first friend in Long Island. I mean, *on* Long Island.

"I'd love to try your juice," I say.

Janice perks up a little, and I follow her to the kitchen. Not surprisingly, her kitchen is immaculate. The floor looks cleaner than my countertops. She has a kitchen table like I do, and it has place settings and coasters on it. Janice reaches into the refrigerator and pulls out a giant pitcher of something thick and grainy and green. She pours two brimming glasses of it and slides one across the table to me.

"Don't forget to use a coaster," she tells me as I bring my glass to the kitchen table.

As Janice settles down at the table across from me, I examine the liquid in my glass. Well, it's almost a liquid. It has some properties of liquids. "What is it, exactly?"

"It's *juice*," she says, like I have asked a very stupid question.

I want to ask what she put in it that made it this vivid shade of green. I can't think of any green fruits that I enjoy eating. Well, there's honeydew, but I don't know if I would want to have honeydew in drink form.

But she's watching me, and I realize that I have got to take a sip of this alleged juice. Well, maybe it's better than it looks—it almost has to be. I wrap my fingers around the glass, lift it to my mouth, and then bottoms up. I take a mouthful of it and…

Oh my God.

This is not better than it looks. Somehow it's worse. This might be the grossest thing I've ever had in my mouth. It is taking all my self-restraint not to spit it right back into the glass. It tastes like she took the grass outside in the backyard, dirt and all, and then turned it into a drink.

"Delicious, right?" Janice takes a healthy swig. "And believe it or not, it's very nutritious too."

I just nod because I'm still working on trying to swallow the current mouthful.

"So," she says, "how are you liking your new house?"

"I love it," I say honestly. "It needs a bit of work, but we're very happy with it."

"Most houses do when you buy them," she says. "And I'm sure you got a very good price on it."

I lick my lips and am immediately sorry because they taste like the green substance. "Why do you say that?"

"Because nobody else wanted it."

Janice's words make me forget all about the bitter taste of juice in my mouth. "What do you mean?"

She shrugs. "Only one other person put in a bid. And they withdrew it."

That's not what our real estate agent told us. She made it sound like there were other bids, but they were on the low side. Was she lying to us? Were we really the only ones interested in this cozy but gorgeous house in an excellent school district?

How could that be?

"Why wasn't anyone bidding on it?" I ask Janice, trying not to let on how curious I am.

"I haven't the faintest clue," she replies. "It's a fine house from the outside. Well built. Good roof."

Well, that's a relief.

"It must be something on the *inside*," she adds.

Something on the *inside*? What's inside my house that scared off the dozens of other couples who must have visited the house?

I can't help but think of that horrible scraping noise that kept me awake at night. I was so happy when we got the call that the house was ours. But there hasn't been a day that has gone by since we moved in when I haven't wondered if I've made a horrible mistake...

"So," Janice says, crisply changing the subject, "how was dinner with Suzette and Jonathan the other night?"

I jerk my head up, feeling a flash of irritation. Okay, now it makes sense why she wanted me to stay. She wants to pump me for gossip about the neighbors. *That's* why I'm here—not to sample her juice concoction.

"It was good," I say. The last thing I want is to trash-talk Suzette and let it get back to her.

"Good? That's hard to believe."

"They seem nice."

She purses her lips. "They're *not* nice people. Trust me. I've lived next door to them for the last five years."

I have to bite my tongue to keep from telling her about how Suzette said the exact same thing about her. Clearly, there's a lot of bad blood between these two. And anyway, the truth is Suzette doesn't seem like a terribly nice person. As much as I tried to get to know her at the dinner, I disliked her even *more* by the end of the evening. "Jonathan seems nice at least."

"She's horrible to him," Janice says.

She didn't seem like the most attentive wife on the planet, but I wouldn't go so far as to say Suzette was horrible to him. "Really?"

"Any time he tries to touch her, she pulls away from him," she says. "She puts him down whenever she can. I can only imagine what their sex life is like."

I'm trying not to imagine that, actually.

Janice's gaze locks with the kitchen window, which has a perfect view of the front door of 12 Locust Street. She can see anyone entering or leaving the house from her kitchen. "Suzette Lowell is the worst person I've ever met."

Wow. I didn't like Suzette either, but that's quite an extreme statement.

"She seems..." I swish the green liquid around in my glass in lieu of drinking it. "She's friendly at least."

"Do you know that your husband is at her house right now?"

I did *not* know that. And Janice can tell from my face that I didn't know it, which seems to give her immense pleasure.

"She opened her door to him about an hour ago," she tells me. It makes sense she would know that, giving the stunning view she has of the front of Suzette's house. "He is still there."

"That's fine." I force a smile because I don't want to give Janice the satisfaction of knowing that this information upsets me. "He told me he'd be working on her yard in the near future, so I guess he decided to do it today."

"On a Sunday? That doesn't sound like a working day."

"Enzo works all the time. He's very busy."

Janice takes a drink from her glass and then licks away the green mustache it leaves behind. "Okay. Well, as long as you trust him."

"I trust him."

She smirks at me. "Then you have nothing to worry about."

Janice is trying to stir up trouble, but I try to ignore her. I do trust Enzo. I mean, yes, for whatever reason, it didn't cross his mind to tell me that he was heading over to work in the backyard of our attractive neighbor. But I'm not going to let myself be bothered by that. Maybe there are things I don't know about my husband, but I know for sure that he is a good man. He has proven that to me time and time again. And even if he weren't, I still don't think he would cheat on me.

He wouldn't dare.

*I am scared of you, Millie Accardi.*

And he should be.

# TWELVE

"Were you at Suzette's house today?"

I ask Enzo the question as casually as possible while he's brushing his teeth. If I'm trying not to seem like a jealous wife, during the toothbrushing process seems like a good time to bring it up. It doesn't get more casual than that, right?

He glances at me, pausing mid-brush. He waits a beat, then he starts scrubbing his teeth again. "Yes. I was helping in her yard. Showing her gardening tips. Like I said I would."

"You didn't tell me you were going over there."

"Is it important I always tell you where I go?"

He spits toothpaste into the sink. I think of all the times he has watched me spit toothpaste into the sink—too many to count. And then I think of all the times he has watched Suzette spit toothpaste into the sink—never.

"It would be nice," I say, "if you tell me where you go on the weekend. Isn't that supposed to be family time? Isn't that what you always say?"

He gives me an exasperated look. "Millie, this is a job. We need money—badly. What do you want?"

"Is she paying you?"

He doesn't answer. Which means the answer is no.

"So you went over there on a Sunday. And she didn't pay you. How is that a job?"

Enzo rinses his mouth out, then spits in the sink again, more aggressively this time. When he looks up, he does not seem pleased. "Millie, she already got me two new jobs. She is helping me. She is helping *us*." He waves his arms around. "How do you think we are supposed to pay for this house?"

It's an extremely fair point. Building a business is all about word of mouth. And Suzette can help with word of mouth.

His shoulders sag. "Look, I am sorry I did not tell you where I went. But you were doing the play-dating with Nico. And Ada always just wants to read. So I thought this is a good time to go over there because nobody needs me."

Again, he's right. Everything Enzo is saying is a hundred percent right. And as hard as he works, Enzo has always been around for our family. He used to participate in tea parties with Ada and her stuffed animals when she was little. Even I couldn't bear those boring teddy bear tea parties, but he sat through a million of them. He used to do different silly voices for the bears, although all the voices had an Italian accent.

"I'm sorry," I say. "I know you're just trying to build your business. I didn't mean to give you a hard time."

He smiles at me. "It is a little cute when you are jealous. You are never jealous."

It's funny because it's true. Women hit on him all the time, but I've always trusted him. I don't know why Suzette manages to push my buttons the way she does. Especially since she's married, so it's not like she expects him to run off with her.

"I am sorry," he says. "You forgive me?"

I don't answer right away, so he comes closer to me and then kisses me with his minty fresh breath. Predictably, the last residues of my anger melt away. I'm terrible at staying mad at him.

"Mom! Dad!" a voice shouts through the door. "Little Kiwi is molting! You gotta see it! Come quick!"

There is literally nothing that kills romance quicker than being told that a praying mantis is molting in your house. Enzo and I exchange looks.

"Later, Nico!" Enzo calls out. "I am…talking to your mom. We are having…important conversation. I will see later, okay?"

But Nico is not to be put off. "When?" he calls through the door.

Enzo sighs, recognizing the potential for sexy time is over. "Just a minute." He winks at me. "You want to see the molting?"

"I'll pass, thanks."

"But…" He glances at the bedroom door, then back at me. "We are good?"

I only hesitate for a moment. "Yes."

"From now on," he says, "I will tell you when I go over to Suzette's house. I give you my promise."

"You don't have to," I say quickly. "I trust you."

And I do. I trust him completely.

But I don't trust Suzette.

# THIRTEEN

My eyes fly open in the middle of the night.

It's that scraping sound again.

I haven't heard it in a few nights. I had hoped the house had finished "settling" or whatever it was that was making such a terrible noise, but there it is, as loud as ever.

I roll my head to look over at the clock on the night-stand next to the bed. It's two o'clock in the morning. Why is there a scraping sound inside our house at two o'clock in the freaking morning?

I hold my breath, listening as hard as I can.

I don't think it's an animal. I don't think we have rats scampering around behind the walls. I mean, I *hope* we don't. It almost sounds like…

It sounds like somebody is trapped and trying to get out.

Janice's words still haunt me. *It must be something on the inside.* There's something wrong with this house.

*Inside* this house. Something that scared off every other person who came to see it.

I can't stop thinking about it. It's driving me out of my mind.

Enzo is lying sound asleep beside me. The sound wasn't enough to wake him. Although to be fair, I could be playing the tuba right next to him, and he would sleep right through it.

If I wake him up, he is not going to be happy. He already told me he's got an early job in the morning that's a forty-minute drive away. But on the other hand, he acts like this sound is something I'm making up. I'm the only one who seems to hear it.

Finally, I crawl out of bed. I'm certainly not going to be able to sleep with that scraping going on. May as well investigate.

The hallway outside the bedroom is dark. I debate if I should turn on the light, my fingers lingering over the switch. I don't want to wake up everyone in the house, but I also don't want to fall down the stairs. As much as I love all the space in this house, I feel a jab of nostalgia for the small apartment in the Bronx where I could pretty much see everything going on if I did a three-sixty turn. There are so many nooks and crannies in this house.

So many places for someone to hide.

My eyes have adjusted to the dark, so I decide to leave the lights out. I carefully feel my way down the hallway to the stairwell. The noise is coming from downstairs. I'm sure of it.

"Hello?" I call down the stairs.

No answer. Of course.

I look back in the direction of the master bedroom.

Okay, there's a scraping noise on the first floor of our house at two in the morning that sounds like it could be created by a human. Am I really going to investigate this on my own? Even though it will make him cranky, wouldn't it be smarter to wake up Enzo so he could go with me?

But I've mentioned the scraping sound to him before. He has repeatedly claimed he doesn't hear it and tells me I'm being silly. He's just going to claim that it's the house settling again, then roll over and go back to sleep. And besides, I don't need a *man* just to investigate the first floor of my own house. I'll be fine.

Anyway, he's within screaming distance.

I grab the banister of the stairwell. For a second, the scraping sound grows louder—loud enough to send a creepy-crawly sensation down my spine. It's like whatever is making that sound is moving toward me.

Nope, that's it. I'm turning back. Enzo needs to wake up. If he doesn't hear this sound, then he needs a hearing test.

Except before I can turn around and go back to the bedroom…

It stops.

I stand there, waiting for it to start again. But it doesn't. The house has gone completely silent.

I'm not sure if I'm relieved or disappointed. I'm glad the awful sound has ceased, but now that the noise is gone, it will be impossible to locate it.

I walk downstairs anyway. I take the stairs slowly, descending till I get to the first floor. The first floor of our house seems incredibly still. I squint at the outline of our furniture, cloaked in shadows. My gaze darts from corner to corner, searching for the source of that sound.

Finally, I reach out and flick on the light switch.

There's no one here. The first floor is completely empty. I guess I shouldn't be surprised. And yet…

There was a noise. There was a noise coming from the first floor of this house. I did *not* imagine it. And as soon as I started down the stairs, the noise stopped. Is it possible whoever made that noise heard me coming and went silent?

No, I'm being ridiculous. Like Enzo said, it's probably just the house settling. Whatever that means.

# FOURTEEN

"Mom."

I am stirring a pot of tomato sauce, and I've got eggplant browning in a pan. Guess what I'm making? Pasta alla Norma. I looked up half a dozen recipes online and chose the one that got the best reviews. Then I took a shopping trip to purchase all the ingredients. And I went to the *good* supermarket—the one on the other side of town. I am working hard on this dish. If it doesn't make Enzo shed at least a single tear, I'm going to be seriously disappointed.

"Mom, Mom, Mom, Mom, Mom. Mom."

I put down the spoon I am using to stir the tomato sauce and turn to look at Nico, who does not do "patient" very well.

He's wearing the same jeans and T-shirt from his Little League practice today, even though I asked him to change when we got home because they were pretty dirty. But you have to pick your battles sometimes. He's been on the team for two weeks, and the coach told me he's one of the star players so far. And I especially liked the way all the other kids cheered for him when he came to bat.

"Mom." Nico's messy black hair flops in his eyes. "Where's Dad? He said he'd practice with me tonight."

"Maybe he meant after dinner?"

He juts out his lower lip. "But I want to practice *now*. Dad said he'd show me how to throw a curveball!"

I raise my eyebrows. "He knows how to do that?"

"Yeah! It's amazing. You think it's going to go right, but then it goes left, then it goes up, then it goes down, and then it goes right again!"

I don't know if this gravity-defying curveball is real or not. Nico hero-worships his father, to the point where I'm sure he imagines that curveball could go backward through time if that's what Enzo wanted it to do. Ada is the same way—both kids think Enzo walks on water. And I'm just an ordinary mom who makes subpar Italian food. But that's okay. Being ordinary has always been an impossible dream for me, so I'm happy to have achieved it. As far as I'm concerned, if my kids think I'm boring, that's great.

"I'm sure he'll be home soon," I say. "And we're going to have dinner in about half an hour."

Nico crinkles his nose. "What are you making?"

"It's your dad's favorite: pasta alla Norma."

"Can I have macaroni and cheese instead?"

If given a choice, Nico would eat macaroni and cheese for every meal, including breakfast. Ada would too. "I'll set aside some spaghetti for you with butter and cheese."

Nico seems happy with this compromise. "Can I practice by myself in the yard until dinner?"

I nod, thrilled that he's satisfied to practice out in the yard without either me or Enzo needing to participate. Nico happily darts out to the backyard so that he can get as dirty as humanly possible before it's time for dinner.

And now back to the pasta alla Norma.

The recipe says to sauté the eggplant until it gets brown, but they are not getting brown. They just seem to be getting mushy and disintegrating. I don't know what I'm doing wrong, because I'm a pretty good cook. It's like I can't figure out this one dish that I have to get right for Enzo. I mean, I don't have to, but…

He always seems to like the food I cook for him. When we sit down at the dinner table and he sees the plate of food in front of him, he always immediately leans over and gives me a kiss on the cheek. It's like a little way of thanking me for making him dinner, even if it's something simple like chicken and rice. But I've never seen him react to a dish like he did to that one he ate at Suzette's the other night.

What am I doing wrong? Why won't the stupid eggplant just get brown already?

*Crash!*

My head jerks up from the stove at the sound of shattering glass. My son is the world's expert at breaking things, so I am very familiar with that sound. And I'm very familiar with the panicked look on his face when he runs back in the house, clutching his baseball bat.

"Mom," he says. "I had an accident."

What. A. Surprise.

I follow him out to the backyard, and I'm expecting

to look up to find one of our bedroom windows shattered, but the reality is much worse. There is a broken window, but it's not in our house. It's next door.

He broke one of Suzette's windows. Great. He hangs his head. "I'm sorry, Mom."

"Don't say it to me," I tell him. "You're going to say it to Mrs. Lowell."

And I'm probably going to have to say it too. Because I have a feeling that Suzette is not the kind of person who shrugs off a broken window.

This is bad. Very, very bad. I don't know how on earth we are going to pay for this.

As I march Nico to the house next door, he acts like I'm leading him to the electric chair. I'm not excited about this either, but he's being *really* dramatic. You would think with the number of times he's broken something, he would be used to apologizing for it.

But as we get closer to the house, I hear voices coming from the back. A female voice and a male voice. And it's not Suzette and Jonathan. I would recognize that accent anywhere. My husband is in Suzette's backyard. *Again.*

What is Enzo doing at Suzette's house in the middle of the evening? Especially after he *specifically* told me he wouldn't go over there without telling me.

I'm so mad, I stomp across Suzette's front lawn to her door. Since Enzo works on yards, I'm pretty anal about never cutting across people's lawns and ruining the grass, but I don't care right now. I'm pissed off. I push my thumb into the doorbell, and without waiting for somebody to answer, I press it again. Then a third time, for good measure.

"Can I press it too?" Nico asks, wanting to get in on the fun.

"Go for it."

By the time Suzette answers the door, looking somewhat hassled, we have managed to ring the bell at least seven times. But when I see her wearing teeny tiny shorts and a tank top that is tied off to reveal her midriff, I feel absolutely no sympathy for bothering her.

Or even for her broken window.

"Millie." She flashes me an exasperated look, which only grows more irritated when she sees Nico. "I could hear the doorbell fine. Once will do."

"Is Enzo here?"

Her irritation vanishes, and a smile creeps across her lips. "Yes. He's just been helping me out in the backyard."

At that moment, Enzo emerges from the back, wearing jeans and a grimy white T-shirt, his hands coated in a healthy layer of dirt. "Can I use the kitchen sink?" he starts to ask, and then he sees me and freezes. "Millie?"

Suzette is eating up this drama, but as much as I hate to disappoint her, I'm not here to catch my husband. We have a more pressing matter. I put my hand on Nico's shoulder and give it a squeeze.

"I broke your window," he says. "I'm really, really sorry."

"My goodness." Suzette clasps a hand to her chest. "I *thought* I heard glass breaking!"

"Nico." Enzo frowns. "I told you to be careful hitting the ball in the backyard, yes?"

I raise an eyebrow at him. "Well, he *thought* you were going to be playing with him."

Now it's Enzo's turn to look guilty. He should have

known better though. When you tell your nine-year-old son that you're going to play baseball with him, it's a good idea to actually do it. Or else bad things happen. Windows get broken.

"Which window was it?" Suzette asks.

"It's on the second floor," I say. "The middle one on the side."

"Oh." She taps a manicured fingernail on her chin. "The stained-glass window."

Stained glass? Oh God, that sounds extremely expensive. Enzo's eyes widen—he's clearly thinking the same thing. There's absolutely no way we're going to be able to afford to pay for a new stained-glass window.

"What if..." I say tentatively, "Nico performs chores around your house until he's paid off the window?"

Suzette clearly does not like this idea. Her whole body goes rigid. "I'm not sure about that."

I need to sell this because we can*not* pay for that window ourselves. "It's the only way for him to learn to take responsibility for his actions."

I look over at Enzo for support. He nods his head slowly. "Yes, I agree. Suzette, I think it would be very good for my son to be able to do the chores for you."

"I *have* someone to do chores." Suzette folds her arms across her chest. "Martha comes two days a week!"

"Then that leaves five days a week for Nico to come," I point out.

I'm fairly sure Suzette would have refused, but Enzo scrunches his brows together, his dark eyes narrowing. "Is there a *reason* why you do not want my son in your house?"

Finally, she throws up her hands. "Fine! He can do a few chores for me."

For the first time since Suzette suggested Enzo teach her gardening tips, the tension drains out of me. Suzette hasn't mentioned money at all. We won't have to pay for the stained-glass window, and Nico will learn to take a little responsibility for his actions. And it also occurs to me that with Nico around, Suzette may refrain from hitting on my husband.

I have solved all my problems. And the sour look on Suzette's face is just a bonus.

# FIFTEEN

I have been tasked with the job of getting Mrs. Green home.

That is what I have been told. Mrs. Green had a mild heart attack, and she's fine. Meaning she's as fine as she was before. But I question whether she was actually fine before, because she has been fairly confused during her hospitalization, and her family told me she's been falling a lot. One of the things I've learned since I started working in the hospital is that a large number of elderly people who live alone probably should *not* be living alone.

And if you want to get really freaked out, I'll tell you how many of those same people are still driving.

Since getting my social work degree, I've worked in a variety of places. I started out working with children, but once I had a child of my own, I struggled to deal with some of the terrible things that happened to kids at the hands of people they were supposed to trust. Every night, I would hold Ada on my lap and sob about the atrocities I saw that day. It was tearing me apart.

It was Enzo who recognized what the work was doing to me and heard about an opening for a hospital social worker. I applied for the job, and it was the best thing that could have happened to me. I work with a primarily elderly population, and they need my help just as much as the kids did, but I don't cry all the way home anymore.

Mrs. Green is lying in her hospital bed. She's a tiny peanut of a woman, ninety-one years old, with a puff of downy-soft white hair and covers neatly tucked up to her armpits to cover the nightgown her family brought her from home.

"Hello, Mrs. Green," I say. "Do you remember me? I'm Millie, your social worker."

She smiles up at me. "Are you here to take out the trash? Because it's very full."

"No, I'm your social worker." I get closer to her and point to the badge on my chest. Then I raise my voice because I suspect that could be the issue. Her chart said HoH, meaning hard of hearing. "SOCIAL WORKER."

She nods in understanding. "Can you mop the floor too?"

"No." I shake my head and point more emphatically to my badge. "I'M YOUR SOCIAL WORKER. I'M HERE TO HELP FIGURE OUT HOW TO GET YOU HOME!"

She points at a pile of clothing that is on the little hospital dresser. "And can you fold my clothes for me?"

I'm not here to clean Mrs. Green's room or fold her laundry, but on the other hand, she's clearly very anxious about the state of cleanliness of her room. Maybe if I fold her clothes, she will trust me. And the truth is, a pile of messy clothes bothers me too. I can imagine being ninety-one years old someday, lying in a hospital bed and being bothered by the dirty floor and unfolded clothes. (Enzo will still be carrying sofas at that point.)

I don't have a mop with me, so I get to work folding her clothes. Unfortunately, all she brought is a big pile of nightgowns. Mrs. Green sort of seems like one of those women who wears nightgowns for all occasions. Again, I can see myself being like that someday. I look forward to a time when I can wear pajamas twenty-four hours a day, seven days a week, and not face any judgment for it.

"Hey!" she calls out. "What are you doing?"

"I'm folding your clothes for you, Mrs. Green!" I say as loudly as I can.

"You're stealing my things!" she gasps. She jams her thumb into the red nurse call button. "Thief! Thief! Call the police!"

Even though I recognize Mrs. Green is a confused older woman, my heart skips a beat in my chest. How could she accuse me of stealing from her? I'm just trying to help her fold her clothes, like she asked me to!

A second later, the nurse supervisor for the floor, a sturdy woman named Donna, comes bustling into the room. By this point, Mrs. Green is screaming at the top of her lungs that I'm a thief and the police need to be contacted. I have dropped her clothing and I'm holding my hands up in the air, just to make it incredibly clear that I am not stealing anything from her.

"What's going on here, Millie?" Donna asks me in

her thick Long Island accent. (Or is it *on* her thick Long Island accent?)

"I..." I swallow hard. "I didn't steal anything. I was just helping her with her clothes. I swear."

"LIAR!" Mrs. Green shrieks. "She was stealing my stuff! You need to call the police right now!"

I stand in the corner of the room, squeezing my hands together while Donna does her best to calm down Mrs. Green. It takes several minutes, but after tuning the television to some show about Christmas caroling (even though it's spring), Mrs. Green finally seems placated.

I, on the other hand, am a disaster.

I follow Donna out of the room, but my knees are still wobbly. Donna is utterly unshaken by the interaction. There's not even one hair out of place in the high bun she keeps on her head. But by the time I get back to the nurses' station, my head is throbbing.

"Are you okay, Millie?" Donna asks me.

"I... I didn't steal anything."

"Of course you didn't." She pulls off the stethoscope hanging from her neck. "You know she has dementia, right? It was all over the chart."

It *was* all over the chart. And anyone else would have shrugged off the interaction, but I can't. Not with my background.

Spending ten years in prison for murder changes the way you look at things.

Donna most likely doesn't know anything about it, and I'm not eager to tell her the story. The short version is that when I was a teenager, a boy tried to rape my best friend. I walked in on them and bashed him on the head with a paperweight. Unfortunately, that didn't stop him. So I hit him again. And again. Eventually, he stopped…breathing.

The boy's parents were very wealthy, and they weren't about to let me off the hook for killing their pride and joy, even though their pride and joy was a rapist. A good lawyer might have been able to get me off, but I only had the public defender, and he wasn't a very good one. I was found guilty of manslaughter and served ten years in a women's prison.

It's not something I go around telling people. Even though I don't regret helping my friend, my time behind bars is not something I'm proud of. But when this hospital hired me a couple of months before I moved out to the island, I disclosed it to them because I had to. I wasn't sure if they would still want me after that, but they did. Social workers are in short supply.

Still, it leaves me feeling paranoid. At my last job, some objects around the hospital went missing, and I was the only one who got called in by the police to be questioned about it. It's not like they brought me into the station or anything serious like that, but it was very clear that because of my background, they were looking at me more closely than anyone else.

Is Donna looking at me that way? Does she think I really stole something from that room? Does she *know*?

"Millie," she says.

A cold sweat breaks out on my forehead. "Yes?"

"You look *really* pale. You should sit down."

Donna manages to grab a chair for me just before my legs collapse under me. She instructs me to put my head between my legs, and then she goes all nurse on me, grabbing one of the automatic blood pressure cuffs.

"Did you eat lunch?" she asks me.

"Uh-huh," I manage.

"You look queasy. Let me take your blood pressure."

Donna insists on wrapping the blood pressure cuff around my arm, even though I'm sure my blood pressure is fine. It's not a blood pressure issue. I'm just scared she knows that I'm a convicted killer. That's all, sheesh.

I sit there while Donna watches over me. The blood pressure cuff tightens around my left biceps, then the pressure eases up, then it tightens again, then the cycle repeats another two times. Donna swears under her breath, but finally, we manage to get a blood pressure reading.

"Whoa," she says.

That is not the response you want to hear from somebody after any kind of medical test. "What?"

"Your blood pressure is high," she says. "*Really* high."

"It is?"

"Yes. What was it at your last doctor's appointment?"

Truthfully, I don't go to the doctor very often. I used to go to my ob-gyn more frequently prior to getting my tubes tied, but given that my childbearing years are over, it doesn't seem like there's much point to it. The last time I went to any kind of doctor was about three years ago, which is ironic since I work in a hospital and I'm around doctors all the time.

"Well, I'm feeling anxious," I say, and it's not any better now that I know my blood pressure is high. "That's probably why."

"It's pretty high, Millie. You should call your doctor."

Great. One more thing to put on my plate. "Is it that big a deal?"

"No," she says. And before I have a chance to relax, she adds, "I mean, not if you don't care if you have a heart attack or a stroke."

That's ridiculous. She is completely overreacting. I'm not old enough to have a heart attack or a stroke. And I'm in pretty good shape. I don't need to deal with this blood pressure issue right now. Obviously, I'm just stressed out from the move. And last night, I got woken up *again* by that scraping sound coming from somewhere within the house, although thankfully it stopped before I had a chance to consider investigating.

I'm sure once everything settles down, my blood pressure will get better too.

# SIXTEEN

After dinner tonight, Enzo helps me clear the table. He's pretty good about doing stuff like that, or at least he's gotten good about it after several snarky comments over the years. But now, he's great. He brings all the plates and glasses into the kitchen without even being told.

"Another delicious dinner," he declares as he drops a couple of plates into the dishwasher.

I look down at the plate in my hand. It's Nico's plate, and it's hardly been touched. I didn't feel like fielding any complaints tonight, so I went with the tried and true macaroni and cheese. It's got his three favorite things: noodles, butter, and lots of cheese. And usually, he eats like a horse. Between him and Enzo, I'm lucky one of them doesn't take a bite out of me.

"Is Nico okay?" I ask. "He didn't eat his mac and cheese."

"Maybe he had big lunch?"

"Maybe..."

"Maybe he is sick of macaroni and cheese?"

"Never."

He grins at me. "Maybe he's been eating Little Kiwi's flies."

That horrible praying mantis has molted again. I have discovered every time it molts, it gets a little bit bigger. And it's already way too big, in my opinion. But Nico loves that insect. He asked to bring it to the dinner table last night after he came back from doing chores for the Lowells. That was a hard no.

I look down at the plate, resisting the urge to eat the leftover macaroni myself. I don't need the calories though, especially since I'm now having *health* issues. Although I still don't believe that I need to see a doctor. I looked it up, and automatic blood pressure cuffs are notoriously inaccurate.

"By the way," I say. "When I was at work today, this nurse checked my blood pressure while I was all keyed up over something, and it was apparently really high. She was making such a big deal out of it."

Enzo is usually sympathetic when I tell him stories about my day at work. But this time, he frowns at me. "Why is your blood pressure high?"

"I don't know." I scrape the mac and cheese into the garbage disposal and stick the plate in the dishwasher. "Hey, let's get the dishes going."

"But the dishwasher is not full."

"Yes, but Martha is coming tomorrow, so I want to get these dishes washed and put away before she comes."

He scratches his chin. "I do not understand. Why do we have to clean the dishes to get ready for the cleaning person? And before dinner, you were vacuuming."

"I just want to make sure everything is clean for her."

"But she is *coming to clean*!" He shakes his head. "Maybe this is why your blood pressure is high, yes?"

"Whatever," I mumble. "It wasn't that high."

"You said 'really high.'"

"No, I said *pretty* high." I try to push past him to get to the dishwasher. "Can we please get these dishes clean for tomorrow?"

Enzo reaches into the cabinet that contains the dishwasher detergent. He fills up the cup, then slams it closed and presses the button to start the cleaning cycle. When he's done, he turns to look at me, his muscular arms folded across his chest. "Okay, now we do not have dishwasher excuse. We can talk about your blood pressure."

"Oh God." I roll my eyes. "Look, I wouldn't have said anything if I thought you were going to make such a big thing about it."

"Why *wouldn't* I make a big thing about it?" he retorts. "You are my wife, and I want you to be healthy and live forever."

"That's...sweet, I guess," I admit. "But you're making too big of a deal out of this. I was just stressed out, and that's why my blood pressure was high."

"Fine. Then you go to a doctor and get it checked out."

"But—"

"You *never* go to the doctor, Millie," he points out.

"Neither do you. And you're even older than I am."

He looks like he's going to protest, but then his shoulders sag. "Fine. We both go see doctors. Okay?"

Fine. *Fine.* Enzo is obviously going to nag me about

this until I agree, so I'll go to the doctor and let them check my blood pressure, but I'm sure it will all be fine.

"Also," he says, "we should get life insurance policies for each other."

I don't like the turn this conversation is taking. It's bad enough I have to find a new doctor to see and make an appointment. "Life insurance policies? I don't know about that. Why would we get those?"

"Why wouldn't we?" He glances out the window, where we have a spectacular view of the Lowells' much larger house. "What if something happened to me? You would be alone with the children. You should have money."

I close my eyes, not wanting to imagine the death of my husband. It's almost unthinkable. "Okay, so take out a life insurance policy on yourself then."

"And you should have one too."

"So you get a payoff if I die?"

He presses his lips together. "Millie, you know this is not for me. This is for our children. So they have a roof over their heads. You know we are barely able to pay the mortgage as it is."

He's not wrong. A lot of people with children have life insurance policies. Several years ago, we were talking about it, but we both got so upset at the idea of one of us dying that we never ended up getting them.

I'm not sure if my blood pressure is high or not right now, but it *feels* high.

"I know this is a sad thing." Enzo picks up my hand in his. "I would not want to ever lose you. But this is responsible."

"Yes, that's true."

"Also," he adds, "Suzette recommended a very good insurance agent. I could give him a call tomorrow."

Oh. Suzette was behind this. Now it all makes sense.

"So for eleven years, you don't think we need life insurance," I say. "And Suzette says one word about it, and now we have to call this guy *tomorrow*?"

"Millie." His face flushes slightly, although it's hard to tell because of his olive skin tone. "I am *trying* to take care of my family, no matter what happens to me."

"Fine. Okay!"

God, why is he making me feel like *I'm* the one being difficult? Life insurance is a big deal, isn't it? I know it's important, but I don't want to rush into buying something, especially when we don't have a lot of disposable income.

It's not like I'm dying *tomorrow*, after all.

# SEVENTEEN

"Are you dying, Mom?"

Ada asks me the question as I'm saying good night to her. She's lying in her twin bed, the blanket covered in pictures of dogs pulled up to her chin, her little face scrunched up with worry. Ada has always worried too much. That girl keeps the weight of the world on her shoulders. Even as a toddler, she used to fret over everything, especially Nico. When Nico had so much as a sniffle, she used to cry over it.

"I'm not dying!" I swipe a few strands of black hair from her face. "Why would you say that?"

"I heard you and Dad talking about it."

Oh great. In our old apartment, we were acutely aware that the kids could hear through the paper-thin walls. Somehow, we have been under the misapprehension that it's different in this big house. But apparently, they can still hear everything.

"I'm not dying," I assure her.

"Then why are you getting life insurance?"

I sense that "in case we die" is not the right answer. Although technically, it is the right answer. "It's just in case some weird, unexpected accident happens. But that won't happen."

"It might."

Ada has the same crease between her eyebrows that Enzo gets when he's worried. She looks a lot like him—same eyes, nose, skin tone, thick black hair—but she doesn't have his personality. And honestly, for better or worse, she's not much like me either. She's one of those kids where you're not entirely sure where she came from. Maybe she's like one of her grandparents. My mother and I are estranged, but she always seemed very anxious.

And her intelligence is a mystery too.

"Ada." I climb into her small bed, curling up beside her warm body. In a few years, she won't let me do this, so I'm going to enjoy it for now. "I'm going to live a long time, probably after you have kids, and maybe even after your kids have kids. And your dad… Well, he's probably going to live forever."

If anyone in this world is immortal, it's Enzo, so it could very well be true.

"Then why do you need life insurance?"

This conversation could potentially go on the rest of the night. "Ada," I say, "you need to stop worrying and get some sleep."

She squirms under the covers. "Is Dad coming in?"

Right now, both of our kids require *both* parents to say good night before they can fall asleep. It's a routine that is simultaneously sweet and exhausting. After I'm done with Ada, my next stop will be Nico's room. That's probably where Enzo is now. We can trade off.

"I'll send him in next," I say.

That gets a smile out of her. As much as I hate to admit it, Ada is a total daddy's girl—from the moment she was born. I remember when she was an infant, there was one day when she was screaming her head off for two straight hours, and the second Enzo came home from work and held her, she quieted down in an instant. So if anybody can make her feel better, it's him.

When I arrive at Nico's room, I expected to see Enzo and Nico together in the room, feeding some flies to the praying mantis or something horrible like that. But Enzo isn't in the room. Nico is alone in his bedroom, and the lights are already out, although his eyes are still open.

"Tired?" I ask him.

"Kind of."

I squint through the darkness at his face. He also has similar features to Enzo, although I suppose he looks more like me between the two of my children, which isn't saying much. We named him Nicolas after Enzo's father. "Is everything okay?"

"Mm-hmm."

Nico has the praying mantis right by the head of his bed. It's a little hard to see in the mesh enclosure, but when I finally spot the long thin insect, I can see its little hands rubbing together. That bug definitely looks like it's plotting something. I know boys are into bugs, but why would *anyone* want something like that inside their bedroom? Is there something wrong with him?

No. There's nothing wrong with Nico. He is the happiest, most well-adjusted kid ever. Everyone loves him.

I cringe as I lean past the enclosure to kiss my son on the forehead. Tomorrow, I'll have to talk to him about moving it. Maybe to the other side of the room, or possibly out of the house entirely.

"Good night," I say.

"G'night, Mom," he says sleepily.

As I pull away, I glance out the window. It's close to a full moon tonight, illuminating our perfectly trimmed backyard. By the summer, I bet we will have the best yard in town. Enzo will make sure of that.

But my eyes are drawn to something outside our own backyard:

The Lowells' yard.

I thought Enzo was in the house, saying good night to the children like I am, but he isn't. For some reason, he is in the neighbors' backyard. But he's not working. He's standing next to Suzette, and they're talking.

I watch them for a moment from within the darkness of my son's bedroom. It could be entirely innocent. After all, they're neighbors and they have been working on the yard together. But there's something about it that hits me wrong. After all, it's ten o'clock at night. Why would my husband be out in the backyard with another woman?

He doesn't touch her. He certainly doesn't kiss her or anything like that. They seem to just be talking. But there's still something about it that makes me uneasy.

I can't shake the feeling that Enzo is hiding something from me.

# EIGHTEEN

It's six in the morning, and someone is breaking into our house.

It's not the scraping noise this time, which I have heard a handful more times since I tried to investigate. I've convinced myself that the scraping must just be a branch somewhere, which scrapes against one of the windows downstairs, but this is a very different kind of sound. These are loud noises. Footsteps. A door slamming. It's loud enough to make me sit up in bed, even though my husband is still snoring softly in the bed beside me. This is supposed to be a safe neighborhood. Stuff like this isn't supposed to happen here.

A resounding thump from downstairs has me sitting bolt upright. Is this one of those home invasions? If it is, what do we do? We don't have a gun. Enzo used to keep one in our apartment, but after Ada was born, he got rid of it. He was terrified of her finding it and hurting herself.

I'll just have to call 911 and hope they get here quickly.

Enzo is sound asleep beside me, completely unaware of the home invasion in progress. He came to bed so late last night, I never had a chance to ask him what he'd been doing with Suzette in her backyard. And now it's the last thing on my mind.

I shake my husband awake, more aggressively than necessary. "Enzo," I hiss. "Someone broke into the house. I'm calling the police."

"*Che?*" He rubs his eyes. His accent is heavier first thing in the morning. "Broke in?"

"Don't you *hear* them?"

He listens for a moment, while I practically want to scream. "Is Martha? No?"

"Martha? How did Martha end up in our house at six in the morning? How did she get in?"

"I give her key."

I stare at him, horrified. "You gave her the *key*? Why?"

"Why? So she will not wake you up when she comes in to clean!" He groans and throws his head back against the pillow. "Go to sleep, Millie!"

And now I hear the distant sound of a vacuum running downstairs. Okay, fine, I guess he's right. Most burglars don't take the time to vacuum the living room, so it must be Martha.

But even now that I know my home isn't being invaded, I can't go back to sleep. My heart is still racing. So instead, I get up and take a shower. I may as well start my day, especially since Nico usually takes some persuading to get out of bed.

I come down the stairs about half an hour later, freshly showered and dressed. I'll grab another banana from the kitchen so I don't get in Martha's way. She does an extremely thorough cleaning of the kitchen.

Except Martha isn't in the kitchen.

She's next to the desk we keep in the corner of the living room. And she's not cleaning the desk. She's looking through one of the drawers. I watch her for a moment, and all I can think to myself is, *What the hell is she doing?* I never rifled through any drawers like that when I was cleaning for people.

"Martha?" I finally say.

She raises her eyes. I may not know Martha very well—she rarely speaks to me unless absolutely necessary—but I know a guilty expression when I see one. I've got to hand it to her though; she composes herself very quickly.

"I needed to leave you a note, so I was looking for a pen and paper," she tells me. "We are almost out of cleaning spray."

Are we? That could be true. I suppose.

But I'm willing to bet she wasn't looking for a pen and paper.

Martha disappears back into the kitchen. I can't believe I caught her going through my desk drawers. That's a fireable offense. Granted, Suzette highly recommended her, but it's not like Suzette is high on my list of people I trust. There's something about Martha that I don't like. I wish we could get rid of her.

I don't know what to do. How do you even fire someone? I mean, it's been done to me before, so I understand the general concept, but my heart speeds up at the idea of it. My blood pressure is undoubtedly through the roof.

I start to sit down on the sofa to contemplate my next move, but it's a good thing I'm wearing slippers, because it turns out there is broken glass all over the floor in front of the couch. It takes me a second to realize that the vase I usually keep on the coffee table has been knocked over. A pile of lilies as well as endless shards of glass are scattered all over the floor.

Okay, now I'm pissed. And I have another reason to fire Martha.

I march to the kitchen, trying to avoid the glass, which seems to be just about everywhere. I'm surprised I didn't hear the shattering of glass from upstairs, only the usual thumps associated with cleaning. In the kitchen, Martha is spraying down the counter with a bottle that looks pretty much full to me.

"Martha," I say, "you could have warned me about the broken glass all over the floor."

She doesn't even bother to look up from the counter. "What broken glass?"

"You knocked over a vase on the coffee table," I say tightly. "And it broke. And there's glass *everywhere*."

Martha finally puts down her sponge. She faces me with her dull gray eyes. "I didn't break any vases. I haven't even started cleaning in the living room yet."

Seriously? First, she was going through my drawers. Now she's pretending she didn't break a vase when she obviously did. I can't believe Suzette recommended this woman.

"Martha," I say sharply. "If you break something, you should at least have the courtesy to admit it. I'm not going to charge you for it." *But I am going to fire you.*

She blinks at me. "I don't break things," she says stiffly. "But if I did, I would admit it."

"Then who broke it?" I shoot back. "Did it just walk off the table and break itself?"

This is unbelievable. It's not like I didn't break my fair share of glasses and vases and whatever when I was cleaning houses. But I always admitted it. It was obvious that I did it, so what would be the point of lying about it? But Martha is stubbornly refusing.

"What is going on here, ladies? What is the shouting?"

Enzo is standing at the entrance to the kitchen. Apparently, I was shouting. I didn't think I was, but I feel a little vein throbbing in my temple like it sometimes does when I raise my voice too loud.

Martha places her hands on her sturdy hips, on either side of her immaculate white apron. "Mr. Accardi, can you please tell your wife that I did not break the vase in the living room?"

Wow. Now she's turning my husband against me? This just gets better and better. "I found it broken when I came down here this morning. Who else would have done it?"

Enzo snorts. "That sounds exactly like the work of Nico."

Granted, Nico does break a lot of things. But when he does, he always tells me about it immediately. He's not one to break a vase and then just leave all the broken glass behind in the living room. I know him well enough to know he wouldn't do that.

"It wasn't Nico," I insist. "Besides, he's still asleep."

Enzo looks down at his watch. "Well, is time to wake up, I think."

Before I can stop him, he goes to the foot of the stairwell and starts shouting Nico's name. It takes a good minute of him shouting for Nico to get his butt down here until my son descends the stairwell with sleepy eyes and tousled hair.

"What is it?" Nico mumbles, still rubbing his eyes. "Why are you bothering me?"

"Nico," Enzo says sternly. "Did you break the vase in the living room?"

There's a long pause while all three of us stare at Nico.

"Oh," he says. "Yeah."

I stare at him, astonished. "Seriously? Why didn't you say anything? I could've cut my foot open on the glass."

He shrugs. "You were asleep. In the middle of the night, I got hungry so I went downstairs to get some food, and that's when I bumped into the table and it fell."

Great. I knew he was going to be hungry after not finishing his dinner. Also, it disturbs me that the sound of shattering glass didn't rouse me from sleep. What else am I sleeping through?

"You could have tried to clean it up," I point out.

"You told me not to touch broken glass."

That is true. But still. I would have hoped Nico had more of a sense of responsibility, especially now that he's doing chores for the Lowells.

"Martha," Enzo says. "We are so sorry we thought you broke the vase. Clearly, we were mistaken."

He's being generous. *I* was the one who accused

her of breaking the vase. In my defense, it really seemed like she had broken it. But I know the feeling of being wrongly accused, and I feel terrible that I did it to Martha. Moreover, I have been accused without any sort of apology plenty of times. A woman I was cleaning for once accused me of taking a ring she left in the bathroom, and when she found it behind the toilet later that day, she didn't even tell me she was sorry. I do not want to be *that* woman.

"I'm so, so sorry," I say to her. "I just… I jumped to conclusions, and I was completely wrong. I hope you can accept my apology."

Martha doesn't say anything.

"And we will clean up the broken vase," Enzo adds. "Of course."

She rests her gaze squarely on my face. "I did not appreciate being made to feel like a *criminal*."

I suck in a breath. Why did she look at me like that when she said the word "criminal"? That was *not* just my imagination.

Is it possible Martha knows about my past? Does she know that I've been to prison? Oh God, has she told *Suzette*? The idea is unthinkable. Suzette would have a field day with that information.

But she couldn't possibly know. My last name is different now, and it's not like she has my Social Security number to do a background check. I'm just being paranoid.

"I am sorry we made you feel like a criminal," Enzo says, oblivious to the edge in her voice. "Will you please accept our apology?"

Finally, she nods. And without another word, she

does an about-face, marches back to the kitchen, and starts cleaning again.

"Come on," Enzo says to me. "We need to get this cleaned up before the kids get downstairs. There is glass everywhere."

I can't help but feel irritated that even though I now have a cleaning woman, I will be spending the beginning of my morning cleaning broken glass. Not that I haven't cleaned my fair share of it over the years. The irony is that if I hadn't accused her, Martha would have probably cleaned it for me.

So fine, she didn't break the vase. But I didn't imagine the look on her face when she said the word "criminal." She was *definitely* snooping in the drawer of that desk—I saw that with my very own eyes. And I'm not sure I believe her excuse.

Why was Martha going through my drawers? What was she looking for? Has the woman been digging into my past?

I can't shake the feeling that I don't trust this woman who Suzette sent to work for us.

# NINETEEN

It's not as easy as it seems to make an appointment with a new primary care doctor.

I called half a dozen practices in the area, and none of them said they were taking new patients. Honestly, I would have given up except Enzo kept asking me every night before we went to bed if I made that appointment yet. Finally, on my seventh try, I booked an appointment with Dr. Sudermann, but I had to wait three weeks to get in.

But here I am, wearing one of those gowns that opens in the back as I sit on the examining table, waiting for Dr. Sudermann to enter the room. I have already had my blood pressure taken, and the nurse made a surprised sound when she saw the number, which didn't make me feel great about the whole thing. So now I'm sitting here nervously waiting, and there's this breeze from the vent that is hitting me exactly where my gown opens up in the back.

After what feels like an hour of waiting, Dr. Sudermann knocks once, then enters the room. I saw a picture of Amanda Sudermann online when I booked the appointment, but I was not fully prepared for how *young* she would look. If someone told me she was still in college, I would believe it. Thankfully, she at least looks older than Ada does. But not by much.

Still, she has a confident air about her. And presumably, she finished medical school and residency, so she's got to be at least…thirty? Unless she's one of those child prodigies you hear about. But she has a sweet face, and that in itself is comforting. I can't imagine this woman giving me really bad news.

"Mrs. Accardi?" she says.

I nod.

"I'm Dr. Sudermann," she says. "It's nice to meet you."

I nod again. Maybe I can get through this appointment without saying a single word.

"I hear you have some concerns about your blood pressure," she continues.

"I had it checked at the hospital where I work," I say. "They told me it was a little high."

"It's *very* high." She sits down on the stool next to the computer in the room, logging in to access my file. "I'd like to do an exam and some tests to see if there's an underlying cause, but either way, I'd like to start you on a blood pressure medication today."

"I've been under a lot of stress," I say, hoping that could change her mind. "I recently moved, I have two young kids, and my job can be really stressful. If I weren't under so much stress, my blood pressure would be fine."

"Stress definitely contributes to high blood

pressure," she concedes. "Working on stress management is a great idea. A lot of my patients say that meditation has helped them."

I tried meditation once and found it impossible. How are you supposed to just sit there without thinking for five entire minutes? That's like not *breathing* for five minutes. But I don't say that.

"But either way," she says, "you need to start medication for your blood pressure. It's *way* too high."

Great.

Dr. Sudermann goes ahead with her exam, and the whole time, I'm seething with resentment. I'm not *that* old. I shouldn't be taking medication for my blood pressure. That's something my father did when I was a teenager, and he was *old* then. I am…well, at least five years younger than he was. I think.

I leave the office, promising to pick up the prescription at the pharmacy on my way home, and she also puts in orders for blood tests, a mammogram, and something called a renal ultrasound. All *this* because my blood pressure is a little high. Okay, very high. But Enzo will be upset if I don't do everything she tells me to do. (He, incidentally, got in to see a doctor a few days ago, and he has absolutely no medical problems whatsoever. He is a perfect specimen of good health.)

When I get back to the house, I notice Jonathan Lowell sitting out on the front porch of 12 Locust. They have a swing mounted there, and he is rocking slowly on it, looking down at his phone. When he sees me get out of my car, he raises a hand in greeting.

"Millie!" he calls out. "Do you have a minute?"

Not really. I don't feel like having a conversation with

my neighbor, but I also don't want to be rude, especially since Jonathan always seems extremely pleasant. I hope whatever he wants to speak to me about will be quick. I'm already feeling extremely stressed out since it took almost an hour for the pharmacy to get my medication ready when I stopped in on the way home.

Jonathan hops off his front porch and sprints across our respective lawns to talk to me. Enzo would hate him walking over the grass, but I'm not about to give him a hard time.

"How are you doing, Millie?" he asks me.

"Oh, fine," I lie.

He flashes me an apologetic smile. "Listen, we have enjoyed having Nico over helping out these last few weeks, but..."

Oh no, now what?

"Yesterday, he was putting some dishes away for us," Jonathan says, "and he dropped one of the plates on the floor. It wasn't a big deal, but he just left it there. He didn't tell anyone."

"Oh my God." I cover my mouth. I'm simultaneously surprised and not at all surprised. "I'm so sorry."

"Anyway." Jonathan runs a hand through his thinning light brown hair. "We're all set with him doing chores around our house to pay off the window. I think it's better if he stops coming."

"Right. Sorry. If I owe you anything..."

I hope to God he doesn't tell me I owe them money. Even though Enzo is getting extra business thanks to Suzette, we are still on a very tight budget.

"It's fine," Jonathan says. "Really."

I look over Jonathan's shoulder at the house behind

him. I see movement from one of the front windows, and I catch a flash of butterscotch hair. It's Suzette. And she's observing our interaction, for some reason.

Does she not trust me with her husband?

It occurs to me that this is my chance to give her a taste of her own medicine. She's been flirting with Enzo since we got here. How would she like it if I do the same with her husband? And while I'm not attracted to Jonathan, there's nothing wrong with a little harmless flirting, right?

I take a step closer to Jonathan. I tuck a strand of my dark blond hair behind my ear and offer him what I hope is a come-hither smile. It's been a while since I've flirted—I'm a bit out of practice.

"I really appreciate that." I slide my hand onto Jonathan's slim shoulder. I don't squeeze it or do anything suggestive, but I'm hoping it looks that way from the window where Suzette is watching. "You guys have just been *wonderful*."

"Uh, thanks." Jonathan flashes me an uncomfortable smile, and then he takes a step back from me, out of my reach. He takes a quick look over his shoulder, then glances back at me. "Anyway, you have a good day, Millie."

And then he runs back into his house as fast as he can, slamming the door behind him.

Wow. That was a quick rejection. Slightly humiliating, if I'm being completely honest.

Jonathan didn't even play along for a split second. The moment I touched him, he couldn't get away from me quickly enough. And the first thing he did was check back to make sure Suzette didn't see anything.

He knew she was watching him.

What is going on at 12 Locust Street? What does Suzette Lowell want from us? It feels like even though we have our shades down, she is always keeping an eye on us.

# TWENTY

I'm late getting home from work.

I usually make it out of the hospital by five-ish, and depending on traffic, I am walking in the front door by five thirty. But today was one of those days when nothing went right. We had a patient who was supposed to go home today, but the patient's daughter suddenly decided that she couldn't take care of her mother, so I spent the afternoon scrambling to make other plans.

I tried to convince the daughter that she could handle her mother, but she wouldn't budge. I then called three other family members, hoping one of them could provide a small amount of assistance my patient needed after her heart attack. I called a rehab hospital, but they rejected her insurance. At this point, I'm not sure what will become of this poor woman.

She is such a nice woman too. I would take her home if I could. Of course, I always say that. If I had my way, my entire house would be filled with patients whose families didn't want to take them home.

In any case, it's almost six o'clock by the time I pull into the garage. Enzo's truck is parked in front of the house, so at least he's home with the kids. Despite the fact that Janice is overprotective, I hate for my kids to be alone at home for any longer than an hour or two.

I unlock the front door to the house, trying to shake off the tension of my workday. I step into the foyer, and right away, I notice the silence. When the kids are home, especially Nico, it is never silent like this.

"Hello?" I call out.

No answer.

I walk around the first floor of the house. It's not nearly as large as the one next door, but it still takes me a minute to get through all that space. I step through the kitchen, which looks identical to the way it did when I made the kids bowls of cereal before I left this morning. (Janice recently expressed her horror and shock at the notion that I made the kids breakfast that did not include some sort of meat protein.)

Nobody is on the first floor. I'm sure of it.

I head out to the backyard next, assuming Nico is tossing around the baseball, trying to break a second window. But when I get out there, all I see is the perfectly trimmed, vividly green grass.

Okay, the kids aren't in the backyard either.

I climb the stairs to get to the second floor. The kids have taken to leaving their doors closed when they go to school, although our master bedroom door is open and the room is empty. Next, I tap on Ada's room door.

No answer. No sound coming from inside.

I turn the knob and push the door open. As always, the bed is perfectly made. I never have to tell her to do that. Frankly, I think it would bother her if she left for school with her bed unmade. Her bookcase is stuffed with paperbacks and hardcovers. And there's one shelf that has a few trophies she won on it. For a science fair and also something called a math fair, whatever that is. But no Ada.

Maybe they are all playing in Nico's room.

My son's room is the last stop. I tap on his door, my stomach clenching as I wait to hear his childish voice calling for me to come in. (Or not to come in.) But yet again, there's no answer.

I open the door so abruptly, I almost fall into the room. Unlike my daughter's room, it's a mess. The blankets are in a big messy lump in the center of his bed, and he's got laundry strewn everywhere. And that awful praying mantis is still in the enclosure next to his bed. Little Kiwi is here, but Nico is not.

Where are they?

# TWENTY-ONE

Okay, there's no reason to panic.

Enzo's truck is in front of the house, so he has been home. He must have taken them somewhere. Of course, it's not like our town is walkable. Where could he have gone without his truck?

I reach for my phone in my pants pocket. I tap out a message to Enzo:

Where are you?

I stare at the screen, waiting for a response. Nothing. It says the message has been delivered but not read.

I don't feel like waiting for him to answer my text at his leisure, so I click on his name from my favorites to call him. The phone rings once, twice...half a dozen times. Then it goes to voicemail.

Again, that in itself should not be concerning. When Enzo is on a job, he never picks up his phone. The equipment is painfully loud, and he's often wearing thick gloves that won't allow him to operate a phone. But then again, he can't be on a job, because his truck is in the yard.

I have this uneasy feeling in the pit of my stomach. Like something has happened.

I sprint back down the stairs, practically tripping on them. I check the living room and the kitchen one more time, looking for some sort of note from Enzo, saying he took the kids out for ice cream or something along those lines.

But there's no note. There's *nothing*.

I grab my phone again, wondering if I need to call the police. That seems like an overreaction though. It would be one thing if just the kids were gone, but since my husband is gone too, the assumption is that they are all together. Enzo will think I have lost my mind if I call the police on him. Besides, I don't trust the police—after spending a decade in prison for reasons I still think are a bit unfair, you can't help but feel that way. There's only one police officer that I trust, but I wouldn't call him unless it was an absolute emergency. And this isn't an emergency—yet.

Okay, I need to think logically. Enzo and the kids are not here, but his truck is here. That means wherever he went, he went on foot. The most likely thing is that he is still in the cul-de-sac.

I exit the front door, trying to calm my rapidly beating heart. This can*not* be good for my blood pressure. I took a pill this morning like I have every day for the last week, and Enzo bought me a blood pressure cuff to monitor it daily, but it's still high. It's not even a tiny bit lower.

My first stop is 12 Locust Street. As I get to the

front door, I can hear noise coming from the backyard. It sounds like Enzo's equipment, which is a good sign. He went over to work in Suzette's yard, and he brought the kids with him.

I press the doorbell, and after what seems like an eternity, Suzette comes to the door. She smiles when she sees me, but there's something in her smile that makes my skin crawl. I just want to collect my family and get the hell out of here.

"Millie!" she exclaims. "You look positively disheveled! Are you all right?"

"Fine," I mutter. "Um, are Enzo and the kids here? I need to get everyone home and start dinner."

"Enzo is here in the backyard," she confirms. "He's got so many helpful tips for gardening. Honestly, he is a genius, Millie."

"Are the kids out there too?"

She shakes her head, puzzled. "No, just Enzo. I haven't seen the kids. I think Nicolas has broken enough things in my house, don't you?"

The relief I felt a minute ago completely evaporates. "The kids aren't here at all?"

"No..."

When I got home, I felt secure in the fact that the kids had to be safe with Enzo. But if he isn't with the kids, then where are they?

I search Suzette's face, wondering if she's messing with me. I don't think making a mother scared that her children have vanished is a funny joke, but who knows with this woman. Except I don't think she's joking around. She hates the kids, so it's not like she would want them over here.

"Can you please go get my husband for me?" I croak.

Her voice softens. "Of course. Just a moment."

A second later, Enzo comes out from the back of the house, walking quickly. He has that same crease between his eyebrows that Ada gets.

Ada... I hope she's okay. Where could she be? That girl would *never* go off anywhere without telling me.

"Millie?" He frowns at me. "What is going on?"

I squeeze my hands together. "I just got home, and the kids aren't there. I...I thought they might be with you."

Enzo looks down at his watch and his eyes bulge. "You just got home *now*?"

I don't appreciate the judgmental look on his face. "Well, *you* weren't home either."

"Because I thought *you* would be," he shoots back.

I don't understand him. He got home before I did, so he had to have known I wasn't there based on the fact that my car wasn't in the garage. Yet he still left.

"Did you check the backyard?" Suzette asks unhelpfully.

"Yes." My face burns. "I checked *everywhere*."

Enzo looks over my shoulder at our house. "I'm sure they're hiding in there somewhere. We will go look. Ada would not have run off."

I can barely keep up with Enzo as he sprints across the yard to our front door. He stomps across the grass, smashing the blades with his boots—he must be *really* worried. Which in turn makes me even more worried. He's generally the more laid-back parent between the two of us.

I trail behind him, and coming up from the rear is

Suzette. Why is she following us? This is none of her business! I am tempted to whip my head around and tell her to get lost, but I've got bigger problems than Suzette right now.

Where the hell are my children? If they are gone...

The front door is still unlocked, and Enzo pushes it open. Just like before, the first floor of our house is completely silent except for the sound of my heart thudding.

"Was the door unlocked when you got home?" he asks me.

"No." I distinctly remember pulling my keys out of my purse. "I unlocked it."

"It's a very safe neighborhood," Suzette insists. "I always tell my clients that the crime rates are some of the lowest in the country."

*Shut up, Suzette. This is not the time for a sales pitch!*

"Ada!" Enzo calls out. "Nico!"

No answer. My heart is beating so fast, I feel dizzy.

"Millie, can you call the school?" he asks. "Maybe we find out if they got on bus to go home."

"The school will be closed," I remind him. "But I can call the...the police..."

"The police?" Suzette bursts out, her blue-green eyes widening. "That seems extreme. You really want to bring the *police* over here? The kids are probably just out riding their bikes somewhere."

Enzo gives her a sharp look. "Ada does not have a bike. And they would *not* have left without telling us. They would never."

"Nico would," she mumbles under her breath.

"Ada!" he calls out again. "Nico!"

I reach in my pocket again to pull out my phone.

We have to call the police. Part of me doesn't want to, because that will make it all real. They will not be two kids who just wandered off for a moment and are quickly found in a neighbor's yard. They will actually be *missing*. But then again, the first few hours after children go missing is crucial. We don't want to waste that time.

Suzette grabs my arm, her fingernails biting into my bare skin. "You're being ridiculous. Don't call the police."

I look up at her perfectly made-up face, and for a moment, I see a flash of real fear. Why doesn't Suzette want me to call the police?

Enzo is standing by the stairwell, frozen, as he stares at the wallpaper, his eyes narrowing. He is looking below the stairwell, although I can't tell what has caught his attention. I shake off Suzette's grip and join him. That's when I see it.

There is a crack in the wallpaper.

No, it's more than a crack. The wallpaper has been completely ripped in a straight line. And the pattern of the tear in the paper is the exact shape of a small door, the top of which comes up to Enzo's shoulder. We usually keep a large house plant in that exact spot, but it's been shifted over to reveal the outline of the doorway.

"*Che diavolo?*" he mutters.

He reaches out and pushes against the defect in the wall. To our surprise, the wall shifts and starts to push open. It takes him some amount of effort, and a terrible scraping sound fills the room.

And that's when it hits me.

"Oh my God!" I cry. "That's it! That's the scraping noise I've been hearing!"

I wasn't imagining that scraping sound haunting me during the night. That was *real.* That was coming from my own home. From this hidden door opening and closing.

Except who was inside my house, opening and closing this door while the rest of us slept?

# TWENTY-TWO

I grab Enzo's arm before he can wrench open the door. As much as I want to find the kids, I'm suddenly terrified of what's behind that door.

"Please be careful," I beg him.

He glances at me for a second, acknowledging my warning. Then he pushes the door the rest of the way open.

It's a small room, not too much bigger than a closet. There are no windows, giving the room a stiflingly claustrophobic feel. I stare into the small space, dimly lit by a single flickering bulb.

And in the corner of the room are Ada and Nico, crouched on the floor, staring up at us.

"Ada! Nico!" My eyes fill with tears of relief. "What are you guys doing in here? How did you find this room? Your father and I were worried sick!"

The kids scramble to their feet, wearing identical guilty expressions. I'm not even sure which one of them to hug first, but Enzo hugs Ada, so I go for Nico. He stiffens at first, but then he buries his face in my chest. As I cling to him, I take a better look around the small room. It's about half the size of either of the kids' bedrooms, and it's extremely dusty, like nobody has been in here for years. I'm surprised the light still works. In one corner of the room, there's a little pile of rusty nails. In another corner, there's a small stack of Nico's comic books.

"I'm sorry, Mom," Nico says. "I found this clubhouse to play in. I didn't know it wasn't allowed."

Only my son would rip through the new wallpaper of our house to find some dirty, disgusting room filled with tetanus-riddled nails and then make it his clubhouse. And apparently, he's been sneaking down here several nights a week to do this, based on how often I've been hearing that scraping sound, which nearly gave me a heart attack several times over.

"We were calling your names!" I say. "Didn't you hear us?"

Ada pulls away from Enzo, wiping her eyes. She is crying hard now. And when I touch my own face, I realize that I'm crying too. "We didn't hear anything!" Ada sobs.

Suzette has stepped into the tiny room, and she is examining the door. "It looks like there's a very thick layer of insulation here. It would've been hard for them to hear anything."

"We didn't hear a thing," Nico confirms.

Suzette is looking all around the room, like she's appraising it for when the house goes back on the market when we inevitably can't afford the mortgage. "I had no idea this little room even existed in this house. They must have wallpapered over it when they were renovating." She lifts her eyes to look at the ceiling. "Maybe they felt it wasn't stable."

I flash the children a stern look. "I cannot *believe* you've been hiding in some mystery room in the house that doesn't even have a stable ceiling."

"I'm sorry," Ada sniffles.

Nico doesn't apologize again, but he drops his eyes.

"All right." My heart rate seems to have decelerated to something normal. And my blood pressure… Well, I'm sure it's still high because it always is. But at least I don't quite feel like I'm about to have a stroke anymore. "Let's all leave this dangerous room under the staircase, please."

I evacuate the kids out of the room first, then Enzo goes, ducking down to avoid hitting the frame of the door, and I follow. Suzette lingers behind, looking around the tiny space. I swear to God, if she suggests we turn this room into some sort of playroom or something else along those lines, I might smack her. I do *not* like enclosed spaces like this. I had a bad experience that I'm not sure I'll ever entirely get over.

"I'm sorry," Ada says again as she wipes her eyes. "We won't ever go in there again. I promise."

She looks really upset. Ada takes everything so hard. "I know you won't, sweetie."

Ada is still crying, gulping to try to get it under control. But here's the weird part: When we came into the room, her eyes looked red and swollen. Like she'd already been crying when we busted into the room.

But why would Ada have been crying?

# TWENTY-THREE

After the scare this evening, Enzo won't leave the kids alone for a millisecond. He spends two hours playing baseball in the backyard with Nico, and he even convinces Ada to play the catcher. By bedtime, both of them are worn out, but Enzo seems to have tons of energy as he strips off his T-shirt and work pants.

"Did you check your blood pressure tonight?" he asks me.

You know what? I am getting super sick of him fretting over my blood pressure. "Yes," I lie.

I checked it this morning. After all the excitement this evening, I don't even want to know what it is now. I got the full workup my doctor recommended, and everything was negative. I'm just unlucky/defective.

"Did you try meditating?" he asks me.

He looked up a bunch of relaxation techniques that are supposed to lower blood pressure, and then he printed out a bunch of articles. Meditation topped the list, so he bought me a book about it, which is now collecting dust in one of our bookcases.

"Did *you* try meditation?" I shoot back. "It's so boring."

He laughs. "Okay, so we do together?"

"Maybe some other time."

"Okay. How about massage?"

I laugh at the way he wags his eyebrows. Enzo gives very good massages. If he's up for it, it's tempting, but I am so tired. And a massage is never just a massage. Not with him.

"Maybe later," I say.

He climbs into bed beside me and gets under the sheets. "I can't believe we have an extra room we didn't even know about," he muses.

"That's not an extra room. That is a hazard."

"Maybe it is not safe right now, no," he says. "But I bet with a little work, we could make it up to code."

"We are *not* doing that, Enzo."

"Why not?"

I throw up my hands. "You seriously need to ask me that question? You know how I feel about tiny enclosed spaces."

He knows. He knows everything I've been through in the past and how I've been locked in a place like that, which I could not escape. Something like that gives you permanent claustrophobia.

This would be a good time for him to drop it, especially if he's worried about my blood pressure. But for reasons I don't understand, he doesn't shut up.

"We could fix it up," he insists. "Suzette says that—"

"Oh? What does *Suzette* say? Please tell me everything *Suzette* thinks."

He presses his lips together. "You know she is a real estate agent. This is what she does. She is offering her expertise."

"You know," I say, "maybe you would make more money if you spent more time *working* and less time in her yard."

"I am only in her yard a little bit."

"You're always there!" I burst out. "In the middle of the night, no less!"

I hadn't yet confronted him about finding him in Suzette's yard at ten at night, and there's no time like the present, especially when I'm already angry.

He blinks at me. "I do not know what you are talking about."

"A few weeks ago, I saw you on Suzette's lawn talking to her while I was putting the kids to bed," I say. "What were you doing there?"

"I do not remember." He truly looks like he means it. It's very tempting to believe him. "She had some question. I think…she wanted a rose bush."

"At *ten at night*?"

He shrugs. "Is not so late."

Maybe not for him, when he's up until all hours of the night.

"Look," he says. "This is not about Suzette. It was *my* idea to convert the room. I thought the extra space would be nice."

"Extra space?" I burst out. "Enzo, the last place we lived was a two-bedroom apartment in the Bronx. This place still feels like a palace to me."

"It's just…it is a lot smaller than Suzette and Jonathan's house." He frowns. "You do not want that extra room?"

"I never want to go inside that room again." I shudder at the thought of it. "And I thought you, of all people, knew me well enough that you wouldn't even ask. If you want to do something with that room, you can buy some new wallpaper and seal it up so that I never have to look at it again. Okay?"

He opens his mouth as if to say something, but then he shuts it again. He does know me well enough to know I'm not going to budge on this. But at the same time, I can tell he still wants it. He wants to turn that tiny terrible room into some sort of playroom or office.

"Okay," he says. "We discuss it later."

Or never.

# TWENTY-FOUR

When I get home from work the next day, the whole house smells like glue. It's not pleasant.

"Enzo?" I call out.

I'm pretty sure he's home. Once again, I saw his truck parked outside the house. But maybe he's at Suzette's again. Maybe he's hidden in some passageway behind the wall where I'll never find him. After yesterday, I have no idea what to expect.

"Am here!" he miraculously calls back.

I follow the sound of his voice around the side of the stairwell. And there he is, painting glue on the wall below the stairwell. There's a tarp beneath his boots as well as a roll of what looks like wallpaper on the floor.

"I called the Realtor," he tells me. "I asked her where the old owners bought the wallpaper, and I got another roll."

"Why?"

He lowers the paintbrush as he turns to look at me.

"You said you want the room sealed up. So that is what I will do."

I am astonished. I thought for sure we were going to have to have five or six more arguments about this room before he agreed to seal it up. And somehow, here he is, doing it of his own free will. I haven't had to nag him once.

"I'm sorry I argued with you yesterday," he says softly. "I understand how you feel. And the truth is..." He looks at the crack in the wall that is the only remaining sign of the fact that there is a door concealed within; even the hinge is on the inside. "It makes me nervous too."

At his words, a shiver goes through me. That room is so tiny and stifling. I can't imagine what it would be like to be trapped inside there. Well, actually, I *can* imagine it. That's the problem.

He reaches for my hand with the one that isn't holding the glue. "Is better now?"

I take his hand and start to say yes, but then a terrible fear grips me. We haven't looked inside this room since yesterday. What if one of the children went inside again? What if we sealed the room up with them trapped in there? It is, after all, soundproof.

"Can you open the door?" I ask him.

He frowns. "But...is covered with glue."

He makes a good point. There is glue completely coating the wall, which would make it exceptionally hard to open. Yet I can't stop thinking about the idea that somebody could be trapped in there. And next time I hear the scraping, it will be that person trying to escape.

"Millie?"

I swallow a lump in my throat. "I just… I'm worried that…"

"The kids are upstairs," he says gently. "I asked them if they wanted to help before I got started." He adds, "They did not."

Okay, I'm being ridiculous. There's no reason to wrench open this door and make a huge mess just because I'm paranoid. "I can help you."

He beams at me. "I would love your help."

So we get to work spreading the pieces of wallpaper over the hidden door. I can't quite rest easy until the door is completely covered. And even then, I can't shake the feeling that this hidden room will come back to haunt me.

# TWENTY-FIVE

I'm in my office at work when I get the call from the kids' school.

There is nothing more frightening than being called by your child's school. There is nothing they could possibly want to tell me at one o'clock in the afternoon that is *good* news. The principal isn't interrupting my workday to tell me that my kid has won a spelling bee.

They only call for bad news. Like two years ago, when Nico fell off the jungle gym and broke his arm. That was a call at one in the afternoon.

I'm in the middle of a phone call with an anxious family that I can't seem to break away from, so I just stare at the cell phone screen, my panic mounting. By the time I manage to disentangle myself from the phone call, the call from the school has gone to voicemail. I listen to the message:

"Mrs. Accardi, this is Margaret Corkum, the principal

of Frost Elementary School. Can you please give me a call back right away at..."

The principal's voice is flat and unfriendly. This is *not* a call about winning a spelling bee. I quickly dial the number she gave me with a shaking hand.

"Margaret Corkum," the voice on the other end of the line answers.

"Hi?" I say into the phone. "This is Millie Accardi... I got a call..."

"Thank you for calling me back, Mrs. Accardi," she says in that same stiff tone as in the voice message. "I'm the school principal. I believe we met briefly when you took the tour of the school before your children started here."

"Oh yes." I vaguely remember Principal Corkum to be a pleasant, middle-aged woman with gray hair cropped short. "Is everything... What's wrong?"

"I'm calling about your son, Nicolas." She clears her throat. "He's fine, but I'm going to need you to come down here right away."

I grip the phone more tightly; my fingers start to tingle. "What happened?"

She hesitates. "You really should come down here so we can talk in person. Your husband is already on his way."

They called Enzo too? Oh God, this is not good.

I check my watch. I'm supposed to be meeting with a patient's family in twenty minutes, but my own family has to take precedence. I can get somebody to cover for me.

"I'll be right there," I tell her.

# TWENTY-SIX

I speed all the way to the school. I can't think straight, and I nearly go through a red light. I've gotten a fair number of calls from the kids' schools over the years, but this is the first time I've been told to come in without any explanation of what went wrong. But the principal said that Nico is fine. He's not dead, and he's not in the hospital. She said he's fine.

But what if somebody else isn't fine? That thought haunts me.

When I get to the school, I am comforted by the fact that there are no ambulances or fire trucks lined up outside. They make me sign in at the front desk, and it takes forever for them to make me a little temporary ID sticker to plaster on my chest. I follow the directions to the principal's office, where I find Enzo already sitting outside in one of those uncomfortable plastic chairs. He stands up when he sees me.

"They said for me to wait until you got here," he says.

"Do you know what's going on?" I ask.

He shakes his head. Even though he is as clueless as I am, I am really glad he's here. Enzo can be incredibly charming, and if Nico is in some sort of trouble, that could come in handy. Although I wish he didn't have quite so much dirt on his boots. He's left a trail leading into the room.

We sit back down on those plastic chairs. Enzo keeps tapping his foot on the ground, and after a minute, he reaches out to take my hand. We exchange nervous looks.

"I'm sure it's nothing serious," I say, even though I am sure of no such thing.

"I did not see any ambulance," Enzo agrees. The exact same thing I had been thinking. "Is nothing."

"This school is so snooty," I say. "He probably just, like, had too many rips in his blue jeans."

"He does have many rips in his jeans," he agrees.

He squeezes my hand. Neither of us really thinks that.

Finally, the principal opens the door to her office, looking much like what I remember. She's even wearing a white dress shirt and tan slacks like she was during the tour. But unlike during the tour, she's not smiling.

"Please come in," she tells us.

Enzo gives my hand one last squeeze, and we follow her into the office. Nico is already sitting there, and when I see his face, I gasp. He has what is definitely going to be a black eye, and his shirt collar is torn. He also looks like he's been rolling around in the dirt.

"As you can see, Nicolas was fighting during recess today," she says.

Nico won't even look at us. He's hanging his head, as well he should be.

I can't believe he was caught fighting. How could he do something like that? He's gotten into trouble for a lot of different things, but never anything violent.

"Who started the fight?" Enzo asks.

Principal Corkum's lips tighten. "Nicolas did."

"Nico!" I cry. "How could you do that!"

"I'm sorry," he mumbles into his torn shirt.

"Why?" Enzo addresses the principal. "What is reason they are fighting?"

"The other boy was making fun of a girl on the playground," Corkum says. "Obviously, that was not good behavior on the part of the other boy. But Nicolas's response was completely inappropriate. He could have told a teacher, or if he did not want to involve the teachers, he could have used his words. Instead, he punched the other boy in the nose."

"So," Enzo says shortly, "my son sticks up for girl, and now he is in trouble?"

"Mr. Accardi," she says tightly. "Your son is in trouble for fighting on school grounds. The other boy is at the emergency room and might have a broken nose."

"I broke my nose once." He waves his hand like it's no big deal, which makes me cringe. "It still works."

I thought Enzo was going to charm our way out of this, but he's just making things worse. I don't know what he thinks he's doing, but we should be groveling right now. "We are so sorry this happened," I say to the principal. "He will definitely be disciplined."

"I'm afraid that's not adequate given the circumstances," Corkum says. "We are going to have to suspend Nicolas for the rest of the week."

I was afraid of this the second I saw Nico's face, but

now that she is saying the words, I want to burst into tears. Suspended? How could that happen? How will this affect his future? Do colleges find out about third-grade suspensions?

No, that's not the issue. The issue is that for some reason, Nico took it upon himself to punch another boy in the nose when he's old enough to know better.

"Fine," Enzo says. "We go home then."

Nico won't even look at us as we make the walk of shame out of the school. He doesn't have the best impulse control in the world, but he's never done anything like this before. He never even pulled my hair when he was a baby. He's not violent.

At least he never was before.

As soon as we get out of the school and down into the parking area, Enzo lays a hand on Nico's shoulder. "Who was this other boy you were in the fight with?"

Nico's shoulders slump. "Caden Ruda. He's a jerk."

"It doesn't matter if he's a jerk," I say. "You can't start a fight like that."

"I *know*," Nico mumbles.

"Your mother is right," Enzo says. He pauses. "But I also do not want you to think it is not okay to stand up for someone who is being bullied."

Nico's dark eyes widen at his father's words.

"Enzo," I snap at him. "Nico is in a lot of trouble. He punched a kid in the face!"

"A kid who deserved it."

"We don't know that!"

He narrows his eyes at me. "I would think you of all people would be understanding about how important it is to stick up for someone in trouble."

He's right. I have always stuck up for people in trouble. And where has that gotten me? I went to prison because I stuck up for a friend in trouble—I kept her from being raped but then went too far and gave up ten years of my life. Enzo also sticks up for people in trouble, but he's always been smarter about it. After all, he has never been to prison like I have.

I had hoped that Nico took after him. I don't want my son to take after me.

"It was the wrong thing to do," I say stubbornly. "Nicolas, you're grounded."

"Fine," he mumbles.

"And you're coming home in my car," I add. I don't want to risk Enzo telling Nico again that he is a hero for breaking that other kid's nose.

I hate the way Nico won't look at me and won't offer a sincere apology. It's not like him. Nico isn't perfect, but when he gets in trouble, he's always quick to say he's sorry. When did that change?

It seems like my son is growing up, and I'm not sure I like what he's becoming.

# TWENTY-SEVEN

I check on Nico after dinner to make sure he's doing all right. He was quiet during dinner, pushing his food around his plate instead of actually eating it. Meanwhile, Enzo acted like nothing at all was wrong. He truly doesn't think our son deserves to be punished.

When I get into Nico's room, he's reading a comic book. As part of his punishment, we have taken away all his devices, but he loves comic books. He is sitting up in bed, his black hair disheveled, his eyes pinned on the page in front of him. His left eye is already turning black and blue, but when I sit at the end of his bed, I notice both eyes are bloodshot.

"Hi, honey," I say. "How are you doing?"

He doesn't raise his eyes from the comic. "Okay."

"Are you feeling upset about what happened today at school? It's okay if you are."

"Nope."

"Nico." I sigh. "Would you look at me?"

It takes him a few seconds to drag his eyes away from the comic. "Nothing's wrong. I'm fine. I just want to read."

I squint at him, not sure I believe him. "Does your eye hurt?"

"Nope."

I look over at the enclosure where Little Kiwi has resided ever since Enzo inflicted him on our family. I try to catch a glimpse of the praying mantis, but I don't see him. I look among the twigs and leaves inside, but he doesn't seem to be anywhere. Just a bunch of flies.

Oh my God. Did that horrible thing *escape*? This day can't possibly get any worse.

"He died," Nico says.

"What?"

"Little Kiwi died," he repeats. "He was molting and… I guess he got stuck in the molt, and he died."

"Oh!" I'm not quite sure how to feel about the death of an insect that I hated with every fiber of my being. But Nico seemed to really like him. "Where did you put him?"

"I flushed him down the toilet."

My jaw drops. That does not seem like a proper burial for a beloved pet, even if that pet is a horrifying praying mantis. I had assumed we would have to have some sort of somber ceremony in the backyard complete with a commemorative rock whenever Little Kiwi passed. "You flushed him *down the toilet*?"

"He's an *insect*, Mom," Nico says in an exasperated voice.

I'm not sure what to say to that. But something about it is highly upsetting to me. "What do you think you're going to do all week while you're suspended?" I barely know myself. He'll have to come to my office or go with Enzo on his jobs.

"I don't know."

"Maybe I can make a playdate for you one afternoon with Spencer when he's done with school," I suggest. The two of them have had a few playdates since that first one, and they both seemed to enjoy it a lot. "At least that way you'll have some social interaction. Would that be okay?"

Nico shrugs again. "Okay."

Then he picks up his comic book and starts reading again. I guess our conversation is over.

I wander back to our bedroom, but there is a sick feeling in the pit of my stomach. I don't know what is going on with Nico. He's always been impulsive, but it's at a new level recently. Moves are hard on kids though. Hopefully, this is just a phase and he'll bounce back soon and be his old happy self. And stop punching other kids in the face.

When I get back to our bedroom, Enzo is sifting around in the drawer of our nightstand, a frown on his lips. "Millie," he says when I come in. "Did you take any money from this drawer?"

"No, why?"

"I had fifty dollars in here," he says. "I think so, at least. But now...is gone."

"Maybe Martha took it," I blurt out.

He raises his eyes. "Martha?"

I still remember the way I caught her looking through the drawer of the desk in our living room. If she was going through that drawer, why not in our bedroom? I knew I should have fired her. "She was cleaning in here, so..."

"Maybe you should accuse her then. That went well last time, no?"

One more false accusation against Martha will be the end of her tenure here. And she *is* very good at cleaning. She's so...efficient. She works her butt off and never complains, even that one time I left dishes in the sink.

But I also don't want her here if she's stealing our stuff. There are other people who are good at cleaning and *don't* steal your money. Plus, I've never felt quite comfortable around her.

"Maybe I took the money out," Enzo says thoughtfully. "I think I did. I am just not sure."

"Enzo," I say. "Can we talk about Nicolas?"

He slides the drawer closed. He juts out his chin in a defensive expression, and I can already see how this conversation will go. "What is there to talk about? This is unfair."

"It's not unfair. He punched a kid in the face."

It bothers me that this makes Enzo smile. "A boy is being mean to a girl, and he stood up for her. Good for him!"

"He shouldn't be breaking other kids' noses."

"The principal says the nose is not broken," he reminds me. We did get an email from the principal, informing us of this. Thank God, because we can't afford a lawsuit. "Just bruised, right? Is nothing."

It also bothers me that Enzo seems a little disappointed that the kid's nose wasn't broken. "That's not the point."

"He's a boy. This is what boys do. They fight. I did this all the time when I was a boy."

"You punched kids in the face when you were a boy?"

“Sometimes.”

Okay, well, that’s interesting to hear. I don’t know if he is exaggerating or if he really means it. Like I’ve said, Enzo has studiously avoided talking about his life before he came to this country. But I do know one thing: he had to flee Italy because he beat a man half to death with his bare hands.

Although in his opinion, the man very much deserved it.

Even so, I have always looked at my husband as the more stable one of the two of us. I can be hotheaded, but he thinks things through. When he assaulted that man, he didn’t do it in a fit of passion. That man was his brother-in-law and used to beat his sister regularly until he finally killed her. He found the man, beat him to a bloody pulp, then hopped on a plane to LaGuardia that evening. Enzo knew exactly what he was doing.

He was exacting revenge.

“He got suspended, Enzo,” I remind him. “This is a big deal.”

“Third-grade suspension is not a big deal.”

It’s frustrating that Enzo is refusing to acknowledge that this is a big deal. It makes me wonder even more about his younger days and what he used to be like. Did he really used to get into fights like that all the time? Maybe he did. After all, he managed to assault his brother-in-law without any injury to himself. You don’t do that the first time you ever throw a punch.

Enzo Accardi is a good man. I believe that with all my heart. He has taken good care of our family.

But more and more, I wonder about his past. I wonder what he has done and what he is capable of doing.

# TWENTY-EIGHT

I don't want Nico moping around the house. He might be grounded, but I also want him to have some socialization aside from tagging along with Enzo to a few of his jobs or sitting in my office at work. So the next morning, while Nico stays behind in his room, I walk Ada to the bus stop so that I can arrange a playdate with Spencer.

As expected, Janice shows up to the bus stop with Spencer, who has his leash firmly attached to his backpack. She nods cordially at me, although I recognize I'm not her favorite person. But the boys are good friends at least.

After the kids board the bus and it zooms them away to school, I clear my throat and offer Janice my best smile. "Hey, any interest in a playdate after school today?"

She snorts. "A playdate? You have got to be kidding me, Millie."

Based on the vehemence of her response, I should probably just drop it. But I can't help myself. "Why not?"

"Nico was *suspended*." She is wearing a bathrobe on

top of a long nightgown, and she wraps it more tightly around her bony frame. "For *fighting*."

"He was defending a girl who was being bullied." I sound like Enzo, but he did have a valid point.

"I'm sure." Janice sneers at me. "Honestly, Millie, even if this hadn't happened, I hadn't planned to allow your son back at my house again."

"Why not? Spencer loves him."

"Spencer is a *child*." She pushes her horn-rimmed glasses up the bridge of her nose. "I did not appreciate Nico's behavior in my house. He was very rude. And I found him extremely aggressive. It doesn't surprise me one bit that he punched another boy."

As much as I hate hearing her talk about my son that way, part of me wants to get more information out of her. What was Nico doing at her house that she found so unacceptable? Is there something else that I should be worried about? Janice is a little strange, but she's very observant—I'll give her that.

"I hate to say it," she adds, "but this is what happens when you go to work all day and leave your kids alone. There's a price to pay for having a career while also trying to be a mother."

"Nico is a good kid," I say through my teeth. "The move has just been hard on him."

"I'm not so sure about that," she retorts. "His behavior has been reprehensible. And frankly, I don't approve of your husband's behavior either."

"Enzo?" I say. "What did he do wrong?"

"Don't you think it's *troubling* how often your husband goes over to visit Suzette?" Her eyes meet mine over the rim of her glasses. "And I suspect it's more than you think."

My face gets hot. How dare she imply that my husband is messing around behind my back? "He's helping her with her yard work so she'll recommend him to new homeowners. It's completely innocent."

"He's helping her with her yard work *inside her house*? When her husband isn't home?"

I hate the way a smile spreads across Janice's lips when she realizes that her words have finally hit home.

"You're mistaken," I finally say.

"No," she says, "I'm not. I catch glimpses through the windows, Millie."

I glance over at 12 Locust Street. At that moment, Suzette emerges from her house, wearing a skimpy robe. Between her and Janice, it feels like I'm the only one who decided to get dressed this morning. Suzette grabs the mail out of the box mounted next to their front door and waves to us. Janice waves back, and I somehow will myself to do the same. I hold my breath until Suzette has gone back inside the house.

When I look back at Janice, she's got a smirk on her face. I want to smack it off her.

"So…what?" I say. "You're just watching the cul-de-sac all day? Spying on the other two houses?"

"Somebody should," she snips back at me. "You might be better off if you did the same."

I follow Janice's gaze, which is directed at the front of my house. The front door swings open, and my husband comes out to collect the mail. He is still wearing his pajama pants, but he doesn't have on his shirt. He flashes us a broad smile and waves, and all I can think is, *Would it kill him to put on a shirt?*

"After all," Janice says to me, "*she's* watching too."

# TWENTY-NINE

I can't believe I forgot my phone at home.

It's a testament to how frazzled I have been lately. My phone is practically fused with my hand, yet I made it nearly all the way to work before realizing that I forgot to bring it. I am stunned that I did that. I may as well have gone to work without a shirt on.

I spend a few minutes debating if it's worth going back to get it. Nico is back at school this week, and if I don't have my phone, I'll spend the whole day worrying if something is going on that I don't know about. So I turn around and drive back home to grab it. Thankfully, I don't have any meetings until ten and traffic is light.

I manage to make it back home in a record twenty minutes, and I enter the house through the garage. Martha is cleaning today, which means the house is filled with the scent of her citrus-scented cleaning fluid. She has started bringing her own products, and I love the way they smell. I should ask her where she gets them for future reference.

I have to admit, Martha is amazing. I am still not convinced she isn't a cyborg, but I'm grateful Enzo insisted on hiring her. I'm also grateful he's talked me out of firing her.

I check the kitchen and living room, but there's no sign of my phone. If Enzo were here, I would ask him to call it, but nobody seems to be home except for Martha. I hear her upstairs, running the vacuum. I suddenly recall noticing my phone battery was low and sticking it on the nightstand's charging station as I was getting dressed. It must still be there.

I climb the stairs, and just as I get to the top, the vacuum stops. I walk down the hallway to my bedroom, my flats nearly silent on the carpet, and I can just barely make out the sound of a drawer opening. I freeze, wondering why Martha is opening a drawer. I do the laundry myself, so that isn't something she's responsible for. What could she possibly need from a drawer?

I quicken my steps, but I try to avoid the places where I've learned the floorboards tend to creak. I reach the master bedroom, and as quietly as I can, I peek inside.

Martha is in the bedroom, as expected. One of my dresser drawers is hanging open, and she's peering inside. I hold my breath as I watch her lift out the jewelry box I keep in the drawer. She pries open the lid, and as I watch, she removes a necklace and drops it into the pocket of her slacks.

Wow. I don't know if I would have believed it if I didn't see it myself.

"Excuse me!" I speak up.

Martha jumps away from the dresser, letting the jewelry box fall back inside as she slams it closed. "Oh! Hello, Millie. I…I didn't realize you were still here!"

Is she really going to try to pass this off like she didn't just steal a necklace out of my drawer?

"I saw what you did," I say. "I saw what you took."

Martha always seems so utterly cool and collected. But she doesn't seem that way now, as her watery gray eyes dart around the room. "I don't know what you're talking about. I'm just folding your clothing for you. I thought I would organize your drawers."

Yeah, right. "Empty your pockets."

"Millie," she says, "remember how you were wrong about the vase? I would never—"

"*Empty your pockets.*"

Martha squares her shoulders. "I don't have to tolerate being spoken to this way. You can consider this my resignation."

She starts to walk past me with her head held high. *Not so fast.* Before she can get out of the room, I step in her path, blocking her.

"I swear to God, Martha," I say. "I saw you put my necklace in your pocket, and you are not leaving this house until I get it back."

Martha is about two inches taller than me and has at least thirty pounds on me. But I am younger and faster, and more importantly, I'm willing to fight dirty if I have to. My son isn't the only one who knows how to throw a punch. One way or another, I am getting my necklace back.

Her gaze rakes over me, and it takes her a minute to figure out I am dead serious. Silently, she reaches into her pocket and pulls out the necklace studded with tiny diamonds that Enzo bought me for my birthday two years ago. Actually, they're cubic zirconia, and it's not worth much aside from the sentimental value—but that's a lot.

"I'm sorry," she mumbles. "I was just borrowing it so that—"

"Get out."

She wipes her shaking hands on her stiff skirt. Up close, the lines on her face are etched deeper than I thought, and for the first time ever, her gray hair is coming loose from her sensible bun. "Are you… Will you tell Suzette about this?"

"Maybe."

It would give me some degree of satisfaction to let Suzette know that her cleaning woman has been stealing. God knows why Martha decided to steal from me when everything Suzette owns is better than anything that I own.

She takes a moment to gather her composure, and when she speaks again, her voice does not waver. "If you tell her about me," she says, "I will tell her about *you*."

A vein in my temple throbs. "About *me*?"

"Suzette would be very interested to know that her new neighbor is an ex-con."

I take a step back, my heart pounding. My blood pressure right now is probably a billion over a million. It turns out I didn't imagine it the other day when I thought she emphasized the word "criminal." Somehow, Martha knows all about my dark past. "How did you find out?" I manage.

"Don't worry," Martha says in a maddeningly calm voice. "Nobody else will know your secret. Not unless you talk to Suzette about me."

I hate that she's blackmailing me this way, but I have to go along with it. What choice do I have? If Suzette finds out about my past, she'll tell *everyone*. I can't even imagine the awkward PTA meetings.

And what if the kids hear about it? That would be horrible. I don't want them to know about my past. Not until they're old enough to understand it, and maybe not even then.

"Fine," I hiss at her. "I won't tell Suzette."

"I'm pleased we have an understanding," Martha says flatly.

My cleaning woman brushes past me, jostling my shoulder as she heads toward the stairs. I follow her down the stairs and to the front door, just to make sure she leaves without stealing or destroying anything. It's only as she turns the lock to get out that I notice her hands are shaking.

# THIRTY

"You fired her?"

Enzo seems surprised when I tell him about what happened with Martha earlier while I'm making dinner. Since my pasta alla Norma all those weeks ago was not a raging success, I'm making macaroni and cheese for the gazillionth time because the kids will eat it. It's just easier that way.

"She was *stealing* from us," I say. "What was I supposed to do—give her a raise?"

He grabs some dishes from the cabinet next to the sink. He's not much of a cook, but he's always game to set the table and load the dishwasher after. "I am just saying, she had a good job here. And with Suzette and Jonathan. Why would she steal?"

"I don't know," I say irritably. "Do you think I have an insight into the psychology of a thief? Maybe she's a kleptomaniac."

He grins at me. "She never tried to corner me in the bedroom."

"Not a *nymphomaniac*. My God." I roll my eyes. "A *klepto*maniac. Like, those people who have a compulsion to steal."

"That is a thing?"

"I read about it in my psychology class."

"Yeah…" He pulls a handful of silverware from the drawer, although he never, ever seems to grab the right silverware. Somebody always ends up with two forks instead of a fork and a knife. I'm not sure how he manages that. Even if it was wrong when he took it out of the drawer, wouldn't he notice that while putting it on the table? "So did you give her a final paycheck?"

"Enzo." I turn away from my simmering macaroni and cheese to look at him. "She *stole* from us. She took the necklace you gave me, and she probably took that money you had in the drawer by the bed."

"It was only fifty dollars."

I haven't told Enzo what Martha said to me before she left. About the way she threatened me. I can't quite bring myself to divulge all the details, and I'm not sure why. The children might not know about my time in prison, but Enzo knows everything. Yet he doesn't quite understand the shame I feel over it. He doesn't understand why I don't want the kids to know and was in favor of telling them "before they find out on their own."

Anyway, I'm not handing over a paycheck to a woman who stole from me and threatened me.

Enzo notoriously has a soft spot for women. Possibly because of his sister, Antonia, and how he felt that he could have prevented her death if he had protected her better. That's why he defended Nico for standing up for that girl. He doesn't seem to think that women are capable of doing anything bad, but he's dead wrong about that one.

Frankly, after what we have been through together, he should know better.

"Look." I take a deep breath. "I don't know why Martha stole from us. But it doesn't matter. We already have enough financial problems on our own without somebody stealing from us. Whatever her issues are, I can't deal with her right now."

He cocks his head to the side. "What was your blood pressure this morning?"

"Enzo! That's not the point."

He hangs his head. "I know. I must do a better job bringing in money for our family. That's why I'm working so hard to build my business, and then we will have no money worries."

I feel terrible how much he beats himself up about our money issues. We're not doing that badly. I wish he wouldn't dwell on it so much. And I worry the kids will overhear and get nervous too—especially Ada.

"We're doing fine." I turn down the stove so I can put my arms around him. He quickly envelops me, and I rest my head on his firm shoulder. "You're doing a great job. And I bet in another year or two, we'll be fine."

"Yes," he murmurs. "Or maybe…sooner."

I don't know what he's talking about. Even though his business is growing, it's not growing *that* fast. One or two years is optimistic. We're going to be pinching pennies for at least the next several years.

Sometimes I wonder if it was all worth it.

# THIRTY-ONE

The whole family is at Nico's Little League game.

Ada doesn't usually want to go, but today she was agreeable to tag along. I'm glad she's here, because Nico hasn't quite been himself since his suspension a few weeks ago. But she's very clearly not interested in the game, based on the fact that she is sitting in the stadium with us, holding a paperback on her lap. Ada doesn't go anywhere without a book in her hand.

"What are you reading?" I ask her.

Her long dark eyelashes flutter. She has olive skin like Enzo, which doesn't show embarrassment the way mine does. But I can always tell when I've made her uncomfortable. "Sorry," she says. "I'll put it away."

"It's okay," I say. "I think baseball is pretty boring too." I nod my head at Enzo, who is quite literally at the edge of his seat, watching the game. He loves sports, but even more, he loves to watch Nico play sports. "*He* likes it though."

"I'm reading *Stranger with My Face* by Lois Duncan," she says.

"Oh, I loved that one when I was a kid. All her books, actually."

I feel a twinge of sadness, thinking about my childhood and how it all went wrong. What might have happened if I hadn't attacked that boy and ended up killing him? Then again, I have a good life now. I love my husband, and I have two amazing kids. If I had to suffer a little hardship (or a *lot* of hardship) on the way to get there, that's just how it had to be.

I take a swig from the water bottle I brought. It's only the middle of May, but the weekend is shaping up to be extremely hot. My phone says it's in the high eighties today. The kids look uncomfortable and listless.

Nico comes up to bat, so I nudge Ada to put down her book. He hasn't had a hit all day, and he's got that frustrated look he gets on his face sometimes. He is a pretty good hitter, so he must be getting in his head or something like that. I hope he gets a hit this time.

The pitcher throws the ball right over the plate, and I hear a crack as the bat makes contact. Enzo shouts with excitement. *Yeah, Nico!* It bounces once and rolls into the field. Nico tosses his bat to the side and makes a run toward first base.

The pitcher manages to grab the ball. With lightning-fast speed, he whips it in the direction of first base. Nico slides onto the plate just as the first baseman catches the ball. I cross my fingers and toes that he's not out, but then the umpire shakes his head.

"No. No!" Enzo is suddenly on his feet, yelling. "Not out! No!"

Apparently, Enzo thinks this was an unfair call. Which doesn't necessarily mean it *was* an unfair call.

Nico isn't any happier about this decision. The other kid is saying something to him, and he takes off his baseball cap and throws it on the ground. Nico is yelling something—I can make out the word "bullshit." I hold my breath, willing my son to back off and return to the dugout.

And that's when Nico throws the punch.

I could tell he was prone to getting angry—he's gotten riled up during Little League games before. But I never saw him get violent before. He punches the first baseman right in the gut, and the poor kid goes down hard. My heart drops into my stomach as I watch it happening and scramble to my feet.

Enzo witnesses it too. He freezes, falling suddenly silent. He was defending Nico about what happened on the playground, but this is harder to defend. That other kid didn't do anything wrong, and Nico punched him.

I don't understand much Italian, but I can tell he's cursing under his breath.

"Millie." He turns to me, his brow furrowed. "Nicolas just punched that kid."

"I saw."

"*Cazzo*," he mutters. "What is he thinking? We have to get him out of here."

The two of us make our way down to the field. The other kid is on the ground, sobbing. Nico is standing over him, breathing hard. The coach, a man named Ted who is the father of one of the other boys, does not look thrilled. He's got pit stains under both his arms, and he looks like he is not enjoying being out here in the heat and now having to deal with my son punching another kid.

"You gotta get him out of here," Ted says to Enzo in his thick Long Island accent. "We got a no-tolerance policy about violence between the boys."

"I am so sorry," Enzo says. "It will never happen again."

"Yeah, it won't." Ted holds up his hands. "Sorry, Enzo. He's off the team."

Enzo opens his mouth to protest, but then he shuts it again. He argued Nico's case in the principal's office, but this is different. We saw what happened. He punched that kid over *nothing*.

Instead, Enzo turns to our son, who is standing on the side, kicking his sneaker into the dirt. "Come on," Enzo says. "We go home now."

# THIRTY-TWO

We don't talk much in the car, partially because Ada is there. Enzo is the one driving, and his knuckles are bloodless on the steering wheel. Every time I glance over my shoulder, Nico is staring out the window. He doesn't even seem upset over getting kicked off the team just a few weeks before the end of the season. It's like it doesn't even matter.

What is wrong with my son?

When we get into the house, Enzo instructs Nico to stay in the living room. Nico drops onto the sofa and reaches for the remote, but Enzo shakes his head. "No TV," he says. "You sit there and be quiet. I will talk to your mother."

I follow my husband to the kitchen, and when we get inside, he turns to face me. He takes a shaky breath. "Okay, that was not so good."

"You think?" I sputter.

"He is good kid," Enzo insists. "He just…"

"He just punched another boy in the gut for no reason."

"Not for no reason. That was unfair call! He was not out!"

I grit my teeth. "That doesn't matter, and you know it. You don't punch another kid just because you don't like what the umpire said."

"He was upset..."

"He's nine years old—not three. It's unacceptable."

"Boys are aggressive." He runs a hand through his thick black hair. "That is normal boy behavior. Is good for him to fight."

I stare at my husband in astonishment. Given his reaction at the game, I had hoped we were finally on the same page about Nico's fighting, but clearly we are not. The fact that Nico's behavior has gotten him both suspended and kicked off the Little League team is a sign that things are out of control. Yet Enzo is still defending what Nico did.

"This is not normal behavior for a boy," I say firmly.

Enzo is quiet for a minute. I want him to agree with me that punching other kids is not okay for a boy to do, and it bothers me that he won't do that. He always seems very controlled in his behavior, especially compared with me. I've never seen him throw a punch, even when someone deserved it.

But he's done it—that's a fact. His fists are the reason he's in this country to begin with.

"Tell me," I say, "is this how *you* behaved when you were nine?"

Again, he hesitates. "Yes, I had fights with fists back when I was a kid. Sometimes I did. It was not a bad thing. Makes you tough."

That is *not* the right answer.

"Okay, okay." He shakes his head. "Is different here in America. I see this now."

I'm not a hundred percent sure we are a united front, but we go back out of the kitchen to where Nico is sitting on the couch in the living room. He is leaning back on the pillows, staring at a crack on the ceiling. He rolls his head to the side when we walk into the room.

"Am I grounded again?" he asks.

He's already been grounded. He was just grounded, like, five minutes ago. It didn't seem to make the slightest difference. I sit beside him on the sofa, and Enzo takes the chair next to the sofa.

"Nico," I say, "you have to learn to control yourself. What you did today was really wrong. You know that, don't you?"

"I'm sorry," he says, although he truthfully doesn't sound very sorry. "Grayson was being a jerk."

"It doesn't matter if he's the biggest jerk in the world. You can't hit him."

"Fine."

It disturbs me that Nico doesn't seem more upset over all this. Why isn't he crying? Why isn't he begging for forgiveness? Isn't that normal behavior for a nine-year-old boy who's done something wrong?

I look over at Enzo, trying to gauge if he thinks this seems normal. But I'm sure if I asked him, he would say something like, *Boys aren't supposed to cry*.

But there's something wrong. Lately, Nico has just become so…

Cold.

"What's my punishment?" he asks, like he's impatient to get it over with.

"Well, you are off the team," Enzo says. "So no more baseball."

Nico shrugs. "Okay."

Enzo seems thrown by how casual Nico's response is to being barred from baseball. The two of them used to practice every day. Nico used to beg for it. *When is Dad going to get home? We gotta practice!*

"And no devices for a month," Enzo adds.

Nico nods. He clearly expected that. "Is that it? Can I go?"

"Yes," Enzo says.

Nico doesn't waste a second. He leaps off the couch and runs up the steps to his room. He slams the door behind him—a very angsty move for a nine-year-old boy.

Enzo is staring at the steps after him. His expression is unreadable. But he doesn't look happy.

"I think," I say, "we might want to consider getting him in for therapy."

He looks at me blankly. "Therapy?"

"A talking therapist," I clarify.

His eyes widen like I've suggested we toss our son off the roof to see if he could fly. "No. *No*. That is ridiculous. He does not need that."

"It might help."

"For what?" Enzo throws up his arms. "He is just acting like a normal boy. It is all your uptight American rules. Nico is fine. He is *fine*."

I can't argue with him when he's acting like this, but he's wrong. I'm afraid there's something wrong with Nico that won't get better without professional help. I'm afraid that between me and my husband, Nico has inherited a combination of genes that has given him a propensity for violence much stronger than other kids his age.

So when dinner is over and the kids have gone upstairs for the night and I've got a moment to myself, the first thing I google is: *Is my child a psychopath?*

Amazingly, there are quite a few posts about it. Apparently I'm not the only woman whose child is having issues. One website has a list of common characteristics found in kids with psychopathic tendencies. I skim the list, growing increasingly concerned.

*A lack of guilt after misbehaving.* Nico barely apologized after punching either of those two boys. He didn't seem at all upset over what he did.

*Constant lying.* He used to tell us when he broke something around the house. But he didn't say a word about breaking that vase until we confronted him. And I get the feeling there's more he's not telling us.

*Cruelty to animals.* What happened to that praying mantis? After claiming he loved that pet, all of a sudden, he flushed it down the toilet.

*Selfish and aggressive behavior.* Well, what's more aggressive than punching a kid in the gut because you weren't called safe on first base?

Enzo might not be worried, but I am. And it makes me feel even worse to imagine there's a chance he might have inherited some of these tendencies from me. I mean, I don't think I'm a psychopath, but I didn't go to prison for picking daisies.

I'll give the dust a chance to settle, but I refuse to do nothing. If my son needs saving from himself, I'm going to save him.

# THIRTY-THREE

I'm walking back to my house from the bus stop when Suzette emerges from her front door to collect her mail.

She must be leaving for a house showing soon, because she is dressed to the nines in a skirt suit with red heels that are so high, I would fall on my face if I tried to walk in them. Her hair is so perfectly coiffed, it almost looks plastic. She waves to me, and it's hard to smile when I wave back, but I force it. I'm not in the mood for Suzette, so when she comes down her steps to talk to me, I almost consider making a run for it. But she's pretty quick, and before I can reach my front door, she has overtaken me.

"Millie!" she says. "How are you doing?"

"Fine. How are you?"

As Suzette smooths her hair, I notice a diamond-studded bracelet around her wrist that catches the sun. It looks a little like the necklace that Martha tried to steal from me, except I assume that *hers* is made from real diamonds. I hope Suzette is keeping that bracelet somewhere safe.

"Nice bracelet," I comment.

"Thank you." She gazes down at the bracelet. "It was a gift from someone very special. And I absolutely love your…" She rakes her gaze over me, clearly struggling to find something to compliment me on. "Have you lost some weight? Your face doesn't look nearly as puffy."

Apparently, that is the best she can do. Also, I don't think I've lost any weight. I'm just as puffy as ever. "Maybe" is all I say.

"Anyway," Suzette says, "I've been meaning to speak with you."

"Um, sure. What's up?"

She flashes me a blindingly white smile. I wonder if she has caps on her teeth. "So here's the thing," she says. "On the day before trash pickup, would you mind putting your trash out a little later in the evening?"

I stare at her. "What are you talking about? Nico doesn't put it out until after dinner."

"Right," she says. "And you guys must eat dinner super early. Because when *we* are eating dinner, we can see your trash out in front of the house. And it's there the entire evening. There's trash sitting on the sidewalk from, like, seven in the evening until the next morning." She sniffs. "Honestly, Millie, it's *unsightly*."

"Did you mention this to Enzo?" I ask. She seems to speak with him constantly, so I'm not sure why she's telling *me* about all this.

"He just seems so busy. I wouldn't want to bother him with something so trivial."

"Okay…"

"Plus, Nico takes care of the trash, doesn't he? The kids are more your domain, I assumed."

Suzette somehow assumes I am a 1950s housewife. But I don't feel like getting into it with her.

"Fine," I grumble. "What time would you like him to take out the trash?"

"Well, no earlier than eleven, certainly."

"His bedtime is ten," I say through my teeth. "He's *nine*."

"Oh." She taps her chin. "Perhaps *you* should take out the trash then?"

She has *got* to be kidding me. I'm tempted to tell this woman where she can shove that trash can, but at that moment, a truck pulls up in front of my house. A man with a big shaggy mustache and potbelly climbs out of the truck, a sour expression on his face. It takes me a second to recognize him as the plumber who came by a few days ago. I called him to fix our downstairs toilet, which was taking about an hour to flush. Enzo kept insisting he could fix it and we didn't need professional help, but it seemed like every time he tried to fix it, the flush took ten minutes longer. I didn't even tell him I called the plumber. He thinks the toilet magically fixed itself.

"Hey!" The plumber, whose name completely escapes me at the moment, ambles down the walkway to where I'm standing with Suzette. "I was here a few days ago to do a job, and you wrote me a bum check!"

*What?*

"I…I did?" I stammer. I don't know how that's possible. I keep track of every penny that goes in and out of our checking account. We don't have a lot of excess cash, but I'm certain we had more than enough to cover the $300 check I wrote for the plumber.

The plumber is not a small man. He's well over six feet, towering over me, and I have to take a step back as he comes closer. "You sure did, lady!" he growls.

Suzette seems entertained by this interaction. Why can't she go back to her house? This is *so* embarrassing.

"I'm so sorry," I say. "I thought there was enough in the account to cover it. Can I… Do you take credit cards?"

"I don't," he spits at me. "I told you when I fixed your toilet: only cash or check. And now for you, only cash."

Well, that's a problem. I don't have $300 in cash just lying around. I probably have forty dollars in my wallet if I'm lucky. Enzo has already taken off for the day, but he doesn't carry much money either. "Um," I say, "if you wait, I can go to an ATM…"

The plumber hikes up his pants and plants himself squarely on the sidewalk in front of my house. "I'm not moving one step until I get paid, lady."

"You know what," Suzette pipes up. "I might have some cash in the house. Give me a minute."

She dashes back into the house, walking admirably well in those four-inch heels. A minute later, she bursts from the front door with a wad of cash. She holds it out to the plumber, who immediately starts counting it.

"It's all there," Suzette assures him.

The plumber finishes counting the cash and nods at her. "You got that right, pretty lady." He tips his grimy baseball cap in her direction. "Thank you muchly."

He gives me one last dirty look and then climbs back into his truck. I'm pretty sure I am blackballed from that plumbing service. Hopefully, Enzo can get better at fixing the pipes.

Suzette watches the plumber drive away, then turns to me with an expectant look on her face. I know what she wants, and I'm going to have to give it to her.

"Thank you so much, Suzette," I say. "I…I promise I'll pay you back every penny."

"Oh, take your time." She toys with the diamond bracelet on her wrist, which glints in the sunlight. "Honestly, Jonathan and I have more money than we know what to do with. You can't even imagine how much we pay in taxes!"

Way to rub it in my face. I don't want Suzette to think of me as some impoverished charity case, racking up debts all over town. And I especially dislike the idea of owing anything to her. Technically, we never paid for her broken window, but that was different because Nico agreed to do chores. I'll pay her back today, if I can.

Except…can I? I thought we had more than enough money in the checking account to cover the plumbing bill. But obviously, we don't. Where did the money go? Enzo and I always discuss large purchases. He wouldn't have just taken the money out without telling me.

Would he?

# THIRTY-FOUR

After the plumber leaves, I log in to the computer to check my bank account.

A few days ago, we had more than a thousand dollars in the checking account. I watch the screen, waiting to confirm that the money is still there. My heart sinks when the balance of the checking account pops up on the screen:

$213

What the hell is going on? We're missing about a thousand dollars from our checking account. And we are not extremely wealthy like our neighbors. That's not an amount that we can just shrug off.

I access the transactions in the history. I do see a $1,000 withdrawal from a few days ago. Presumably, that is the culprit. Except who took that out of our account? It certainly wasn't me. I can't imagine Enzo would do that without mentioning it to me.

I'm running late for work, but this is far more important. If somebody stole money from our bank account, I need to do something about it ASAP. So I call the bank and end up on hold with them for fifteen minutes while I glance at my watch and text one of my coworkers to cover me at a meeting that I am definitely going to miss.

"Hello, this is Serena, your customer service representative," a perky female voice pipes up.

"Hi." I clear my throat. "I need your help regarding some money that is missing from my bank account."

"Oh dear," Serena says. I vehemently agree with that sentiment. "Let me see what I can find out for you."

I have to hand over all my bank information, and then I get to wait as I listen to the sound of keys tapping in the background. And then *more* keys tapping. And then more waiting. "Sorry the system is so slow today," Serena says cheerfully. "It's just one of those days, you know?"

I'm not in the mood to make small talk while I'm trying to figure out why money is missing from my bank account. "Uh-huh."

"Ah, okay!" she says triumphantly. "The withdrawal was made two days ago by Enzo Accardi, who is also on the account. Is that your husband?"

"Yes, but..." I frown. "My husband didn't..."

Did he?

"Is he saying he didn't withdraw the money?" she asks me.

"No. I mean, I just... I thought he would've told me. But..."

Serena seems like she's at a loss for words. I suppose family drama isn't her job. "Oh."

"Thank you for your help," I mumble. "I think I… I better have a talk with my husband. He probably… Maybe he forgot."

"I'm sure he forgot," she says in a super patronizing voice. "Is there anything else I can help you with today?"

*Yes, you can tell me why my husband took a bunch of money out of our account without saying a damn word to me about it.*

I hang up the phone and stare at the screen for a good minute. I am now extremely late for work, but I can't focus on anything until I call Enzo and ask him what happened with that money. And I'm not sure why the thought of doing that makes me so uneasy. I *trust* him. If he took that money out of the account, he had a good reason.

Finally, I select his name from my favorites. If he's working, he often doesn't answer his phone, but ever since the incident with Nico getting suspended, he's been answering immediately.

"Millie?" he says. "What is wrong?"

I rarely call him during the day, so he recognizes this is not a social call. "There's money missing from our checking account."

I had been hoping for a string of angry Italian curses. But the way he becomes dead silent confirms that this is not news to him. Even if Serena hadn't already confirmed it.

"I had written a check for three hundred dollars," I continue when he doesn't seem to be commenting. "And the check *bounced*."

"Oh." He sucks in a breath. "So what happened?"

"Suzette lent me the money," I say.

"Well, that is good."

"So I called the bank to figure out where the money went," I go on, "and they told me that you withdrew a thousand dollars."

More silence. He's not planning on making this easy for me.

"So," I say, "did you?"

There's another long silence. "I did," he says eventually.

"Okay. That seems like an awful lot of cash to withdraw from our joint bank account without telling me."

"Yes…" He's silent for a few more beats, and I can't help but think to myself that it sounds like he's stalling while he makes up a lie. "I am so sorry. We were short this month, and I needed the money to replace some equipment that broke. I thought I would have it back in the account before you noticed. I'll have it back tomorrow."

"Some equipment that broke?" I repeat.

"Yes, I need new lawn aerator and rototiller. Is expensive."

I swear, sometimes I think he's just making up these words. But I guess it sounds like a reasonable excuse, so I choose to believe him. It makes sense that if his equipment broke, he'd need to replace it immediately.

It's better than the alternative, which is that my husband is lying to me.

# THIRTY-FIVE

Nico is sneaking out.

Or at least that's what it seems like when I hear the back door opening on a sunny Saturday afternoon. Thank God we never bothered to oil the hinges, because I can hear that door opening and closing all the way across town. I toss aside my book and reach the back door just in time to catch Nico before he takes off.

"Excuse me, mister." I clear my throat. "Where do you think you're going?"

He looks up at me without a trace of guilt on his face. "Spencer's house. You said I could go whenever I want."

I did say that. But I thought he had been banished from Janice's home.

"Spencer's mom is okay with that?" I ask.

"She said it's okay as long as we stay in the backyard."

I'm relieved. I hated it when Janice said Nico couldn't play with her son, so I'm glad he's back in her good graces. Apparently, he's not allowed inside her immaculate house, but that's understandable.

"Fine," I say. "Just be home by dinner."

Nico nods, then hurries off in the direction of his friend's house. I was so focused on my son's imminent escape that I hadn't noticed my husband in the corner of the backyard. Not that it's unusual to see Enzo in the backyard—it's his favorite place—but he isn't working out there. Instead, he's talking quietly on his phone, a smile playing on his lips.

Who is he talking to?

I wave at him to get his attention. He blinks a few times when he notices me, and the smile momentarily drops off his face, but he recovers quickly and waves back. He murmurs a few more unintelligible words into the phone, then shoves it into the pocket of his worn blue jeans.

"Millie." He jogs across the lawn to talk to me. "I have very good news."

"Oh?"

"Yes! There's a potential client with two large estates that need services. Very big job. This is very good."

I glance down at his phone, protruding from his pocket. "Were you talking to the client?"

"Yes." He hesitates. "Well, no. Not exactly. That was Suzette on the phone. The clients…they are friends of hers. She would like me to meet with them tomorrow."

"Oh…" I had been hoping tomorrow could be a family day. "Where are you meeting them?"

He hesitates another beat. "It is informal meeting. At private beach."

Alarm bells sound in the back of my head. "A meeting at the *beach*? Will Suzette be there?"

"Well…yes. They are her friends."

I do not like any part of this. First, Enzo is ducking

out on a family day. Second, a business meeting at the *beach*? Third, I don't want him alone around Suzette in a bikini. Especially after that smile on his face when he was talking to her.

A fleeting thought drifts into my head. The other day, when the plumber showed up to demand his money, Suzette was wearing a new expensive-looking bracelet that she told me was a "gift." And then at the same time, a thousand dollars were suddenly missing from our bank account. Is it possible that Enzo used that money to buy a gift for Suzette?

No, I don't believe that. He wouldn't.

And yet…

"If you're going to the beach tomorrow," I say, "you need to take the kids. The whole family."

"What? No."

"I'm not asking, Enzo."

He shakes his head. "Millie, this is important business meeting."

"*Our family* is important too," I point out. "You've been working nonstop since we moved here—"

"For *us*."

"And we hardly ever see you," I continue. "You haven't taken the kids to the beach yet since we moved here. They would love it. Nico especially could use a day at the beach—he's been so down since getting kicked out of Little League. And I'll keep an eye on them. I won't disturb you until you're done with your meeting."

He's quiet for a moment, thinking it over. "Okay, yes. I see what you say. I will speak with Suzette. But… she will not be happy."

Yes, I'll bet he's right.

# THIRTY-SIX

We are on our way to the beach.

Suzette reluctantly permitted the family to tag along on the beach trip. I didn't hear the conversation, but I'd imagine she did everything in her power to keep us from going. But we're still here.

I'm looking forward to it though. It's a private beach on the coast that only Suzette and her elite group of friends have access to. The beach requires a special card to get in. I've been to a lot of beaches in my life, but this is most likely the snootiest beach I've ever been to. I bet it's really nice.

Enzo is driving, and as usual, he's driving way too fast. I thought he would stop doing that after we had kids, but he still does it. And it doesn't help that the kids love it.

"Can you please slow down?" I murmur as we pass a sign on the expressway that says 55 mph. We are at least twenty miles above that.

"Millie," he says. "*Everyone* is going this fast. We go slower, and they will all be going around us."

"I don't drive this fast," I point out.

He winks at me. "Yes, but you drive like old lady."

"No, I don't."

"My mistake. Old ladies drive faster than you."

I roll my eyes. "Very funny."

"It's true, Mom," Nico chimes in. "People are always honking at you to go faster."

Apparently in (on?) Long Island, you're not allowed to go less than twenty miles above the speed limit.

Except as we're taking the off-ramp from the expressway, the sound of a police siren comes from behind us. Enzo looks in the rearview mirror and swears in Italian under his breath. "You got to be kidding me," he mutters.

He pulls over to the side of the road while I resist the urge to say I told him so. The police officer takes his sweet time getting out of the car while Enzo fumbles around, looking for his license.

"Is Dad going to be arrested?" Ada asks in a worried voice.

"No," I say.

"That would be cool," Nico says.

"Still no," I say.

The cop is a guy in his thirties, who seems like he's not too excited to be doing this in the ninety-degree heat. Enzo rolls down the window and smiles charmingly at him.

"Hello, officer," he says in an accent so thick, it's hard to understand him. "Is problem?"

"License and registration," the officer says in a bored voice.

Enzo hands over the paperwork, waiting to hear what the cop has to say. He inspects Enzo's license and finally says, "You know how fast you were going, Mr. Accardi?"

"I so sorry," Enzo says. "But…see gas dial? Is almost empty! I must go fast to find gas station before we run out!"

The officer stares at him for a second, scratching his head. "It doesn't work like that, you know."

"No?" Enzo flashes him an astonished look, which actually seems pretty genuine. "I did not know!"

"No. It doesn't." He looks down at the license again, then back at my husband and the rest of us in the car. "Okay, I don't want to spoil your afternoon with your family. Go get some gas for your car. No need to go so fast."

"*Grazie*." Enzo smiles up at the officer. "You have good day, sir."

It's only after the police officer has gone back to his car and Enzo has rolled up the window that he winks at me. "Is too easy."

He never gets tickets. He always manages to talk his way out of it. Or *lie* his way out of it, as the case may be. It's astonishing how good he is at saying things that are a hundred percent untrue with a completely straight face.

I've always known my husband is an excellent liar. It just never bothered me until I suspected he was hiding something from me.

# THIRTY-SEVEN

Jonathan and Suzette beat us to the beach. Even though we were likely driving faster, they didn't get pulled over by the cops on the way over.

We park in the special fancy lot for the private beach, and when I get out of the car, Jonathan and Suzette are making their way to the entrance, which is guarded by a tough-looking guy in a black wife-beater T-shirt and swim shorts. He's like the private beach equivalent of a bouncer.

Jonathan is carrying two beach chairs and an umbrella, while Suzette just has a small tote bag slung over her shoulder. Jonathan looks like the typical beach-goer at the beginning of the season—a little too pale, a bit of a gut hanging over his swim trunks, his white feet shoved into a pair of flip-flops, a baseball cap covering his thinning hair. Suzette, on the other hand, looks like she has been going to the beach all winter. She is perfectly tanned, her Cartier sunglasses perched on her nose, and she is wearing a tiny bikini that shows off a spectacularly fit body.

After two children and forty-plus years of gravity taking its toll, my body doesn't look like that. It can't. But even when I was twenty-five, I never felt comfortable prancing around the beach in a bikini the size of a handkerchief, so today I am wearing a modest one-piece bathing suit with a cover-up over it. And much like Jonathan, I am painfully pale. I probably won't take the cover-up off the whole time, since I'm not much of a swimmer.

The beach bouncer is checking out Suzette in her teeny tiny bikini. Actually, a lot of people are checking out Suzette. Even *I'm* having trouble not staring a bit. When does she have time to get her belly that firm? And I'm guessing she doesn't have any C-section scars or stretch marks she needs to cover up.

Enzo has his T-shirt and trunks on, and he is wrangling our own beach furniture he pulled from the trunk. To be honest, I wouldn't have blamed him if he were checking Suzette out in that tiny bikini—he's only human—but I don't catch his gaze dipping below the neckline.

"Millie!" Suzette says. "What an…interesting cover-up you have on. I love how you don't feel like you need to spend a ton of money on a beach outfit. That is *so* you."

That was a backhanded compliment if there ever was one. But I can't really argue with it. I got the cover-up from the discount rack.

And while Enzo has not been checking out Suzette, I can't say the same for her. Her cool blue-green eyes rake over his body, and her lips curl. And he hasn't even taken his shirt off yet.

We're not even on the beach yet, and suddenly I want to go home. But I suppose it's better I'm here instead of leaving him alone with Suzette in her tiny bikini.

"Did you have trouble finding the beach?" Suzette asks. "We were wondering if you guys got lost along the way."

Nico quickly spills the beans. "Dad got pulled over by the cops."

Enzo laughs. "I was going too fast, they said."

"I'm sure you weren't." Suzette shakes her head. "The police around here are so overzealous."

"Well, we're glad you could make it," Jonathan says. Unlike his wife, there doesn't seem to be any overtone in his statement. He seems genuinely glad to see us. "How are you doing, Nico? We miss you coming over to do chores."

It's kind of Jonathan to say that, even though really I know they were sick of having Nico over at their house and breaking half their living room.

Nico shrugs.

I want to tell him he's being rude, but it feels like there's almost no point. His moodiness has gotten even worse lately. I finally called his pediatrician and took him in for a visit, but after listening to his heart and lungs, she didn't have much else to add. She didn't recommend therapy. In fact, she said the same exact thing Enzo said: *Boys can be aggressive sometimes. He's probably still adjusting to the move. Just give it time.*

"Where are the clients we're meeting?" I ask Suzette.

"Oh." She shrugs. "They canceled."

Enzo doesn't seem the slightest bit surprised, which makes me wonder if there was ever a client to begin with. I mean, a *beach meeting*? That sounded so made up.

But no, I'm being paranoid. I'm sure there was a client. People do cancel.

Suzette leads us to the beach to find the perfect spot to set up. Except she can't seem to decide on the perfect spot. We tromp through half the beach, past several spots that seem perfectly fine. Poor Jonathan is struggling with carrying the two chairs and umbrella, so I offer to grab the umbrella for him in addition to our own. Suzette could offer to carry at least one thing, but she doesn't seem inclined to do so. Jonathan is pretty good-natured about the whole thing though.

"Okay," she finally says when it feels like my arms are about to fall off. "This seems good."

Jonathan drops the two chairs on the ground, but just as he's flexing his arms, she says, "Wait, maybe we should go down that way. The sun is better over there."

Jonathan is ready to pick up the chairs again, but I've had enough. "Suzette," I say, "this is perfect. And I'm not walking one more step."

She rolls her eyes. "All right, all right. But, Millie, walking is good for you. It's slimming."

Would punching her in the face be slimming? Because that might happen today.

After we get our chairs and towels set up, I grab the spray bottle of sunscreen from my tote bag. Enzo always refuses it, but I like to spray it on the kids and definitely on myself. I'm the only one who ever gets sunburned, but isn't sunscreen supposed to prevent cancer or something like that? Anyway, the kids don't have a choice.

"Oh, Millie," Suzette gasps as she watches me spray down Ada. "You're not actually *spraying sunscreen* on your children, are you?"

I obviously am. "Yes…"

"Well, you know the spray has all sorts of toxic chemicals in it," she says. "And it's all in the air now. We're basically all *inhaling sunscreen* now."

Should I be more bothered about the fact that I might be inhaling sunscreen? Somehow, I'm not. "Uh-huh…"

"Also," she adds, "it's flammable."

Nico's eyes widen. "You mean we could *catch on fire*?"

"You're not going to catch on fire from your sunscreen," I tell him.

He looks disappointed.

Suzette reaches into her own bag and pulls out a white tube. "This is the best sunscreen on the market. It's all natural ingredients, *and* it has SPF 200! You can't find SPF 200 anywhere."

Why on earth would we need sunscreen that is SPF 200? Does she think we're going to be running through a circle of fire to get to the water?

Enzo has taken off his T-shirt, and I can't help but notice the way Suzette's eyes bulge as she looks over his dark, sculpted chest. I love that I have a handsome, muscular husband. But also, sometimes I wish he would let himself get fat and out of shape.

"Enzo," she says, "would you like to try my sunscreen?"

He laughs. "I do not need. I never get burns."

"Yes, but this is good for you even if you don't get burned," she says. "It prevents skin cancer, you know."

"Yeah?" Enzo says with interest, although I have been saying the exact same thing to him for the last decade.

"Yes, of course it does," she says eagerly. "You should at least put it on your shoulders. Here, let me help you."

My mouth falls open as Suzette squeezes some sunscreen onto her palm and then starts rubbing it onto my husband's shoulders. Is she really doing this? Is she really rubbing sunscreen all over my husband? This seems wildly inappropriate.

I look over at Jonathan, expecting that he will seem as horrified as I feel. But he has his own tube of obscenely expensive sunscreen that is apparently made for people who will be vacationing on the sun, and he's rubbing lotion onto his arms. Then he tries to get some on his back, but he can't quite reach, and of course, his wife is busy rubbing her hands all over my husband.

"I am good," Enzo says after this goes on for far too long. "I have enough. Will come off in the water anyway."

"Oh no," Suzette says, "this stuff is waterproof. You could swim all day, and you will still have SPF 200 protection."

Enzo's eyes widen. "Yeah?"

I am so sick of hearing about this stupid sunscreen.

"Ada," Suzette says. "Would you like to try this sunscreen?"

Ada looks down at the tube but then shakes her head. I don't blame her. She never burns, like Enzo, and I'm sure she doesn't want to smear that white cream all over herself.

"Nico?" Suzette asks.

Nico just stares at Suzette. He doesn't answer, but he gives her this really cold look. I don't know if I've ever seen him look at someone that way before, and the truth is, it sends a chill down my spine. But then he looks away, and I'm not sure if I imagined the whole thing.

The kids want to go in the water, and Enzo is happy to take them. I would have thought Suzette would be the kind of person who would want to sunbathe on the beach all afternoon, especially after the fuss she kicked up about where we were going to park ourselves. But as soon as Enzo says he wants to go in the water, she quickly agrees to follow.

"You want to come, Millie?" Enzo asked me.

I shake my head. "I'm just going to relax over here."

Jonathan rubs at a glob of sunscreen that is still intact on the bridge of his nose. He starts to follow Suzette, but before he can take more than a couple of steps, she turns to look at him. "No," she says. "You stay here. I'm going for a swim."

He nods and, without question, turns around to go back to his beach chair. He settles down and picks up a paperback. I crane my neck to look at the title. *Madame Bovary.*

"You don't want to go for a swim?" I ask him.

He waves a hand. "Not really."

"Because it looked like you were going to go in the water before Suzette told you not to."

"I don't mind."

Maybe he doesn't mind, but I find Suzette's bossiness infuriating, and before I can stop myself, I blurt out, "It just seems like it shouldn't be Suzette's decision whether you go swimming or not."

Jonathan shrugs and smiles. "She likes to have her space sometimes. I don't mind, like I said."

I've asked around, and it turns out Suzette isn't that successful as a real estate agent. Yet she has the biggest house by far in our cul-de-sac, in a town where housing prices are very high. Clearly, Jonathan is the one making all the money to support her lifestyle. Yet she's the one who gets to boss him around. I mean, he isn't even allowed to go in the water at the beach? That's nuts.

"It's a huge body of water," I point out. "It's the Atlantic Ocean. It seems like both of you could swim in it without bothering each other."

He rests his book down on his lap. "Do *you* want to go swimming, Millie?"

"No, that's not what I'm saying."

Jonathan looks at me blankly. Does he really not care at all how much Suzette bosses him around? I'd like to think that Enzo and I are equal partners in all our decision-making, but from what I've noticed, it seems like Suzette is making every important decision in the Lowell household.

Then again, Enzo did take $1,000 out of our joint bank account without telling me. But he's already put the money back. I'm sure he was telling the truth that it was for equipment for his business. Like, 99 percent sure.

The clear blue water is glistening under the sun. Both my kids are strong swimmers like Enzo—he used to take them to the YMCA when they were little, and he taught them both to swim before they could walk. I take stock of both of their dark heads bobbing in the water. Ada is near Enzo, and then Nico is a bit away from them and he's…

Huh. Why does it look like he's talking to Suzette?

What could Nico possibly have to say to Suzette? It seems strange, especially after that seething look he gave her earlier. I wish I knew what they were talking about, but I'm not anywhere close to being in earshot.

"Anyway," Jonathan is saying, "we're not leaving any time soon. I can swim later. This sunscreen will last for hours. Days, actually, if I needed it to."

I manage to tear my gaze away from the water. "Does it really?"

"Oh yes, it's great stuff." He digs into Suzette's tote and pulls out the tube. "Do you want some?"

"Sure," I say.

Jonathan hands it over to me. He doesn't try to rub it into my back and shoulders, which is very appropriate, given he's not my boyfriend or husband. It looks like a pretty ordinary tube of sunscreen, although I have to admit, it smells nice.

I'm about to squeeze some of this magical sunscreen onto my palm when I get interrupted by a sound coming from the direction of the ocean.

Someone is screaming.

# THIRTY-EIGHT

It all happens so fast. Drowning is quick.

There is a huge commotion out in the ocean, but I can't see much. I leap to my feet, and Jonathan does the same next to me. Whatever is happening is happening right where I saw my children swimming just a short time ago. The lifeguard has climbed down from his perch and is running for the shore, but it turns out he's too late.

Enzo is already coming out of the water holding her.

Suzette turns out to be the person who was almost drowning. She's clinging to Enzo's neck as he heroically carries her out of the water. She is still conscious, although her face is pink and she's coughing. As much as I would like to accuse her of fake drowning, she looks like she's in real distress.

Enzo lays her down on the sand and gets on his knees beside her. The lifeguard crouches next to her too, but Suzette's attention is solely on my husband.

"You okay?" Enzo asks her.

"Yes," she gasps, then starts coughing again. "That was just... It was so scary. I'm okay though." She reaches for my husband's hand. "Thank you. Thank you for saving me. You're my hero."

Oh, brother.

I look over at Jonathan, who does not seem the slightest bit bothered that an incredibly sexy Italian man is hovering over his wife, and she is pretty much drooling over him. Or maybe the drooling is from the near drowning.

"You sure you're okay, miss?" the lifeguard asks her.

"I'm fine." She manages to prop herself up on her elbows. "It just felt like my leg got tangled in something, and it was pulling me under. It was...terrifying."

"Maybe some seaweed," the lifeguard suggests.

"Yes," Suzette says, although she doesn't look convinced. I agree that it's not clear how seaweed could pull someone under the water, but I'm not sure what another explanation could be.

Ada and Nico have come out of the water, looking decidedly shaken by the incident. Ada is hugging herself, and Nico has planted himself at the shore, about ten feet away from us, an unreadable expression on his face.

"Suzette, dear," Jonathan says, "I think it would be best if we got you home."

"Perhaps," she says, "but I don't want to ruin everyone's fun."

"Do not worry about fun," Enzo says. That's when I realize she is still holding his hand. Or he is holding *her* hand. Either way, their hands are very much linked. "You must take care of yourself."

"You truly saved my life," she says. "Honestly, I was so scared and you...you saved me."

"Is nothing." Enzo waves a hand, but he's eating it up. He loves being the hero. Who could blame him?

Enzo helps Suzette to her feet, and Jonathan reaches out to assist her, but she doesn't make any moves to go to him. We end up packing all our stuff, because everyone is so shaken and it's too hard to enjoy a day at the beach at this point. I mean, *I* could've still enjoyed myself, but even the kids look like they want to leave.

Unfortunately, Enzo is helping Suzette, who you would think suffered some kind of leg trauma where she can't walk anymore, so we end up having to grab most of the furniture ourselves. The kids take one chair each, I grab two, and I manage to stuff the umbrella under my arm as well. It's not easy going, but somehow we make it back to the cars.

"Thank you again." Suzette gazes up at Enzo as he helps her hobble to Jonathan's Mercedes, depositing her directly into the passenger seat. "You saved my life."

And when she says it, she puts her arm on his biceps. Which, honestly, feels a little unnecessary.

The way she is gazing at him, I feel like if her husband wasn't a couple of feet away, and I wasn't standing there staring daggers at her, the two of them would be making out as we speak. Not that I think Enzo would do that to me. But if I didn't exist, who knows? Suzette is a very attractive woman, and although I dislike her, he doesn't seem to dislike her the way I do.

"Drive home safely," he says to her.

"We will!" Jonathan says cheerfully. "Thanks again, Enzo! I appreciate you looking after my wife!"

Is he genuinely *thanking* my husband for pawing at his wife?

I wish I could say that I'm relieved when they drive away. But it's hard to ever get rid of somebody when they live right next door to you.

# THIRTY-NINE

"What? You think I should let her drown, Millie? Is that what you want?"

I have been moping around all evening, ever since we returned home from the beach. Despite only having been there less than an hour, there is sand all over everything. Every crack of my body seems to have a few grains of sand in it. Even after showering, I still feel a bit sandy.

So yes, I've been cranky. And when we got into our bed to turn in for the night, I couldn't help but remark about Enzo's heroic rescue in the ocean.

"I didn't want you to let her drown," I grumble. "But did you have to save her like *that*?"

"Like what?"

"Like…" I sit up in bed, scratching at my toes, which still feel like they have sand between them. "Like, so… heroically."

His lips twitch. "*Heroically?*"

"I mean, she could have walked back to the car by herself. Or Jonathan could have walked with her."

He shrugs. "She wanted me."

"I'll bet." I grit my teeth. "And how *convenient* that the client canceled."

"No, not convenient." He frowns. "I wanted to meet the client. I want this job."

"You didn't look surprised when they didn't show."

"Because she told me this morning. But I still wanted to have beach day with you and the kids."

"Right."

He grunts. "Millie, this is ridiculous. I do not understand why you are upset."

"Okay, so if some handsome guy pulled me out of the water and was fawning over me, that wouldn't bother you at all?"

"No, it would not."

If that's true, that makes me even more upset. Why *wouldn't* he be jealous if some handsome guy were hitting on me?

"Because I *trust* you," he adds before I can get myself more worked up. "And you can trust me. You know that, yes?"

Do I? Before we moved to 14 Locust Street, the answer would have been a resounding yes. But the amount of time he's been spending with Suzette Lowell has made me suspicious. I mean, a conversation about *rose bushes* in the middle of the night? *Really?*

Yet Enzo is a good man. I believe that with all my heart.

He's staring at me, waiting for me to reply, and there's only one right answer: "Yes, I trust you."

"Good. Now calm down. If Suzette turns up murdered, you will be first suspect."

"Ha ha."

Enzo reaches over to shut out the light. He moves closer to me, his arm encircling my body. He's in the mood—I can tell. But I can't get into it. Even though he has assuaged some of my worries about what happened at the beach, one of them still remains, and I can't quite let it go.

"Enzo," I say.

"Shh," he murmurs, his hand sliding up my thigh. "No more talk about Suzette."

"But…how do you think Suzette got caught under the water?"

His hand comes to a quick halt. "What?"

"I mean," I say, "she said her leg got caught on something and that's what made her go under the water. What do you think she got caught on?"

"Seaweed?"

"So seaweed grabbed her by the leg and pulled her under the water?"

He removes his hand from my thigh altogether. "I don't know. Maybe some kids fooling around?"

"Which kids? Did you see any other kids swimming where she was?"

He is silent for a moment. "I do not understand. What is your worry?"

"I just…" I grip the blanket with my fists. "Did you notice Nico talking to her? Like, right before this whole drowning thing happened?"

He narrows his eyes. "No."

"I saw it."

He sits up fully in bed this time. I wasn't in the mood before, but it's safe to say that he isn't either anymore. "What are you saying, Millie?"

"I'm not saying anything. I'm just trying to figure out what happened."

"Are you saying our son tried to drown Suzette? Is that what you think?"

"No," I say, even though that is kind of what I was thinking. Enzo didn't see the way Nico was glaring at her before they went into the water.

"Well, good. Because he did not."

"You're sure?"

"Yes!" He shoots me an exasperated look. "I saw him. He wasn't near her. Like I said, it was seaweed or other kids."

But he's lying to me. I'm sure of it. Because I saw Nico next to her myself not long before she went under. He's just telling me what he thinks I need to hear. But what I want is the truth.

"Nico is a good kid," Enzo says stubbornly. "You should not worry so much. Is bad for your blood pressure."

Except I can't help but think that right now I have much worse problems than my blood pressure.

# FORTY

I wake up at three in the morning covered in sweat.

I was having some sort of bad dream. In the dream, I was floating in the ocean. And all of a sudden, a hand closed around my ankle and started pulling me down into the water. I was screaming, trying to get free, but the hand kept pulling and pulling, and sure enough, I started going under.

That's when I woke up.

It's been a week since our attempted trip to the beach went sour, and it feels like things haven't been the same since that day, although I can't put my finger on why. Enzo has been acting distant all week, but it's not something I could call him on because he isn't really doing anything wrong. He just seems oddly distracted.

The sky is clear tonight, and moonlight is streaming in through the windows of the bedroom. I roll my head to the side, expecting to see my husband sound asleep beside me. But that's not what I see.

Enzo isn't sleeping soundly. In fact, he's not in the bed at all.

What the hell?

I sit up straight in bed, wide awake. I'm the one who wakes up all the time in the middle of the night, but Enzo is a sound sleeper. I'm not sure if I've ever woken up to find him missing from our bed before. Where could he be? Is he in the bathroom?

But I can clearly see the master bathroom. He's not there.

The sound of a car engine catches my attention. I dart over to the window, and my mouth falls open when my husband's truck pulls into our driveway. What was he doing driving around our neighborhood in the middle of the night?

As he parks in the driveway, the cab of his truck is out of sight, so I can't see him climbing out. More importantly, I can't see if he was alone in there. I don't know what would be worse—if he were driving around in the middle of the night by himself or if he were with somebody.

Who am I kidding? *With somebody* is definitely worse.

My husband's footsteps grow louder as he climbs the stairs leading up to the second floor. He's moving slowly, trying not to make too much noise. He's hoping not to wake me. He's hoping that when he gets back to the bedroom, I will be sound asleep and none the wiser.

He is in for a surprise.

The door to the bedroom cracks open. Enzo peeks his head inside, and his eyes widen when he sees me sitting up in bed. "Millie," he says. "Uh, hello."

"Where were you?" I snap at him.

"I was…" He looks over his shoulder in the direction of the hallway. "I was thirsty. I just went downstairs to get a drink of water."

"In blue jeans?"

Enzo looks down at his jeans and T-shirt. He's also wearing socks, which he would never sleep in. It's very clear that between the time when he went to bed with me and this moment, he put on clothing.

Before he can come up with yet another lie, I say, "I saw your truck pulling into the driveway. So tell me again, where were you?"

"I am sorry." He rubs the back of his neck. "I was having trouble sleeping, so I go for a drive. I did not want to bother you or worry you."

"You went for a drive?"

"I did."

"Where did you go?"

He shrugs. "Just drive around neighborhood."

"By yourself?"

He nods. "Myself."

I remember the way he smiled at that police officer who caught him speeding and lied through his teeth. I've known him a long time, but if I did not already know the truth that day, I never would have known he was lying. And when I look at him now, I truly can't tell. Was he just going for a drive because he couldn't sleep?

Or was he doing something more ominous?

"You should not worry," he tells me. "Is nothing. Just a quick drive. And now I'm back." He lets out a loud yawn. "And it worked. Now I am tired."

He kicks off his blue jeans, then strips off his T-shirt. He takes off his socks one by one and tosses them in the laundry basket. Then he climbs into bed beside me and wraps his arms around me.

"Go to sleep, Millie," he murmurs. "It is late."

I want to go to sleep. I'm tired and I've got a long day at work tomorrow. I wish I could close my eyes and drift off the way he seems to be doing. I wish that more than anything.

But it's extremely hard to sleep when another woman's perfume is tickling your nostrils.

# FORTY-ONE

Enzo is cheating on me.

It's all I can think about as I drive home from work, even though I'm making excellent time on the Long Island Expressway (for a change). It's been two nights since Enzo snuck out in the middle of the night. Two nights since he came home stinking of what I'm pretty sure was Suzette's perfume. And I can't seem to get it out of my head.

Enzo is acting like everything is fine. He's sticking with his story about the random drive in the middle of the night. He hasn't tearfully confessed to a night of passion with Suzette. And I haven't smelled her perfume on him again.

I keep trying to come up with an innocent explanation, but I can't. When Enzo and I went to bed that night, he did not smell like perfume. He obviously got up during the night, went somewhere with her in his car and was gone until three in the morning, and then he came home and pretended like nothing had happened.

When I get home, Enzo's truck is parked in front of the house. Well, at least he's home now. Maybe I should talk to him about this. Even if there isn't an innocent explanation, maybe it's better to just get it out in the open. I never wanted to be the kind of wife who has to pretend like she's clueless about her husband messing around behind her back.

When I get inside, the kids' shoes are strewn about near the front door—they are obviously upstairs. But I don't see Enzo's boots.

So his car is parked outside yet he's not home.

He must be with Suzette.

I grit my teeth. I am *so* sick of this woman. I am so sick of Enzo running over to her house to work in her backyard. I had to watch my husband rescue her from the ocean when she was probably never even drowning in the first place. I bet she made the whole thing up. After all, who gets pulled into the water by *seaweed*?

I'm done being the good neighbor. I'm going to tell that woman what I think of her once and for all. And then I'm bringing my husband home with me.

I don't bother to take my own shoes off. I slam the front door to our house as I walk outside and tromp across both of our freshly cut lawns to get to 12 Locust Street. I press my thumb into the doorbell, letting it ring for far longer than I need to.

No answer.

I press it again for the second time with the same result. It's quiet inside the house. No footsteps coming to answer—nothing. And I don't hear the sounds of Enzo's equipment in the backyard.

What if they don't hear the doorbell because they're

busy? What if they are upstairs in Suzette's bedroom and they're…

Oh God, I don't want to think about it.

On a whim, I put my hand on the doorknob. I didn't expect it to turn, but it does. I turn the knob all the way to the right and lean against the door to push it open.

I step into the foyer of the Lowells' large house. It seems…quiet. I don't hear any beds a-rockin' upstairs, that's for sure.

"Suzette?" I call out. And then in a low growl, "Enzo?"

Again, no answer.

I walk through the foyer. Everything is still quiet. It truly doesn't sound like there is anyone home. But when I get into the living room, I notice something else. It's a distinctive odor. One that I have become very familiar with.

It's the stench of blood.

Why does this house smell like blood? And it's not faint. The house reeks of it. Whereas the last time I was here, it smelled like lilacs or something.

"Suzette?" I call out, and this time, there's a tremor in my voice.

I lower my eyes and that's when I see it, around the corner of the stairwell. A foot sticking out, attached to a lifeless body on the ground. A pair of dead eyes stare up at the ceiling, and a pool of blood spreads slowly across the living room floor. I recognize what I'm looking at immediately, and it takes everything I have not to collapse onto the floor.

It's Jonathan Lowell.

And someone's slit his throat.

# PART II

# FORTY-TWO

I've got to call 911. *Now.*

Of course, there is no saving Jonathan Lowell. He is very much dead. But what scares me even more is that there is still blood leaking from his neck. That means that whoever killed him did it extremely recently.

Is it possible they are still in the house?

A door slams somewhere in the house. It sounds like the back door. Is that somebody leaving the house? Or are they coming back inside to get rid of witnesses?

I pat my pockets, searching for my phone. All I can find are my house keys. And then I remember: I made a call while I was in my car and then dropped my phone in my purse. Which is currently back at my house. I don't know if Jonathan has a phone in his pocket that I could use, but there's no way I'm going to touch him. I've got to get back to my house to call the police.

I try not to think about the possibility that the killer could have escaped next door, to the house where my children live, as I do an about-face and run for the front door. I don't even look behind me. I make a beeline out of the house and back to my own home. I don't stop running until I get to my front door, and then I come inside and slam it behind me.

When I get into the house, the first thing I hear is the sound of running water coming from the kitchen. Then I hear the swears in Italian—my husband is home. At least he will know what to do in this situation.

I've been in scenarios like this before, and he is one of the few people I can trust.

When I get to the kitchen, Enzo is bent over the sink, washing his hands. Again, he swears under his breath. As I come closer, I catch a glimpse of the dark red liquid circling the drain.

What is he washing off his hands?

"Enzo?" I say.

He glances over his shoulder. "Millie, give me one second. I slipped and cut my hand with clippers. *Stupido*."

Except I don't see a cut on his hand. All I see is a lot of blood going down the drain.

"Something is wrong?" he asks me.

I open my mouth to tell him the terrible thing that I just saw. Jonathan Lowell is dead in the house next door. But as he turns around to reveal the blood all over his white T-shirt, I have a horrible feeling he already knows.

"Millie?" he says.

In the distance, the sound of sirens grows louder. Except I never called the police. Somehow, they are coming anyway. Somehow, they know what has happened.

He furrows his dark eyebrows. "Millie? What is going on?"

"Jonathan Lowell is dead," I choke out. "Somebody stabbed him."

"*What?*"

I wasn't sure if he was lying two days ago when he disappeared from our bedroom in the middle of the night. But at this moment, Enzo truly looks astonished. I could almost swear on my life that he is shocked by what I am telling him.

Almost.

Enzo's gaze drops to his shirt, speckled in still-damp blood. When he lifts his eyes again and sees my face, he takes a step back. "I told you, I cut myself. This is my blood. *My* blood."

The sirens are much louder now. The police car will be here any moment.

"Change your shirt," I tell him.

Enzo is frozen for a moment, but finally, he nods. He runs upstairs to get rid of his bloody shirt. And whatever else he needs to get rid of.

# FORTY-THREE

Over the next twenty minutes, more and more police officers arrive at the Lowell household.

We instruct the kids to stay up in their rooms, because we don't want them to see what's going on out there. At some point, they are going to find out that our neighbor was murdered, but I want to postpone that as long as possible. I end up making some pizza bagels in the microwave and let them eat them in their rooms.

I watch the spectacle through the window. Suzette comes home about half an hour after the police arrive, and I watch as a man who looks like a detective breaks the news to her. She covers her eyes and starts to sob, although to my eyes, it looks fake.

She's not at all upset that her husband is dead.

At some point, the police will arrive at our house to ask questions. But it hasn't happened yet. And when they do, I'm not sure what to tell them.

Enzo and I sit at the kitchen table, staring down at

the pizza bagels I made for us. In the best of times, they would be unappetizing. The cheese is unmelted on one side and somehow overcooked on the other side. But even if it were a gourmet meal, I wouldn't be able to eat one bite of it.

"I don't understand," I say to Enzo. "What happened over there? Were you in their house?"

"No!" he cries. "I never went inside. I was outside. Working."

"And you didn't hear a thing?"

"No, but you know my equipment is loud. I never hear anything inside the house."

I look down at Enzo's hands, clasped together on the kitchen table. "Where is the cut?"

"What?"

"You told me you cut your hand," I remind him. "That's why you were bleeding everywhere, *remember*? So where is it?"

He holds out his left hand. I don't even see it at first, but when I look closer, I notice the cut on the palm.

I'm just going to say it: there is no way that cut created that much blood.

"Cuts on the hand bleed a lot," he says defensively. "Lots of blood vessels."

"It's not bleeding now."

"Well, it *stopped*."

I don't know what to say. I want to believe him. I really, really do. Because when I think about Jonathan Lowell lying on the floor of the living room with his throat slashed open, I don't want to think about the fact that my husband could be responsible for doing something like that.

If he did that, he is a very different person than I thought he was.

Before I can formulate another question, the doorbell rings. Even though we were expecting it, we both jump. Enzo looks terrified as he grabs my arm.

"Millie," he croaks. "Do not tell them about the blood on my shirt. Okay?"

I shrug off his grip and get out of my seat to answer the door. I have no intention of telling them about his shirt. Wasn't I the one who told him to change it?

That same detective who broke the news to Suzette is standing at our front door. He's around forty, with neatly trimmed graying hair, wearing a beige trench coat over a white shirt and dark red tie. I've met a lot of detectives over the years, and something in the back of my head tells me not to trust this one. Then again, I feel that way a lot around cops.

"Mrs. Accardi?" The detective's accent sounds more Queens than Long Island. "I'm Detective Willard. You got a minute?"

I nod wordlessly. "Yes."

"Can I come in?" Willard asks.

This is not my first rodeo, and that's how I know it's a mistake to invite a police officer into your house. Once I tell him it's okay to come in, he can look around. And when I think about the bloody shirt my husband just stripped off, I would prefer he didn't look around.

"Actually," I say, "my kids are inside. So I'd rather stay out here on the porch."

"If that's what you want," Willard says.

I flick on the porch light, and we step outside. The mosquitoes are circling, and I wish I had spritzed on some protection, but I'm still not going to invite this man into my home. I'd rather get eaten alive.

"So I don't know if you heard what happened," he says.

He's watching my expression carefully. Whatever else I can say about this detective, he seems smart. I decide to be straight about what happened.

"I, uh… I have a good idea…" I clear my throat. "I went over to talk to Suzette, and I saw Jonathan lying on the floor, and he was…" I have to close my eyes, trying to block out the memory. "I came home to get my phone and call 911, but then I heard the police sirens."

Willard nods. "Your neighbor, Janice Archer, was the one who called them. She said she heard shouting inside the house."

Janice—of course. Always watching. And she has a perfect view of the front of 12 Locust Street.

"She said she saw you enter the house after she called the police," he says. "Then you left shortly after."

Thank God I decided to tell the truth. Janice saw everything, so at least now she has confirmed my story. It will be nice, just this one freaking time, to not be a murder suspect.

"She also told me," Willard continues, "that your husband entered through the front door about two hours before the scuffle. And she never saw him leave, which means that he went out through the back door, which she does not have a view of."

"My husband is a landscaper," I say. "He works in their backyard a lot. It's just a job."

"Mrs. Archer says that he is at the Lowell house frequently," he says. "Especially when Mr. Lowell is not home."

Okay. Wow.

"That's not..." I compose myself, reminding myself that the detective is looking for a reaction from me. I'm not going to give it to him. He didn't even ask me a direct question, so I don't owe him an answer. "Mrs. Archer is a busybody. Nothing is going on between them."

"Yeah? You sure about that?"

"I'm sure," I say tightly.

Willard adjusts his red tie. "You know anyone who might have wanted to hurt Jonathan Lowell?"

"I didn't know him well."

"How about your husband?"

"My husband would never do something like that!" I burst out. "That's the most ridiculous thing I've ever heard!"

A grim smile twitches at the detective's thin lips. "I just meant did your husband know Mr. Lowell well?"

"Oh." My cheeks grow warm. "No. I... I don't think so."

"How about Mrs. Lowell?" The subtext in his words is obvious. "Did he know *her* well?"

"Not that well."

"Even though he was over there all the time?"

"*Working*."

I'm furious at myself for allowing the detective to fluster me this way. Ten years ago, I never would have let that happen. Becoming a wife and mother has made me soft.

"Well," Willard says. "Maybe I better talk to your husband then. You mind getting him?"

I take a calming breath. "Of course. Just a moment."

I return to my house and close the door behind me,

leaving the detective on the front porch. I lean against the door, taking a moment to breathe in and out. Detective Willard has rattled me. When I look down at my hands, they're trembling.

I finally pull myself together enough to enter the kitchen. Enzo is still sitting there, the cold pizza bagels in an untouched pile in front of him. He looks up at me when I enter the room.

"Well?" he says.

"The detective wants to talk to you," I say.

Dread fills his handsome features. He's looking at me like I told him he is being marched to a firing squad. But he gets out of his chair and walks to the front door to talk to the detective.

# FORTY-FOUR

Enzo won't say much to me after his discussion with the detective.

I don't know what they talked about. I pressed my ear against the front door, attempting to listen, but our front door must be just as soundproof as that hidden room, because I could not hear one word. But on the plus side, the detective didn't take my husband away in handcuffs.

After the detective left, I went upstairs to find the T-shirt with the blood stains on it. But I didn't see it in the laundry hamper. I didn't see it anywhere.

I wonder what Enzo did with it.

We have mostly sequestered the children in their rooms, so after they finish eating, we decide to bring them both down to the living room to talk about what happened. After all, it's not like we can hide the fact that our next-door neighbor was murdered. They know something is going on.

The two of them sit down on the sofa. Ada looks up at me intently with her big dark eyes, and Nico squirms, trying to get comfortable. That kid never seems able to sit still. I also can't help but notice he is avoiding eye contact.

I sit beside him on the sofa, and Enzo takes the armchair. I'm not sure which of us should initiate the conversation. But Enzo has this glazed look on his face, like he's still reeling from whatever he spoke about with the detective, so I have a feeling it's going to be me.

"We want to talk to you about what is going on next door," I begin. "I assume you saw the police cars."

Ada nods solemnly while Nico fidgets.

"I'm sorry to tell you," I say, "that Mr. Lowell was… Somebody killed him."

They don't need to hear the details. They don't need to know about how I found him in a pool of blood with his neck gaping open. This sanitized version is bad enough.

Predictably, Ada bursts into tears. Nico drops his eyes and doesn't say anything.

"I don't want you to be scared," I say. "The person who did this to him… That person won't want to hurt our family. It has nothing to do with us."

Of course, we have no evidence of that. We have no idea who killed Jonathan Lowell. But I don't think there's anything wrong with reassuring two children that their lives are not in danger.

"Are you okay?" I ask them gently.

Ada wipes her eyes. "Do they know who killed him?"

I can't say the words in my head, which are, *The police think it might be your father.* I put my arm around her shoulders. "They will soon. Don't worry."

Nico is leaning back on the sofa, and there is an expression on his face I can't quite read. I remember how flat he was when his beloved praying mantis bit the dust. It was…disturbing. But this is a different situation. This is a *human being*. Plus Nico spent some time over there doing his chores. He knew the Lowells. His brain must be a mess right now.

But the truth is he doesn't look even the slightest bit upset.

We send the kids back up to their rooms. Ada extracts guarantees from both of us that we will come in to say good night, but Nico doesn't say much at all.

I wait until I hear both of their bedroom doors closing before I turn to my husband. "Do you think they're okay?"

He has barely said a word to me since the detective left. He still has that glassy look in his eyes.

"Enzo?" I say.

He rolls his head to look at me. "I did not kill him, Millie. You know that, yes?"

I am all the way at the other end of the sofa, and I could scoot down to be closer to the armchair, but I don't do it. "I know."

"I cut my hand," he says. "It was bleeding."

"Right. That's what you said."

"And," he adds, "I was not cheating with Suzette."

"Okay," I say.

The police are already suspicious of him based on what Janice told them. They don't even know the things I know. The blood on his hands. The way he snuck out the other night and returned smelling of Suzette's perfume.

He has given me explanations for all those things, none of which I believe. I won't repeat any of it to the police. But that doesn't mean I can forget it happened.

"Please, Millie." His voice breaks. "I need you to believe me. Is important. I did not do this."

"Okay," I say. "I believe you."

"You swear?"

"I swear," I say softly.

See? I can lie just as well as he can.

# FORTY-FIVE

We are woken up the next morning to the sound of Enzo's phone ringing.

I rub my eyes as he fumbles around to find it on the nightstand. I hear his sleepy, "Hello?" And then his body goes rigid.

"Yes," he says into the receiver. "I can come to the station. I just… I have to reschedule some things, and… Yes, she can come too. We just need to get the kids off to school, but… Yes, okay. I'll be there." Enzo hangs up the phone, looking about as wide awake as I have ever seen him at this hour of the day. "That is Detective Willard," he says. "He wants us both to come to the station. To talk."

And now I am equally awake. "Did he say anything else?"

"No. That is all."

Again, I know from experience that asking us to come to the station isn't a good thing. He wants to make sure whatever we say is on the record.

I wonder if they found out anything else.

"I think," I say, "that we should call Ramirez."

Enzo sighs. "I do not want to bother him. And he is retired, no?"

"He said he was retiring last time we talked, but I bet he didn't."

He hesitates for only a second. "Okay. Call him."

Enzo and I don't have a ton of close friends, but one of our closest is Benito Ramirez, a detective with the NYPD. I met him during a dark time in my life, when I was accused of something terrible that I hadn't done, and he went a long way to make sure that all the charges were completely dropped. We have become good friends since then, and we have helped each other out when we can. When Ada was born, we asked him to be her godfather. He's the biggest workaholic I know—even worse than Enzo—but we've spent a lot of time together over the years, and he's always had presents at the holidays and birthdays for his godchildren.

Also, he's the only person who might be happy to hear from me at this hour of the morning.

I select Ramirez's name from my list of contacts. Enzo keeps his dark eyes on me as I place the call. It rings twice, and then the detective's familiar gravelly voice fills my ear.

"Millie?" he says, sounding as wide awake as I am. "Is that you, Millie Calloway?"

He's the only person who still calls me by my maiden name, even though I have been Accardi for over a decade. "Yes, it is."

"Then I'm guessing you're in some kind of trouble,"

he says. But he doesn't sound angry about it. More like amused.

"We have a bit of a situation," I admit. I drop my voice, even though the only person in the room is Enzo. "We moved out to Long Island, like I told you last time we talked."

"Right! You're a Long Islander now! Are you listening to a lot of Billy Joel? Going to diners every night?"

"My neighbor was just found murdered, Benny."

That stops him in his tracks. "Jesus, Millie. I'm really sorry to hear that. What's going on?"

I tell him the whole story about finding Jonathan dead yesterday in his house. I tell him about Detective Willard and being asked to come down to the station this morning. I start to tell him about the blood on Enzo's hands, but then my husband gives me a look and I shut my mouth. It's not that he doesn't trust Ramirez, but… well, he's a cop.

When I finish telling him what happened, Ramirez lets out a low whistle. "Wow. That's a wild story. But they don't got any real reason to suspect you or Enzo, do they?"

"No…"

"So go down to the station and talk to them," he says. "If anything starts to sound funny, you stop and don't say another word. Then you get a good lawyer."

A good lawyer. I wonder what that would cost. "Benny, I don't know if we can afford a lawyer right now."

"Yeah, but they gotta provide you with one. They can't question you if you say you want a lawyer."

It will be some public defender who might have no idea what they're doing. The last time I had a public defender, I ended up in prison for ten years. But it's better than nothing. I guess.

"Meanwhile," he says, "I'll ask around and see what I can find out."

"You still work for the NYPD?" I ask him. "You were talking about retiring."

He snorts. "Yeah, well, I'm still here. If I had a wife, she would be furious."

I give Enzo a thumbs-up. He nods and heads in the direction of the bathroom. The shower starts up, and it's only then that I blurt out, "Benny, Enzo had blood all over his hands when he came home last night."

There's a long silence on the other line. "Blood on his hands?"

"He says he cut himself."

"Maybe he did."

I shake my head. "I don't know..."

"Millie," he says, "one thing I know about Enzo Accardi is that he is a good guy. I don't think he would kill anyone. But if he did, it would be for a damn good reason."

That is not untrue.

"Don't overreact to this," he advises me. "Your neighbor just got murdered. Of course they're going to want to question you. The sooner they find the person who did this, the sooner it will be over." He pauses. "But don't tell them about the blood on his hands."

If I had a dime for every time I lied to the police, I wouldn't have to worry about mortgage payments.

# FORTY-SIX

I had been considering keeping the kids home from school today, but if Enzo and I are both going to the police station, there's no way to do that. I'm not bringing my children to a police station. My wish is that neither of them ever have to set foot in a police station for their entire lives. (Except possibly for a school trip. That would be okay, I suppose.)

Even Nico manages to get ready for school without much protest or fuss. They are both uncharacteristically silent while they choke down a few bites of cereal, which seems appropriate given the gravity of what happened. I haven't been walking them to the bus stop in the morning, but I do it today, just to make sure everything goes smoothly.

Unfortunately, Janice and Spencer are waiting at the bus stop when we arrive. Janice is wearing her usual nightgown and slippers, and it takes all my self-restraint not to wrap my fingers around her skinny little neck.

This woman basically told the police she thought my husband killed a man. That's not exactly neighborly.

We don't say one word to each other while we wait for the bus to arrive. And that's fine with me.

"Mommy," Nico says. It pulls on my heartstrings because he hasn't called me that in years. "Do I have to go to school today?"

I wish I could keep him with me, close to my side. But that's impossible. "I'm sorry, honey. I have...something I need to do."

"Can I go with you?"

"I... I'm afraid not."

His lower lip trembles slightly. Nico hasn't cried in public in a long time, but I'm worried it's about to happen.

"I'm so sorry," I say quickly. "But I'll be home when you get back from school. I promise."

"Can I play with Spencer?" he asks hopefully.

Spencer's eyes light up at the suggestion. "Can we, Mama?"

Janice looks like she's about to have a stroke. I'm not thrilled about the idea either after what Janice said to the police about my husband, although I'd allow it just to make Nico feel better. But that doesn't seem like a possibility.

"Spencer," Janice says sharply. "I told you after Nicolas was suspended from school for fighting that you were not to spend time with him ever again."

Wait, *what*?

I barely have time to be furious with Janice for talking like that right in front of Nico. Because what she just said can't be right. Nico went over to Spencer's house the day before the beach trip. And a few times since then as well. At least that's what he told me…

"Nico," I say sharply, "I thought Mrs. Archer said you could play in the backyard with Spencer?"

"I said no such thing!" she barks. "Did I, Spencer?"

Spencer nods in agreement, eager to please, and that's when a look of guilt comes over my son's face. Janice never told him he could play in their backyard. And considering how vigilant she is, there's no way he was playing there with Spencer without her knowledge. So that means…

"Nico, come over here." I tug him by the arm until we are several yards away, and he dutifully follows. I drop my voice enough that Janice won't hear me. "Where have you been going when you leave the house?"

"Nowhere," he says quickly. "I've just been playing out on the street. Alone."

Except if that's all he was doing, why did he lie about it?

"I just wanted to be alone," he adds. "I didn't want you to worry."

I don't believe him. There's something more to this story that he's not telling me. But at that moment, the school bus arrives, and this time, Nico is only too eager to climb aboard. I watch as the bus carries my children away, wondering if I will ever get answers to the questions swirling around my head.

# FORTY-SEVEN

Even though I knew it was coming, it's unsettling that the first thing that happens when we get to the police station is that they put me and Enzo in separate rooms.

Of course they want to separate us. They don't want us to be able to coordinate our stories. It makes sense, but at the same time, it gets me panicky. The fact that they feel a need to separate us makes me think that they're not just questioning us as next-door neighbors of the victim. They are considering us actual suspects.

I sit in the poorly lit interrogation room, squirming in one of the uncomfortable plastic chairs. I imagine my husband sitting in a similar room somewhere else in the station, and I wonder what he's thinking. He has barely spoken to me since the phone call I made this morning. I didn't tell him that I admitted to Ramirez that he came home with blood on his hands.

My other piece of evidence that we might be in trouble is that Detective Willard himself is the one who saunters into the room to talk to me. He didn't send one of his minions. He wants to talk to me himself. Personally.

That's not good.

"Mrs. Accardi." He drops into the seat across from me. He has bags under his eyes, and the lighting in the room almost makes them look like bruises. "Thanks for coming by."

"No problem." I try to sound as much as I can like a woman who isn't scared that she and her husband are being accused of murder. "We just want to find out who did this to Jonathan. It's so awful. He seemed like a really nice guy."

"Don't worry," Willard says. "We're going to find out who did this."

Why does it sound like a threat?

"Am I a suspect?" I ask.

"No," he says without hesitation. Despite everything, I feel a flash of relief. "You were at work until thirty minutes before the body was found. Mrs. Archer saw your car pull up to the house, and she said you were in the Lowells' house for only a couple of minutes. And this was after she had already called 911 because of concern of a disturbance. So no, you are not a suspect." He adds, "I can see why you would be concerned though, given your...history."

I shouldn't be even the slightest bit surprised that he knows about my criminal history. I would have lost respect for any police officer in this situation who didn't. But it always feels like a slap in the face when someone brings it up. "Yes," I say tightly.

"Mrs. Accardi," he says, "what do you know about your husband's relationship with Mrs. Lowell?"

"The Lowells are our neighbors, obviously." I lift a shoulder, trying not to let my nerves show. "He was helping her with her backyard in exchange for referrals. They were friendly."

"Did you ever suspect anything more?"

"No. Never."

He flashes me a conspiratorial smile. "Never? Not even a little bit? Especially when he was over there all the time? I mean, Suzette Lowell is a very attractive woman."

My jaw tightens. "I said *never*."

"I see."

This detective is not going to trip me up. I'm too smart for that. He is not dealing with a rookie.

"Mrs. Accardi," he says. "Did you know that your husband recently purchased a gun?"

My mouth falls open. "A...a gun?"

"That's right." He is watching my expression. "He withdrew a thousand dollars from your joint bank account and then used some of that money to purchase a firearm. *Illegally*. But we have contacts."

"I..."

My heart is slamming in my chest. It's hard to imagine it could be true, but I can't deny the money was missing from our account. Enzo claimed it was to replace broken equipment. But if that's all it was, why wouldn't he have told me about it?

But then again, so what if he bought a gun? I mean, I'm not thrilled about it, and I'm most definitely wondering where it is right now and what he intended to do with it. But Jonathan Lowell was not shot. He was stabbed. So whether Enzo bought a gun or not, it's not the murder weapon.

"Also," Willard adds, "did you know that he checked into a motel with Suzette Lowell four nights ago?"

Now I feel like I'm going to choke. I suspected when Enzo told me he had just gone out for a drive that he wasn't being honest. But this information floors me. I desperately want to believe that the detective is making it up just to shake me up, but everything he is saying fits. The missing money, Enzo's disappearance…

Willard doesn't even wait for me to answer his question. He got all the information he needed from the look on my face.

"Mrs. Accardi," he goes on. "You and your husband… Your financial situation is not great, is it?"

"We're doing fine," I say defensively.

"So you didn't recently bounce a check?"

Oh my God, this detective knows *everything*. I squirm in the plastic chair, wondering if he knows what color underwear I'm wearing right now. I wouldn't be surprised.

"That was a miscalculation," I say.

"Do you know," he says, "that Jonathan Lowell had a substantial life insurance policy and Suzette Lowell is the sole beneficiary?"

Again, I am trying not to react. "No, I did not. But I'm not sure what that has to do with me or my husband."

He raises an eyebrow. "Don't you?"

I take a deep breath, remembering what Ramirez told me to say if the questions start going in the wrong direction. I might not be a suspect, but I'm pretty damn sure that my husband is. "Detective Willard," I say, "I am not answering any more questions without a lawyer."

# FORTY-EIGHT

The detective decides he doesn't have any more questions for me.

But the same is not true for Enzo. I wait in the station for him, and they keep him there for *hours*. I doubt they're questioning him the whole time. They're just trying to wear him down and sweat the truth out of him. I'm sure he has asked for a lawyer too, and that will have taken time.

He finally emerges three hours later, looking exhausted. There are circles under his slightly bloodshot eyes. His lips are turned down, and he looks like he wants to throw up.

"What happened?" I ask him.

"We go," he says. "Now. *Please*."

We took my car to the station, which turns out to be a good thing because he does not look like he's up for driving (and I am slightly terrified of driving his truck with its stick shift). He climbs into the passenger seat beside me and stares out the window.

I wonder what they said to him in there.

He's quiet for the first five minutes of the drive as he watches the streets zip by. Finally, he says, "Millie, you know I did not cheat on you with Suzette?"

I grimace. I don't want to have this conversation right now, because between my prior suspicions and everything I heard from Detective Willard today, I can't imagine how Enzo *wasn't* cheating on me. And if he says otherwise, it's all a bunch of lies.

"I would never." He turns away from the window to face me. "I swear to you."

I remember Ramirez's words from this morning: *One thing I know about Enzo Accardi is that he is a good guy. I don't think he would kill anyone. But if he did, it would be for a damn good reason.*

I want so badly to believe that. But he's making it very hard for me.

"So why were you at a motel with her?" I ask.

"I was not!"

"The detective told me—"

"Is not true," he insists.

"Enzo," I say. "I smelled her perfume on you."

He's quiet again, absorbing this piece of information. I glance over at him as I pull over to the side of the road, not wanting to crash the car while we have this conversation. He looks like he's turning things over in his head. Is he going to confess everything?

Do I *want* him to confess everything?

"Okay," he finally says. "I checked into a motel that night. Is true."

I didn't realize until that second just how badly I had wanted him to deny everything. "I see..."

"But not with Suzette. I swear to you. They only know it was a woman and they assumed."

*What?* "So who are you cheating on me with then?" I snap at him.

"Not cheating," he says firmly. "I was… It was Martha. Suzette gives her leftover perfume, I think. Or maybe…she might take it."

"Martha, our *cleaning woman*?"

He nods slowly.

Okay…

Of all the people I would have thought my husband might cheat with, my sixty-year-old cleaning woman was at the bottom of the list. Of course, he is claiming he didn't cheat. But if he didn't, why was he at a motel with her?

"I went over to her house to give her last paycheck," he begins.

I clench my teeth, remembering how I *asked* him not to do that, yet he did it anyway. "Okay…"

"And she had…" He touches his hand to his face. "Bruises everywhere. I had sensed it when I spoke with her before, but that day was when I knew. Her husband… He took her whole paycheck, and that's why she was stealing things—to save up enough to leave. He would have killed her, Millie. Plus he was angry she got fired from another job. I needed to help her get away."

Enzo would never lie about that. *Never.* If he says Martha was getting beat on by her husband, it's the truth. Or at least it's the truth as he believes it.

"Maybe she was manipulating you to get money," I suggest.

"No," he says. "Is real. In fact…"

He stops talking, as if unsure if he should tell me

anything else. But this is not the time for holding things back. "What?"

"She wanted to talk to *you*," he sighs. "She knew about you."

"She…she did?"

I wonder how she knew. I wonder who told her.

The thing is, I have a bit of a…history with women like Martha. Women who are in terrible situations and have no way out. I became the way out for some of those women. So did Enzo. I have to say, I can't help but look back on it all with pride. We have done some good things in our time.

Some bad things too, maybe, along the way.

"Yes. And she was trying to work up the courage because she wanted your help. But then you accuse her of breaking things and then you say she is stealing…"

"She *was* stealing!"

"I told you why!" He shakes his head. "She did not take much from us. Suzette thought she was stealing too, and that is what she was talking to me about that night in the backyard. I had to convince her there was no stealing so Martha would not lose her job."

I can see in his dark eyes that every word of what he's saying is true, and I feel a stab of guilt. Martha wasn't staring at me because she meant me harm. She was staring at me because she thought I was her only hope for escape and she was working up the nerve to ask for my help. What has become of me that I wasn't able to see that?

"So," I say quietly, "you're telling me the gun was for her?"

"She needed it until I could get her away from him, and after she left, she needed it even more. He was coming for her, Millie. I had to help. She's hundreds of miles away right now, but he could still find her."

"Okay, okay." I grip the steering wheel tighter. "I understand what you did. I can't say I wouldn't have done the same, but…why didn't you tell me? You know you can talk to me about stuff like that. I mean, we used to be a *team*. Right?"

We used to help women in trouble all the time. It was how we got to know each other. It's the reason we fell in love in the first place. I could have helped—I would have *wanted* to help. Why did he leave me out this time?

He's silent, measuring his next words. "I was worried about you."

"Worried?"

"You have so much stress. Your blood pressure…"

"Oh my *God*." I hit the steering wheel with the palm of my hand. "So you would rather I wake up during the night, wondering where the hell you are? Do you think *that* was good for my blood pressure?"

He lets out a long sigh, dropping his head back against the headrest. "I messed up. I was stupid."

"Yes. You were."

"But…you believe me?"

"Yes," I say. "I do."

For the first time since leaving the police station, he manages the tiniest of smiles. Okay, this looks bad. Janice's eyewitness testimony puts Enzo squarely at the scene of the crime. But Ramirez is right—my husband wouldn't kill a man over nothing. If he says he didn't do it, then I believe him.

Although deep down, I still get the feeling there is something he is hiding from me.

# FORTY-NINE

When I reach our cul-de-sac, there's a black Dodge Charger parked in front of our house. Before I even look through the windshield at the driver, I recognize it as Benito Ramirez's car. Sure enough, the second he sees us pull into the driveway, he steps out of the car, clutching a cup of coffee.

He waves to me as I get out of the car. Even though it's hot out, he's wearing a black suit jacket and a tie loosely knotted around his neck. When I first met him over a decade ago, his close-cropped hair was salt and pepper, but now it's mostly salt.

"Millie." He comes over to me to give me the obligatory hug and kiss. "Good to see you. You look good."

"Thank you," I say, even though I'm sure I look exhausted.

When Enzo comes out of the car, Ramirez says to him, "And you look like shit, my friend."

"Thank you," Enzo says. "I feel like it."

Ramirez jerks his hand in the direction of our house. "Come on. Let's go inside. I've got a few more reasons for you to feel like shit. You need to hear this."

Oh God. What now?

We lead Ramirez into the house. Under other circumstances, I would have felt compelled to give him the grand tour, but none of us are in the mood for that. Still, he looks around and nods approvingly. "Nice place you got here. Better than the Bronx."

"I'm sorry we left," I say.

"How are the kids?"

"Very good," Enzo says, which I suppose isn't an outright lie.

We settle down in the living room, and I can't stop shaking, wondering what the hell Ramirez is going to tell us. I offer him coffee, even though he's already holding a cup, and he smiles at me sympathetically.

"Okay, let's cut to the chase." He drops his cup of coffee on my coffee table and leans forward on his elbows. "Luckily, I got a contact here on the island, and I did a little digging. You two were right to be worried. Willard is a tough cop, and he thinks you killed Jonathan Lowell, Enzo. He's busy building his case right now."

"Based on *what*?" I say.

"Well," Ramirez says. "Not to be crude, Enzo, but he thinks you were doing Suzette Lowell. He thinks the two of you conspired to off her husband to get his insurance money. She recently increased the insurance payout, and we're talking a lot of money right now."

"That is ridiculous," Enzo mutters.

"That lady across the street," Ramirez says, "is singing like a bird for the police. Not just that, she took pictures."

"Pictures?" I gasp.

"Uh-huh. Nothing outright incriminating, but lots of them at different times, standing a little too close, if you know what I mean."

Suzette was so right. Janice is *such* a busybody.

Enzo groans. "We were just talking."

Ramirez arches an eyebrow. "About what?"

"Nothing. Gardening stuff. Problems with her cleaning lady. The weather. It did not matter—she always had an excuse for me to stay. I get the feeling… I do not know… She did not seem happy in her marriage."

"Do you think the husband was beating her up?"

"No. I did not get that sense."

"Was she flirting with you?"

Enzo casts a worried look in my direction, then throws up his arms. "Yes. She was. Of course she was. But was nothing. Harmless."

"So here's the deal," Ramirez says. "Your neighbor has pictures of you and Suzette Lowell that are very suggestive. A motel about an hour away has a record of you checking in with a woman just a few days ago. You buy a gun using cash. Suzette Lowell ups her husband's life insurance policy. Then the neighbor sees you going into the Lowells' house, and the next thing we know, Jonathan Lowell is dead."

Enzo grits his teeth. "I was in the backyard the whole time. Suzette wanted to plant a garden, so I was getting the soil ready."

"So you expect me to believe that not only did you not hear what happened in the house, but the actual killer went in and out the back door without you seeing."

"I had equipment going… Very hard to hear… And I was back and forth from my own yard."

"Come on, Enzo." Ramirez levels his gaze at my husband. "You can be straight with me. Did you kill him?"

Enzo drops his face into his hands. "No. I swear. Benny, I would never."

"Then you're going to need a really good lawyer."

Enzo punches his fist into the sofa in frustration, and I don't even blame him. A good lawyer? We don't have any money. We can't afford *any* lawyer, much less a good one. We will have to take whoever we can get for free. The court-appointed attorney is going to have to be good enough.

"We don't have much money," I say to Ramirez. "So getting a really good lawyer is off the table."

"I thought you might say that," he says. "So I took the liberty of reaching out to a public defender who is one of the best I've seen. She's based in the Bronx, so not in this jurisdiction, but we can pull some strings to make it happen. She's young—two years out of law school—but really sharp. She has a great winning record, and she's had a couple of murder trials that both went her way. When I told her about you, she was eager to help."

"That's great," I say.

"She's on her way over." Ramirez looks down at his watch. "If she hasn't hit traffic, she should be here shortly. And then you can fill her in on all the details." He gives Enzo a warning look. "You tell this woman everything. No bullshit."

"Never," Enzo agrees.

I shake my head. "That's so nice of her to make the trip on such short notice."

"She moved a few things around, she said."

I narrow my eyes at Ramirez. Something about this

seems a little fishy. This woman is apparently an amazing public defender, yet she's willing to drop everything and drive all the way out from the city to *Long Island* to help some couple she's never even met? Who does that? I look over at Enzo, whose expression is equally skeptical.

There's something going on here that I'm not aware of.

Ramirez reaches into his pocket for his phone. He reads the message on the screen, then swivels his head to look out the front window. A blue sedan has pulled up in front of our house.

"That's her," he says.

I lean forward in my seat to get a closer look at the woman climbing out of the vehicle. She has white-blond hair pulled back into a French twist and a trim build. She looks wispy—not the kind of person you would think would be a shark in a courtroom, but looks can be deceiving. If Ramirez says she's good, I trust him.

Ramirez leaps off the couch to let her inside. I rise to my feet as our new lawyer enters the living room, clutching a briefcase. Enzo stands up as well, and I hear the sharp intake of his breath. "*Oddio!*" he gasps.

Our lawyer isn't just any public defender. Enzo knows exactly who this woman is.

And a moment later, so do I.

# FIFTY

"Cecelia!" Enzo cries.

The second he says her name, I know exactly who this girl is: Cecelia Winchester. I used to sort of be her nanny a while ago. And Enzo also looked after her while some other stuff was going on in her life. I haven't seen her in person since she was ten years old. And now she's…

Oh my God, she's *twenty-seven.* I am horribly old.

Despite everything, Enzo runs over to her. He wraps his arms around her, and she hugs him back. He whispers something in her ear, and she smiles and nods. I couldn't make out what he said, although I heard the words "your mother."

I cross the room to get a better look at this girl. She might be twenty-seven, but she still looks very young. I would believe twenty if somebody tried to convince me. But there is something very shrewd and hard about her blue eyes. She has the eyes of someone twenty years older.

Something about her eyes makes me believe that having her on our side might be the best weapon we can have.

"Hello, Millie," she says. The last time I heard her voice, it was high and childlike. Now it's crisp and businesslike. She seems like the sort of woman who is working even at the dinner table.

I manage a smile. "Hi, Cece. It's really good to see you."

"Same." She smooths out the lapel of her suit jacket. "I wish it didn't have to be under these circumstances."

"Cecelia is a public defender, so officially, we are mortal enemies," Ramirez says. "But I admired her passion when I saw her in action. I ran into her about a year ago at the supermarket when I was picking up that cake you asked me to get for Ada's birthday party, and we got to chatting. When I told her who I was getting the cake for, it turned out she knew you just as well as I did. So when you called me this morning, I gave her a call right away."

"Just as well as I did" is pushing it. We've been friends with Benny for years, and I last saw Cecelia when she was a child. Has she been keeping tabs on us?

But if she has, I should be grateful. She's our only hope right now.

"Benny has been filling me in on all the details while I battled the Long Island Expressway," she says as we return to the living room. "They have been building quite a case against you, Enzo."

He winces. "I know. Is terrible. Cecelia, you need to know, I didn't…"

Cecelia settles down on the sofa, crossing one of her skinny legs over the other. She places her briefcase on her lap and opens it with a snap. She extracts a yellow legal pad of paper and clicks open her ballpoint pen. Clearly, she does not want to waste time on small talk, which I appreciate right now. "Maybe you didn't kill him," she says, "but they are going after you *hard*. I promise you that. I wouldn't be surprised if they've got a search warrant in the works."

Enzo sneers. "Let them search. They will find nothing."

I don't feel the same way. I have had my home searched by the police before, and it's the largest violation I can imagine. They go through *everything*. They rip apart your entire life, and they don't put it back.

"What will they be looking for?" I ask Cecelia.

"A murder weapon," she says without hesitation. "Any traces of Lowell's blood."

I think about that bloody T-shirt Enzo was wearing last night. I never ended up finding it. He must've gotten rid of it.

Except if it really was his blood, why would he get rid of the shirt? It wouldn't be incriminating if it was his own blood.

"They won't find that," he says firmly.

"It would help," she says, "if you tell me everything from the beginning."

And so he does what she asks. He tells her everything while she quietly jots down notes on her legal pad. He talks about his relationship with Suzette, the things he did to help Martha, and finally working in the yard yesterday while Jonathan was being murdered.

"I did nothing," he insists. "*Nothing*. Why would they think I would kill him?"

It's a rhetorical question, but Cecelia seems to be

truly considering it. She has clearly grown up to be a very thoughtful young woman. I wonder if Ada will turn out like her.

Of course, if her father gets locked up in prison, that's going to mess her up forever.

"I'll be honest with you, Enzo," Cecelia finally says. "I believe it might have something to do with Dario Fontana."

At the mention of that name, all the color leaves Enzo's face. "What?" he says.

"My understanding"—Cecelia glances over at Ramirez, who nods—"is that Detective Willard has done some digging into your past, before you came to this country. And that is a name that has come up."

I've never heard the name before in my life. So it's disturbing that the man I have been married to for over a decade has such a violent reaction to it.

"Who is Dario Fontana?" I ask him.

"That was a long time ago," he chokes out.

Cecelia's voice is firm, leaving no room for bullshit. "Not that long."

"Enzo?" I say.

He is squeezing his knees so hard that his knuckles are white. "Dario was my sister's husband."

His sister's husband. Okay, now it makes sense that the name upset him so much. Antonia was abused by her husband for many years, until he finally ended up killing her. He was also a man with dangerous mobster ties, and when Enzo took his vengeance, he immediately had to leave the country. I can understand why he never wanted to say the man's name. But what I don't understand is why Cecelia has brought him up.

"He wasn't just that," Cecelia says. "We need to be honest about the situation we're dealing with."

Enzo shoots me a pained look. "Millie, would you leave us for a moment?"

Is he joking with me? Does he really think I would *leave* right now?

"No way," I say sharply. "What is it that you don't want me to know?"

"Enzo," Ramirez says. "Just tell your wife the truth."

Enzo mumbles something under his breath. There is no way I am leaving this room without finding out what he doesn't want me to know.

"Enzo?" I say again.

"Okay. *Okay*." He clenches his hands into fists. "I worked for him. I worked for Dario Fontana. Okay?"

My jaw drops. That is a piece of the puzzle I never heard before. Enzo *worked* for the guy who used to beat up on his sister? Not only that, but from what I understood, the man was a mobster. So if Enzo worked for him…

"I was a *kid*," he says. "I was sixteen when I started working for Dario. I didn't know who he really was. By the time I realized…"

"How many years did you work for him?" Cecelia presses him.

Enzo looks completely miserable having this conversation. "Eight years."

"And when you were working for him, what did you do for him?"

Enzo closes his eyes for a moment, then opens them again. "Please stop. I…I understand. This is bad. I get it."

What *did* Enzo do for this mobster?

"Okay," Cecelia concedes. "We don't have to talk about this right now. But I need you to see what we are dealing with. If this were to come up in a courtroom..."

"Yes. I understand."

"I will fight for you," she says. "But I don't want to hear lies, Enzo. I can't do a thing for you if you lie to my face. You have to tell me everything. You have to be completely honest so I can protect you."

He looks her straight in the eyes. "I did not kill Jonathan Lowell. You have my word."

"Fine," she says. "But if you didn't, then who did?"

"Suzette Lowell," I blurt out. That has been the thought in my head since the moment I saw that dead body lying on the floor. Suzette never seemed to respect or even like her husband. My first instinct was that she finally killed him.

"But how?" Ramirez asks. "That neighbor—she swears Suzette was out all day."

"Does she have an alibi?" I ask.

"No alibi, no. But it's not like this cul-de-sac is walkable. She would've had to come home with her car. It would have been noticeable."

"There is another way," Enzo says.

Cecelia raises her eyebrows. "I'm listening."

"There's a way to park around the back without going through the cul-de-sac," Enzo says. "Suzette told me about it. She could have parked in the back, gone in through the back door, and Janice Archer would never have seen her."

"And you wouldn't have noticed her?"

"I was back and forth between our yard and theirs. I wouldn't have necessarily seen her."

"Okay, that's a start. Let me look into it." Cecelia looks down at her watch. "All right, I've got a busy afternoon, so I have to run. This is not going to be a walk in the park, but I promise, I'll do everything in my power to keep them from pinning this on you. I'll fight for you."

Enzo frowns at her as she rises to her feet. When did little Cecelia Winchester learn to walk in such high heels? "You have had cases like this before and won?" he asks.

To her credit, Cecelia artfully dodges the question. "We are going to win this one."

I hope she's right.

# FIFTY-ONE

After Cecelia and Ramirez leave, we have thirty minutes until the kids get off the school bus.

Thirty minutes to weasel the truth out of my husband.

"Enzo," I say. "We need to talk."

He bows his head. "Millie, I am so tired. We need to talk right this minute?"

"Yes, we do." I fold my arms across my chest—I am not about to let him off the hook this time. "We have been married for eleven years, and all of a sudden, it feels like there's quite a lot I don't know about you."

"I have told you everything important."

"And you get to decide what's important?"

He stumbles back to the living room and collapses onto the sofa. "What? Do you need to know every detail? Everything I did from the day I was born?"

I follow him back to the sofa and sit down beside him. "No, but if you were some mobster's henchman, yes, that is something worth disclosing."

"I was not henchman."

"So what sort of work did you do for this guy?"

"Nothing. Errands."

I give him a look. "*Errands?* You mean, like you fed his cat when he was out of town and picked up his dry cleaning? Is that what Cecelia was talking about?"

"What do you want me to say?" He sits up straight but won't look at me. "I was just a kid, and I made a terrible mistake working for an awful person. I wanted out, but then he was dating my sister, and it was not so easy to get out. And then he married her, and then what could I do?"

"So what did you do for him?" I ask. "Did you go after people who owed him money and break their kneecaps?"

He snorts. "You watch too many movies. Nobody breaks kneecaps. That is ridiculous."

"Gee, I didn't realize you were so *knowledgeable*," I retort.

"Millie..."

"Okay, so nobody breaks kneecaps. What's better? What do you break when you want to get some deadbeat to pay back a loan, huh?"

He's quiet for a long time, looking down at his lap. Finally, in a low voice, he says, "Fingers."

Oh. My. God.

"Millie." He raises his eyes. "I am not proud of this. Believe me. It is all my fault that Antonia is dead. If I hadn't started working for Dario when I was a stupid kid, she never would have married him. She would still be alive." His Adam's apple bobs. "I have to live with that. It eats at me every day. That's why...when anyone else needs help...I must..."

I have to bite my tongue to keep from saying the terrible thought going through my head. That if he was shaking people down and breaking their fingers (or worse), maybe this is karma coming back to bite him.

"Tell me," I say, "did you ever kill anyone for him?"

"No. Never! I have said that to you."

"Well, you said a lot of things that turned out not to be true."

He flashes me a wounded expression. "I was only trying to protect you."

Bullshit. He concealed so much of his past, and I can't believe I'm only finding it all out now. He had so many opportunities to tell me the truth. And he knows everything about my past, which isn't exactly idyllic. I have plenty of skeletons in my own closet.

He could have been honest. He could have told me everything. He chose not to.

"I never killed anyone." His voice breaks. "I would never. I did not kill Jonathan."

I look into his eyes. The first time I met him, I couldn't believe how dark they were—it sent a chill down my spine. But then years later, when we stood together in the courthouse, vowing to love each other until death did us part, I looked into those same eyes and felt nothing but love for this man. I trusted him. He was going to be the father of my child, and I knew with all my heart that he would take care of us. He would do everything in his power to protect us.

I'm not sure how it all went wrong.

Because I feel more and more certain that Enzo has been lying all along.

# FIFTY-TWO

After everyone is in bed for the night, I decide to slip into the Lowells' backyard with a flashlight.

I wait until after the kids are asleep. Enzo looks like he's asleep as well. I have no idea how he was able to drift off with everything that happened today, but when I looked down at him on his side of the bed, his eyes were closed and he was snoring softly.

I don't bother to get dressed because I'm just going into the backyard next door. I put on a pair of pajama pants and stuff my feet into a pair of slippers. That should be good enough.

The entire front of 12 Locust is cordoned off by police tape, and the inside of the house is dark—Suzette has clearly found another place to stay that isn't stained with her husband's blood. There were a handful of reporters milling about, but Enzo and I stayed inside, and they eventually got bored and left. I called my work and told them that I would need a couple of days off, and they have been very understanding.

Enzo claims there is a way to get into the backyard without parking in front of the house. I want to believe he is right, because if he isn't, he is the only one who could have killed Jonathan Lowell. And I want so badly to believe that he didn't do it.

The Lowells' backyard is enormous compared with ours. You would think that if our house really used to be for the animals, we would at least have a giant backyard, but it pales in comparison to our neighbors'. The grass has been neatly trimmed, courtesy of my husband, and he has planted and shaped shrubbery along the periphery of the yard. He has also sectioned off an area that Suzette apparently wanted to reserve to start a garden.

It is exactly as he said it would be.

I shine my flashlight around the edges of the yard. I checked a map before I came over, but it was not very revealing. There are plenty of things that exist in real life that might not show up on a map—even a virtual one. That's why I'm here to look around myself.

I keep my flashlight trained on the shrubs. Enzo did a great job with them. Every single one is perfectly trimmed, without a stray leaf or branch. He is so skillful. Even without Suzette, he would have been able to build his business here. He didn't need her.

What if what the detective said is true? What if Enzo and Suzette conspired to kill Jonathan and had an agreement to split the life insurance payment?

No. I can't imagine my husband agreeing to something like that. Enzo is willing to bend the law sometimes, but he'd never kill someone for money. But I also can't imagine him breaking someone's fingers.

Enzo has been stressed about the mortgage payments.

They are, admittedly, suffocatingly high. We wanted this house so badly, so it was hard to admit that it was a bit out of our price range. He desperately wanted to give his family a nice home in a great neighborhood.

But no. He would not have killed to get us that. I don't believe it.

I can't.

When I reach the far end of the yard, I hear a sound. A rustling of leaves. I shine my beam in the direction of the sound, and some of the branches move of their own accord. The shadows shift and bend.

It occurs to me that if somebody did come in through the back to kill Jonathan Lowell, they still have access. And here I am, in my pajamas and fuzzy slippers, wandering around the backyard with no weapon whatsoever to defend myself besides my own two hands.

For a second, I imagine Enzo coming into the backyard next door tomorrow morning and finding me with my throat slashed, lying in a pool of blood.

"Hello?" I whisper, aiming the beam of the light squarely at the rustling leaves.

I consider making a run for it. Our own backyard is only a stone's throw away. After all, Nico was able to hit his baseball into this yard from our own and break a window. If I turn off the flashlight, whoever it is won't be able to see me anymore.

Unless they have a flashlight of their own.

My heart races as I debate what I should do next. And as I stand there, frozen, I realize I have waited too long.

The intruder is here.

# FIFTY-THREE

I take a step back, trying to decide if I should shut the flashlight beam off. Is it better to have the element of surprise, or is it better to see who I'm dealing with?

Before I can decide, a figure steps into the backyard. And my shoulders relax.

"Suzette?" I say.

Suzette Lowell is dressed as casually as I have ever seen her, in jeans and a light cardigan. She looks me up and down in my pajamas, my hair pulled back in a messy ponytail, clutching the flashlight for dear life. She laughs, although it's not a happy laugh.

"What are you doing in my backyard, Millie?" she demands to know.

"I, uh…" I hike up my pajama pants. "I heard a noise."

She lifts an eyebrow. It's a weak excuse, and she knows it. "Don't you think your family has done enough to me?"

I tighten my grip on the flashlight until my fingers hurt. "We haven't done anything."

"Seriously?" The shadows cast dark circles under her eyes. "Your husband murdered my husband last night."

"That's not true," I say, even though I have my private doubts.

"Are you kidding me?" she says. "Janice saw him enter the house. He was *there* when Jonathan was killed. Are you really telling me he didn't do it?"

"Why would he do something like that?"

I am curious to hear Suzette's answer, because everything I have heard so far involves some sort of conspiracy between her and Enzo. But clearly, Suzette would deny something like that because she wouldn't admit to being involved.

"Millie," she says, "I hate to be the one to break it to you, but Enzo was obsessed with me."

"Obsessed with you?" I repeat incredulously.

"Do you think I asked him to come over here every minute?" She shakes her head. "He always had an excuse to be here. Always flirting with me. And he was *intensely* jealous of Jonathan."

This is almost laughable. Enzo wasn't flirting with her. I could see with my own eyes that she was the instigator. At this point, I can tell when a woman is throwing herself at my husband.

"After all," she says, "you saw the way he was all over me at the beach. Do you think I wanted him to practically carry me back to the car? I couldn't get him away from me."

"It didn't look like you minded," I comment.

"Well, I did," she sniffs. "And he told me he wasn't

happy. He said he felt trapped into getting married. Because you were pregnant."

*What?*

Her words finally hit home. Because it's absolutely true. Enzo married me because I was pregnant with Ada. Yes, we had been living together, but there was little talk of marriage. Okay, there was *no* talk of marriage.

I certainly never mentioned to Suzette that Enzo and I got married because I was knocked up. That means he must have told her. Why would he say that to her? Unless…

"I'm sorry you have to hear it from me," she says, "but your husband is a dangerous man." She cocks her head to the side. "But maybe you already know."

A sudden cool breeze sends a shiver through me. "There's nothing to know. Enzo wouldn't hurt a fly."

She laughs. "Oh, Millie. I'm sure you don't really believe that."

I do believe it. My husband has never done anything violent to another person during the time I have known him. Threatened it, maybe. But I've never even seen him throw a punch.

Although there's a small chance he may have broken some fingers. Oh yeah, and he did once almost beat a man to death.

"Anyway." Suzette steps out of the beam of the flashlight. "I need to get some stuff from the house without the paparazzi catching wind of me. I figured I'd slip in through the back."

"The reporters are all gone."

"Really?"

She frowns, clearly disappointed by the lack of

attention from the press. Whether Suzette killed Jonathan or not, she does not seem terribly broken up about his death. It's like she doesn't even care. And talking to her has not helped matters. But I have found out one very important thing tonight.

There absolutely *is* a way for somebody to get into the back of the house without Janice Archer seeing them from across the street.

# FIFTY-FOUR

The next morning, we are woken up by the doorbell ringing downstairs and red and blue lights flashing outside the house. I shake Enzo awake, and he is instantly alert and joins me at the window.

"What this time?" he mutters.

Is there a chance that the detective has come to arrest my husband? I can't even wrap my head around that possibility.

I throw on jeans and a T-shirt, and I race downstairs in my bare feet, practically tripping on the stairs. I haven't even showered yet or brushed my teeth, and my hair is greasy. But you can't exactly tell the police waiting at your front door to give you a few minutes to pop in the shower.

When I crack open the door, a sober-faced Willard is standing on our front porch, dressed in a crisp white shirt, his tie cinched close to his neck. "Mrs. Accardi," he says.

"How…how can I help you?"

"I got a search warrant here."

Cecelia mentioned this as a strong possibility, but it still shocks me that they're here. It's been two days since Jonathan Lowell was murdered, and it seems like there should be other more realistic suspects by now. The fact that they are still looking at Enzo scares me.

"Can I wake up the kids first please?" I ask.

"We can start downstairs," he offers.

That is the best I can hope for.

When I get upstairs, Enzo has managed to throw on jeans and a T-shirt. He can hear the officers entering our house, and his face fills with concern. "They are searching? Now?"

I nod. "This will take a while. You stay here, and I'm going to drive the kids to school."

The kids are understandably a bit frightened and confused about what is happening. I tell them to get dressed, and I run to take a quick shower and brush my teeth. It's way too early for school, so maybe I'll take them to a diner for some breakfast. I don't want to be here while this is happening anyway.

When I get out of the bathroom, both the kids are dressed and look like they're ready to go. They are both in Nico's bedroom, wearing identical worried expressions on their faces. Enzo is in there with them, sitting on Nico's bed and talking to them softly. I hang back for a moment, listening to the conversation.

"Daddy," Ada whimpers. "Why are they searching our house? What are they looking for?"

"I don't know," Enzo answers. "But they are not going to find anything interesting. So we will let them finish, then this will be over."

"Are you in trouble?" she presses him.

"No." His voice is firm. "Not at all."

Then he speaks to the two of them in Italian, which they both understand but I do not. I don't know what he says, but whatever it is, he manages to coax a small smile out of Ada. Nico, on the other hand, just has a troubled look on his face.

"All right!" I clap my hands together. "Who wants to go out for chocolate chip pancakes?"

There was a point in time when Nico would have sold his Nintendo for chocolate chip pancakes. But now they just stare at me, utterly unenthusiastic about the possibility of eating chocolate for breakfast.

Before I can get them out of the house, Enzo grabs me. He leans in close to me and whispers in my ear, "Do not worry. This will all be over soon."

I wish I could believe him.

The kids barely talk on the way to the diner, and even though we do get the obligatory chocolate chip pancakes, they both just stare at the little brown circles and push them listlessly around their plates. Ada has bags under her eyes, and Nico has some dried drool in the corner of his lips.

"Do you want more syrup?" I ask them.

I lift up the container of maple syrup, ready to douse both of their plates in it if that's what it will take to get them to eat.

"Mom," Ada says, "do the police think Dad killed Mr. Lowell?"

"No," I say quickly.

"Then why are they searching our house?" Nico asks.

"Well," I say, "they are searching to prove that he *didn't* kill Mr. Lowell."

"That makes no sense," Ada says. Nico nods in agreement.

"Okay, fine." It was so much easier when they were little and accepted everything I said. Oh wait, that never used to happen. "Here's the thing. We all know that your dad would never hurt anyone. Not unless he had to to protect us, right?"

I'm proud of how quickly they both nod their heads.

"So it doesn't matter if they're searching our house," I say. "Because your dad didn't do anything wrong, so there's no way they're going to find anything."

As I say the words, I try my hardest to believe them. If I let my doubts seep into my voice, the children will hear it. And I need them to believe that their father is innocent right now.

"Everything is going to be okay," I tell them.

But even as the words leave my mouth, I know that they are not true. And that things are about to get much worse.

# FIFTY-FIVE

After I drop the kids off at school, I make a stop on the way home.

Partly because I don't want to come home in the middle of the search. And partly because there is something I need to know. Something that is tugging at me, and I won't be able to stop thinking about it until I make this pit stop.

I find the address I'm looking for in my inbox. It's located about two towns over, in a neighborhood where Enzo and I looked at houses. We found a beautiful house that was closer to being within our price range than where we ended up, but the neighborhood was terrible. At least it's safe here during the day. Mostly.

I park in front of a weather-worn white house that looks like it is badly in need of a paint job. I climb out of my car, debating if it's safe to leave it on the street. It's okay though. I won't be long.

I walk toward the front steps of the house, looking

around for some sort of guard dog racing out at me. This somehow looks like the sort of house that would have a terrifying dog guarding it. And possibly a man with a sawed-off shotgun.

Well, I would still rather be here than back at my house with the police.

I march up the steps to the front door. I press my finger against the doorbell, but I'm fairly sure it's broken. So instead, I rap my fist against the door. When there's no answer, I knock harder. There's a Pinto in the driveway, so I assume somebody is home.

Finally, I hear footsteps growing louder behind the door. A scratchy voice calls out, "Okay, okay, hold your horses."

A second later, the door is yanked open by a man in his sixties. He's got sparse white hair and veins of spider webbing around his bulbous nose. Even though it's early in the morning, he stinks of whiskey.

"Um, hello." I offer a smile. "I'm looking for… Is Martha here?"

The man narrows his bloodshot eyes at me. "How do you know my wife?"

For a moment, I allow myself to imagine the proper, efficient woman I came to know in my house being married to this man. It doesn't seem like a good fit, but I've learned that people change a lot after they say "I do." What was it like for her to go home to this man every night?

I can't help but feel a rush of sympathy for the woman I accused of stealing from me. Although to be fair, she *did* steal from me.

"She, uh, she used to clean my house." I silently

curse myself for not having a story ready. "She left her coat behind, and I wanted to return it to her."

Never mind that I'm not actually carrying a coat. I'm counting on the fact that this guy is too blitzed to notice. I just want to talk to Martha so I can confirm Enzo's story. I need to know if he was telling the truth.

"You may as well keep the coat," the man says. "Because that bitch took off on me earlier this week. After all I did for her..."

He lets out a hacking cough, and I take a step back. "You mean she moved out?"

"Well, do you see her anywhere?" he grunts. "If you see her, you tell her she's got some groveling to do when she drags herself back here."

For Martha's sake, wherever Enzo took her, I hope she never does drag herself back here. I hope she's gone for good.

The man slams the door in my face, and I walk back to my car, which miraculously has not been stolen in the two minutes I was away from it. But this time, my step is a little lighter. I hadn't been entirely convinced of Enzo's story about Martha, but now it looks like it all checks out. If he showed up here, he would have been concerned. And if she answered the door with bruises on her face, he would not have been able to walk away without trying to help her. Because he couldn't help his sister in time, and it's eaten at him for the last two decades. His desire to help women in danger is something I always loved about him and a passion I shared.

I want to trust him. I want to trust my husband so badly.

# FIFTY-SIX

The police search our house for hours.

When they finish, the house is in shambles. As expected. Neither of us are working today—I've taken a personal day, and Enzo is trusting his work to his staff—so we get to cleaning it all up. I'm just hoping we can get it done before the school bus delivers the kids back home. If they walk into this mess, they will panic.

Enzo and I clean together in silence. We're working on the kitchen now, putting away pots and pans that were thrown on the kitchen floor. It's almost like unpacking our boxes all over again.

Even though I shouldn't say it, there's a question running through my head, and before I can stop myself, I blurt it out. "Enzo, did you tell Suzette that you only married me because I was pregnant?"

His body goes rigid. "What?"

"Did you tell her you knocked me up?"

"No, I did not say that to her." He rubs his jaw. "Why would you think I would tell her that?"

"Because she knew about it. And I sure didn't tell her. So how did she know?"

"Ada is eleven. We are married less than twelve years." He lifts a shoulder. "She did math?"

Maybe. It's entirely possible I might have mentioned that we were married eleven years. I should have been more careful about what I said around somebody like Suzette. She was surely analyzing every word.

He narrows his eyes at me. "When were you talking to Suzette about this?"

I can't very well tell him that I snuck into their backyard last night. He would be furious. "This was a while ago. I just started thinking about it."

"Believe me, Millie, I do not say our business to anyone." He frowns at the kitchen counter. "They broke three plates. You know that?"

"I told you they were not going to be gentle."

"This is allowed? They just break things?"

I don't know what to say. What are we supposed to do? Call the cops on them?

"Do you know if they found anything?" I ask him.

"No. They did not find anything because there is nothing to find." He clenches his fist in frustration. "They broke a mug too! Is ridiculous!"

"Enzo," I say, "why don't you let me finish up in the kitchen? You can go clean up the bedrooms, okay?"

"Fine," he grumbles.

He stalks off, leaving me alone to clean the kitchen. Good thing, because I'm pretty sure there's a lot more that they broke in here. There are fewer things to break in the bedrooms.

While I am throwing away the remains of the broken

dishes, my phone rings. It's a 718 number, which means it's not somebody on the island. I take the call.

"Millie?"

It's Cecelia's voice—I recognize it from yesterday. I still can't get over how different she sounds from the little girl she used to be.

"Hi, Cecelia," I say. "I…I guess you heard what happened."

"Yes, I spoke to Enzo this morning. He wasn't happy."

"We were just surprised," I say. "We were hoping it wouldn't come to this. That they would find another suspect."

"Oh no," Cecelia says. "They are laser-focused on Enzo right now."

"Did you check out the backyard at the Lowell house?" I ask her. "I looked around, and there is definitely a place where you can get in without passing the front of the house."

"Yes, I was able to confirm that. But it might be a moot point."

"What do you mean?"

"I mean, when they were searching your house, they found something."

What? Enzo was so emphatic that nothing would be found that would incriminate him.

My stomach sinks. "What did they find?"

"I don't know." She sighs. "They are being incredibly difficult about sharing any information at this time, but I was able to ascertain that from one of my contacts. They are doing some tests right now, but my contact said they think it's a 'slam dunk.'"

A slam dunk?

Oh my God, what if they found that bloody shirt? Enzo swore it was his own blood, but if they say it's a slam dunk…

"Does Enzo know this?" I ask.

"Yes, I just got off the phone with him, but I wanted to let you know as well because it didn't sound like he was going to tell you." She hesitates. "This is all in confidence, of course. I'm not supposed to know this information at all, and I'm certainly not supposed to tell either of you. Can I trust you to keep this between us, Millie?"

"You can," I confirm.

"Benito and I both have our ears to the ground." Despite the fact that my world is crashing around me, Cecelia doesn't sound the slightest bit rattled. And her confidence makes me calmer. "If we hear anything at all about an arrest warrant, I'll call you immediately."

The idea of my husband being arrested is almost too horrible for words. Suddenly, I'm too choked up to even respond.

"Millie." Cecelia's voice is firm. "We are going to figure this out. I promise you that. Do you believe me?"

"But…" I manage. "What if…"

I can't even complete the sentence. Anyway, I don't know what I'm going to say next.

*What if my husband really was having an affair with Suzette Lowell?*

*What if Enzo really killed Jonathan Lowell?*

*What if they lock him up? What the hell am I going to do? What will I tell our children?*

"Millie," Cecelia says in that confident, capable voice of hers. "You need to trust me on this. Because I trust you. I trust *Enzo*. We will get through this."

"Okay," I agree. "I trust you."

Except how exactly will we get through this? If they found that shirt, covered in Jonathan's blood, Enzo is in deep trouble. I have to hope that he got rid of that shirt. That he put it somewhere they'll never find it.

It doesn't even occur to me that they have found something far worse.

# FIFTY-SEVEN

I don't mention my conversation with Cecelia to Enzo.

The truth is I'm scared to talk to him about it. When he comes to the kitchen to help me set the table, I open my mouth a dozen times, but the words never come out. Something terrible is coming, and it almost feels like talking about it will make it real.

When the kids get home, we act like everything is normal. We act like our home didn't just get torn apart by police officers looking for evidence of murder. If there's a chance he's going to get arrested soon, it's all the more reason to cling to normal while we still can. Enzo even manages to coax Nico out into the backyard for some baseball—the first time since the Little League incident.

But Enzo spends much longer on the bedtime routine than usual. I was going to let him go first, but when he's already been in with Ada for half an hour, I decide to go in to say good night to Nico. It's late enough that he might drift off soon if I don't go in there.

But when I get into Nico's bedroom, he doesn't look like he's about to drift off anytime soon. He is sitting up in bed, reading a comic book. The enclosure where Little Kiwi used to reside is still by his bed, but of course, now it's empty.

"Bedtime." I tug the comic book out of his hands and lay it down on his desk. "Time to go to sleep."

"I'm not tired."

"I bet you're more tired than you think."

"I bet I'm not."

But he obediently puts his head on the pillow. I turn off the lights, but the moonlight is still streaming through the window by his bed. Even though we have shades, he usually keeps them up. The whites of his eyes almost seem to be glowing in the moonlight.

"Mom?" he says.

I perch myself at the edge of his bed. "Yes?"

"Do you think that if a person does a bad thing, that makes them a bad person?"

"Well, what kind of bad thing?"

His eyes grow larger. "A *really* bad thing."

He must be thinking about his father. It must have been so jarring for him to wake up this morning to the police in our house. What will he think if they arrest Enzo?

He is watching me, waiting for my answer. After everything I have been through in my own life, I have a unique perspective on this. I have done some bad things. Some *really* bad things. I have killed somebody. Actually, more than one somebody.

Nico doesn't know about that though. We have kept that secret from our children. One of these days, they will almost certainly find out. And I am terrified that when it happens, they will hate me.

"I think," I say, "that a person can do bad things and still be a good person. As long as they were doing the bad thing for the right reason."

"You can do bad things for a good reason?"

"Absolutely. Like, we both know lying is wrong, right?"

He nods.

"Well, what if Ada got a haircut and it looked bad. And she asked you how it looked, and you told her it looked pretty because you didn't want to hurt her feelings. That would be lying, but it would be for a good reason. Does that make sense?"

"Yes..."

"Does that answer your question?"

"Not really," he says. "Because lying about a haircut isn't something *really* bad."

A chill runs down my spine. "Well, what sort of thing do you have in mind?"

*Where were you all those times you swore you were with Spencer Archer?*

I watch my son's face, waiting to see what he's going to say. But he just shrugs. Whatever he's done, he's not talking.

Before I can probe further, there's a knock at the door. It's Enzo, ready to take his turn saying good night. I'm still not sure what Nico was asking about. It seems like he has something very specific in mind, but it doesn't look like he's going to tell me what it is. Maybe Enzo will answer his questions better than I can.

# FIFTY-EIGHT

It's a rare thing that all four of us are gathered around the breakfast table.

Since the kids didn't eat their pancakes yesterday, I am making chocolate chip pancakes again today. It's nothing amazing. I am using the pancake batter that comes from the grocery store, where all I have to do is add water and mix. Then I pour little circles into the frying pan with lots of oil. I use way too much oil for my pancakes. I am basically deep frying them, but the kids love it. Actually, Enzo does too.

And then my final touch is the chocolate chips. I put about eight or nine chips in each pancake. I try to make the chocolate chips look like happy faces. It is only partially successful.

"Smells good, Millie," Enzo says. His voice sounds cheerful, but he must be at least a little panicked inside after what Cecelia told him yesterday.

Finally, I lay out four heaping plates of pancakes on

the table. The kids dig in with more gusto than yesterday. For all they know, this mess with the police is all over.

"It is raining now but it will stop this afternoon," Enzo comments. "Nico, we should practice baseball again when I get back from work."

"Do you think they would let me on a Little League team again next year?" Nico asks around a mouth full of pancakes.

I'm not sure about the rules, but after punching a kid in the gut, Nico might be banned for life. "I am not sure," Enzo says, "but maybe over the summer, we practice soccer instead. We get you just as good as at baseball. Okay?"

Nico nods. "Okay!"

It's this perfect calm family moment that I dreamed of when I first saw this house. The four of us, sitting around the breakfast table in the kitchen, eating pancakes. If I could take a family photo, it would be at this very moment.

And then the doorbell rings, spoiling everything.

"I get it." Enzo leaps out of his seat so quickly, I'm worried he already knows who is at the door. "Will be right back."

Of course, I follow him. Whatever is going on, I want to know what it is. At this point, I'm fairly sure nothing good is waiting on the other side of that door.

When I get out to the foyer, Enzo has already opened the front door. Cecelia is standing there, her pants suit drenched, her blond hair plastered to her head from the rain. If she were wearing any makeup, it would be running down her face.

"Come in," Enzo tells her. "You are soaked!"

Even though Cecelia is dripping wet, she barely seems to notice as she pushes past us into the foyer. "I'm glad I got here in time. We need to talk."

I look over at the kitchen, making sure the kids aren't standing at the entrance, listening in. I have a feeling whatever Cecelia has to say, I don't want the kids to hear it.

"Do you want to sit down?" I ask her. "I can get you a towel or—"

"The police are on their way here to arrest you, Enzo," Cecelia interrupts me.

Even though she warned me yesterday, this revelation knocks the wind out of me. Enzo looks equally shaken.

"The police gave me a heads-up this morning as a courtesy." She pushes a few strands of wet hair from her face. "They are obtaining a warrant for your arrest, and I would expect they will be here shortly. I got here as fast as I could so we could talk before it happens."

"Why?" he cries. "What do they have? They have nothing."

"Benito had some information for me," she says. "We talked while I was driving here. As I told you yesterday, they did find something when they were here. They found what they believe is the murder weapon."

"Is ridiculous!" Enzo rants. "Murder weapon? What—one of our kitchen knives?"

"No, a pocketknife," she says. "It had your initials on it—EA. They found it stuffed in a drawer."

I turn my head to look at my husband. I know that knife—the one his father gave him. He always carries it around.

"And," she adds, "it looked like it had been wiped clean, but there were still traces of blood on it. They did a rush DNA analysis that came back this morning with a match for Jonathan Lowell."

Enzo's mouth falls open. He slumps against the wall, looking like his legs are about to give out. Of all the evidence they had against him, this is by far the most damning. But he must have a reason. There must be a reason why his knife has Jonathan's blood on it. I need to hear his explanation.

I need to hear it now.

"Enzo?" I whisper.

"I..." He blinks a few times. "I thought I wiped it all off."

*What?*

He stands up straight and takes a shaky breath. "I'm so sorry, Millie," he says. "I was not honest with you. I am the one who killed Jonathan."

# FIFTY-NINE

*I am the one who killed Jonathan.*

I will hear my husband saying those words in my head until the day I die.

Until this moment, Cecelia has seemed utterly confident and in control of the situation, but this confession has shaken her. "Enzo, are you saying…"

"I am so sorry," he says quietly. "I did a terrible thing. I am sorry that I lied about it. But…now I will make it right. I will confess."

"What are you talking about?" I am nearly shrieking—loud enough for the kids to hear—but I can't help myself. "Why would you do that?"

He drops his eyes. "I am so sorry. I did it for us…for the insurance money. We were so broke and…"

Cecelia is at a loss for words. And, for that matter, so am I. I have so many questions. If he did this for the insurance money, does that mean Suzette was involved? Will she be arrested too? I can't even think of where to start, but then the doorbell rings and I realize that I don't have time to ask even one question.

Cecelia snaps back to attention. "That's the police," she says.

Enzo's face fills with panic. "Millie, can you please bring the children upstairs? I do not want them to see."

The doorbell rings again, followed by pounding on the door. I don't want the kids to see either. But it doesn't seem like I have much time.

*Oh, Enzo, what were you thinking?*

I nearly trip over my feet on the way to the kitchen, where the kids are still eating their pancakes. God, I wish I could let them finish those pancakes. But there's no time. "You guys," I say. "I need you both to go to your rooms and shut the doors. Now."

There was a time when a request like that would have been met with whining and objections. But right now, they get it. They abandon their plates and run upstairs. Two doors slam in succession.

When I return, Enzo and Cecelia still have not opened the door—they're waiting for me to give the all clear. Enzo looks like he's going to be sick, but he squares himself and opens the front door. It's no surprise that Detective Willard is standing there, that same grim expression on his face that I have come to despise.

"Enzo Accardi," he says. "You are under arrest for the murder of Jonathan Lowell."

When the detective snaps the cuffs on my husband's wrists, I am so glad the kids are upstairs so they don't witness this. I know how it feels to have handcuffs on your wrists. I remember the way the metal bites into your skin, and when you walk, you almost feel off balance. I know what it feels like to be taken away by the police in handcuffs. I see that pain in Enzo's eyes.

And he has a lot more handcuffs in his future. A lifetime.

"I love you, Millie," Enzo calls out to me just as they are taking him away.

He doesn't make excuses. He doesn't pretend he's innocent anymore. All he has to say for himself are those four words.

"Enzo!" Cecelia calls after him, sticking her head out into the rain. "Do not say one word to them without me there! Do you hear me? Not one word! I'm going to meet you there!"

I watch the detective lead my husband to the police car. They shove him in the back seat, and something inside me just breaks. I'm never going to come home to my husband again. The next time I see him, he will be in custody.

He will almost certainly spend the rest of his life behind bars.

Cecelia closes our front door and leans against it, shaking her head. She brushes a strand of wet hair out of her eyes. "I can't believe that just happened. I am stunned."

"Yeah," I manage.

"We're missing something." She stares intently out the window at the police car carrying my husband away from us—as if that might somehow hold the clue. "He's not telling us everything. He wouldn't kill someone for money. I don't believe that for one second. He had another reason."

"Maybe..."

Except she doesn't know how badly we wanted this

house. Even at 10 percent below asking, it wasn't in our price range, but we bought it anyway. We celebrated when our mortgage got approved, but now I wish the bank had rejected us. We could have kept looking. We could have found something just as good where we weren't constantly struggling to pay our bills.

"Do not panic, Millie," she says to me. "I will handle this."

I shoot her a look. "My husband just confessed to murder, Cecelia."

It's hard to gauge what the worst part of this is. It's awful in every way imaginable. But the hardest part is imagining Enzo doing that to Jonathan. It's not like Jonathan was shot from across the room. Enzo walked right up to him with his pocketknife and slashed his throat from ear to ear. What kind of person does that?

But there's a lot Enzo has done in his life that I would not have believed. I couldn't have imagined my husband breaking fingers for a mobster, but it turns out that's part of his history too. He's apparently very much the sort of man who could cut another man's throat.

After all, he did it. He confessed.

A door slams upstairs. One of the kids must've come out of their room to witness their father being taken away by the police. Now I have to deal with that. I have to tell both of them what happened.

"I better get over to the police station," Cecelia says. "Will you be all right, Millie?"

Absolutely not. But there's nothing she can do for me right now. "Go to the station."

She nods. "Remember—this is not over. I will help him."

"Thank you," I say, although what can she really do for us at this point? It wasn't self-defense. It was either first-degree or second-degree murder. Either way, he's lost his freedom for good.

Cecelia hugs me goodbye, and she promises to stay in touch with any updates. Once she's gone though and the house is silent once again, I take in the reality of my situation.

Enzo is gone.

And now I have to tell the kids.

As I walk up the creaky stairs to the second floor of our house, it hits me that there is no way we will be able to afford the mortgage payments anymore. The first thing we are going to have to do is put this house back on the market. I don't know where we will be able to afford to live on just my income.

I start for Nico's room first, because he has been the more troubled of my two children, but then I hear the sobs coming from Ada's room—that girl always takes everything so hard. And in this situation, I can't blame her. I knock on the door, and when she doesn't answer, I come in anyway.

Ada is lying on her bed, sobbing into her pillow, her narrow shoulders shaking violently. Actually, her whole body is shaking. I saw somebody have a seizure at the hospital last year, and this looks not entirely dissimilar to that. Ada has always been a daddy's girl, and it's going to destroy her world to find out what he did. Just watching her cry makes the tears I've been holding back spring to my eyes.

*Enzo, how could you do this to us? How could you?*

"Ada." I sit on the edge of her bed and stroke her soft black hair. "Ada, honey… I told you not to come down."

She says something into her pillow that I can't quite make out.

"It's okay." I stroke her hair again. "It's going to be okay."

I don't know who I am trying to convince. If I'm trying to convince her, it's not working. And I'm not convincing myself either. I should just shut up.

Ada shifts on the bed, turning to look at me with her puffy, bloodshot eyes. "They think Dad killed Mr. Lowell."

My instinct is to lie, but what is the point? "Yes. They do."

Tears stream down her cheeks. "But he didn't!"

This next part is going to be hard for her, but she's going to hear it sooner or later. Better she hears it from me than reads it online or hears it from a friend. "Ada, honey, he confessed," I tell her. "He admitted to them that he killed Mr. Lowell."

"He didn't though!" she cries. "I know he didn't!"

I try to put my hand on her shoulder, but she shrugs me away. "How do you know?"

"Because," my daughter says, "I was the one who killed him."

# PART III

# SIXTY

## ADA

My name is Ada Accardi, and I am eleven years old.

I have black hair and eyes that are actually brown except some people say they look black as well. I have one brother named Nicolas, and he is nine years old. I speak two languages fluently: English and Italian. My favorite food is macaroni and cheese, especially the way my mom makes it. My favorite book is *Daughters of Eve* by Lois Duncan. My favorite flavor of ice cream is cookie dough.

Also, I killed my next-door neighbor, Jonathan Lowell.

One more thing:

I'm not sorry.

# HOW TO KILL YOUR CREEPY NEXT-DOOR NEIGHBOR—A GUIDE BY ADA ACCARDI, GRADE FIVE

## STEP 1: LEAVE BEHIND YOUR HOME AND EVERYTHING YOU LOVE

Tomorrow, we are moving.

Mom and Dad are really excited about this. Especially Dad. He keeps talking about how we are going to live in this great new house and we are going to love it. They act like they are doing this wonderful thing for us, except I don't want to move. I like it in the Bronx. All my friends are here. I even like this apartment that they say is "too small."

But when you are eleven years old, you don't have a choice. If your mom and dad tell you that you need to move, you have to move.

Anyway, that's why I can't sleep.

I've been lying awake in bed for the last hour, staring up at the ceiling. I like my ceiling. It has a lot of cracks in the paint, but the cracks look familiar. Like, there's this crack right in the center that looks just like a face. I named it Constance.

I'm going to miss Constance when we leave.

"Nico?" I whisper into the darkness.

One thing my parents say is bad about our home is that Nico and I have to share a room. And because he's a boy and I'm a girl, we shouldn't have to share. Except Dad hung a curtain in the middle of the room, so it's fine. I don't mind sharing with Nico. I like knowing that when I go to sleep, he is in the room with me, on the other side of the curtain.

"Yeah?" Nico whispers back.

He's awake. Good. "I can't sleep."

"Me either."

"I wish we didn't have to move."

Nico's mattress makes that loud squeaking noise that it always does when he rolls over. "I know. It's not fair."

Somehow, it makes me feel better that Nico also doesn't want to leave. Because Mom and Dad are so excited. You would think we were moving to Disneyland.

But it's not as bad for him as it is for me. Nico has always made friends more easily than me. Everyone likes Nico right away. But I have had the same two best friends—Inara and Trinity—since I was in kindergarten. Also, I am only three months away from graduating from elementary school, and I am going to miss my graduation. Instead, I'm going to graduate with a bunch of kids I don't even *know*.

"Maybe it will be awful," Nico says, "and Mom and Dad will want to move back."

"Probably not. I think this new house was really expensive."

"Right. They said they can't even hardly afford the garage."

"You mean the mortgage?"

"Is that different?"

I don't understand what a mortgage is, but I know it's not the same as a garage. Like, I'm pretty sure. "We are stuck living in this new house until we go to college."

He's quiet on the other side of the curtain. "Well, maybe it won't be so bad. Maybe we'll get to like it."

I can't imagine that. I can't imagine making all new friends and getting used to a big scary house.

"Nico?" I say.

"Uh-huh."

"Can I pull the curtains open?"

The curtains separating the two sides of the room are really meant for me. When Dad put them up, Mom told me that we were doing it because "you are a young lady now and you need your privacy." But I always sort of want to open the curtains at night.

"Okay," Nico says agreeably.

I climb out of bed and pull the curtains back. Nico has his Super Mario Bros. bedspread pulled up to his neck, and his black hair is messy. He waves to me, and I wave back.

I remember the day Mom and Dad brought Nico home from the hospital. Mom says I can't possibly remember that because I was only two years old, and my brain couldn't make memories yet, but I swear I remember it. Mom brought him into the house in his little baby carrying case, and he was just so tiny. I couldn't believe how tiny he was! Even smaller than my dolls.

I asked if I could hold him, and Mom said that I could if I was very careful. So I sat down on the couch, and Mom laid him down on my lap. She told me I had to support his head, so I did. He looked really happy being held, although he mostly looked like an old man. And then I put my finger in his little tiny mouth, and he sucked on it. And I said to him, "I love you, Nico."

I will miss my brother being my roommate.

# SIXTY-ONE

Today is moving day.

Dad got a big truck, and he's mostly moving everything with a couple of his friends that he works with. Mom keeps yelling that he's going to hurt his back and telling him to be careful, and he says he will, but he never gets hurt, so I don't know why she's so worried. I can tell he thinks it's silly too, but he usually gives in when she gets upset like that.

My mom is a really good mom. She's, like, the kind of mom where if you forgot you were supposed to bring in a tray of Rice Krispies squares for school tomorrow and it's already almost bedtime, she will go out and get the Rice Krispies and marshmallows, and she'll make it for you and make sure they're packed and ready for school the next day. (This happened to Nico recently, so I know it's true.) She's just kind of your average good mom who loves us and takes care of us.

But Dad is different.

My dad can basically do anything. Like, Mom could go out and get stuff to make Rice Krispies squares and have them ready for school tomorrow. But if I said to Dad that I needed Rice Krispies squares that came from, like, I don't know, *China*, then he would have them for me. I don't know how, but he would get them by the time I needed them for school the next day.

Also, he drives this big truck, and he used to let me ride in front with him, but then Mom found out and got mad. So now he doesn't let me, because he says she is really smart, and if she says it's not safe, I can't do it.

My room in the new house is big. It is about twice the size of the room that Nico and I used to share. Dad told me that I get to pick my room first, because I am the oldest, so I picked the one on the corner. It has lots of windows that I can look out while I read.

Except right in the middle of unpacking books in my new room, I start to cry.

I cry too much. Everybody says that about me. I can't help it though! When I'm sad, I cry. What I don't understand is why everybody else doesn't cry more often. Even Nico hardly ever cries anymore.

Dad passes by my bedroom while I am sitting on the bed crying. He immediately drops the box he is holding and comes to sit next to me. "What is wrong, *piccolina*? Why are you sad?"

I raise my eyes to look at him. I am almost as tall as Mom, but Dad is much taller than both of us. When he comes to pick me up from school, the other girls at school say that he is very handsome. Also, Inara's mom has a crush on him. But I don't think of him that way.

"I want to go back home," I say.

He frowns. "But this is home now. And much better home."

"I hate it."

"Ada, you do not mean that."

He looks so disappointed that I don't tell him that I do mean it. If I could snap my fingers and be back home in our tiny little apartment again, I would do it in a second.

"I will tell you what," he says. "You give our new house a chance. And if in one year, if you still hate, then we move back."

"No, we won't."

"We will! I make you a promise."

"Mom won't let us do that."

He winks at me and says in Italian, "So we do it anyway."

I don't believe him, but it makes me feel better. Plus, when I think about it, he is probably right. Everything will be different in a year. Maybe I really will love it here by then.

# SIXTY-TWO

## STEP 2: TRY TO FIT IN—BADLY

I've never been the new kid before.

I always felt bad for the new kid standing in front of the classroom, having to tell us all about themselves. And now it's me. I'm standing up in front of a room full of fifth graders, wearing the itchy, uncomfortable pink dress my mom put out for me. There was a beautiful white floaty dress at the department store that I wanted to buy for my first day of school, but for some reason, my mom never, ever lets me wear white, so that's how we ended up with this one. And now I don't know what to say.

"Go on, Ada," my teacher, Mrs. Ratner, says to me. "Tell everyone a little about yourself."

I don't like Mrs. Ratner. My old teacher, Ms. Marcus, was young and wore these cute purple glasses all the time, and she used to bring candy for us every Thursday. Mrs. Ratner is about a million years old, and I think her smile muscles might be too old to work anymore.

"My name is Ada," I say, "and I'm from New York City."

I look over at Mrs. Ratner, checking if this might be enough. It isn't.

"I like to read," I say. "And I used to take ballet lessons." I haven't taken ballet lessons since I was nine years old, but I'm hoping that might be enough.

It's not.

"My favorite subject is English," I go on. "And my dad is Italian so I speak Italian."

"Does anyone have any questions for Ada?" Mrs. Ratner addresses the class.

A kid in the class raises his hand. "If your dad is an alien, is he green?"

"He's not an alien. He's *Italian*."

"You said alien."

I don't know what to say to that. Then the second question comes: "If you're Italian, how come your favorite subject is English?"

"My *dad* is Italian," I explain. "I'm from here."

"No, you're not," another kid says. "You just moved here. So how can you be *from* here?"

"I mean," I say, "I'm from New York, which is here."

"This is not New York City," the first kid says.

"But it's New York State."

"So?"

Mrs. Ratner lets the other kids ask me questions for a few more minutes. They ask me some questions that are okay, like what is my favorite movie or my favorite TV show. But they ask me a lot of other questions that are weird. Like, why am I wearing socks with a dress? And that same kid who asked if my dad was an alien asks me if I believe in aliens and if I've ever seen one.

When I go back to my seat, the boy next to me is staring at me. It's pretty annoying, and I finally say to him, "What is it?"

And then he says, "If you are an alien, you are the prettiest alien I have ever seen."

I don't even know what to say to *that*. But then Mrs. Ratner shushes us, so I don't have to think of what to say back.

When it's time for lunch, the boy who was sitting next to me follows me to the cafeteria. Well, I am pretty much following everyone else since I don't know where to go, but I feel like he is behind me the whole time. And then when I get into the line, he is right in line behind me.

"Hi, Ada," he says. "I'm Gabe."

"Hi," I say back.

When I was in kindergarten or first grade, all the kids in our class were about the same size. But in fifth grade, some kids are a lot bigger than others. Like, there are kids that only go up to my shoulder, and then there are other kids like Gabe who are super tall and kind of tower over me.

"So how do you like the school so far?" he asks me.

I don't like it at all. But I can't say that. So I just shrug. "It's fine."

"How come you moved here?"

"My parents think it's a good place for kids to grow up or something."

"Oh, it's not." Gabe's eyes bug out, and for a moment, he reminds me a little bit of the praying mantis that Nico wants to get. "Did you know that this kid disappeared a few years ago? Like, one day he was here, and one day he wasn't."

I don't know what he is talking about. If this town wasn't safe, my parents wouldn't have moved us here. "From our school?"

"No, he lived a few towns away, but we all went to the same camp together." Gabe looks way too excited to talk about this missing kid. "He was really good at archery, but I was a better swimmer. His name was Braden Lundie. And like I said, one day he just never came home from school, and nobody ever figured out what happened to him."

"They say it's usually someone in the family." I heard my mom saying that once to my dad when they were watching the news and thought I couldn't hear them.

"No, it wasn't," Gabe insists. "Braden's parents were working with the police and trying so hard to find him. But they never did." He gives me an ominous look. "He's probably dead now."

"Maybe he ran away."

"He was only eight years old! Where would he even go?"

The idea of an eight-year-old disappearing makes goose bumps pop up all over my arms. I have to make sure to wait with Nico for the bus. If we're together, nothing can happen.

"If you want," Gabe says, "I can walk you home so nothing happens to you."

"I take the bus."

And even if I didn't, I do *not* want to hang out with Gabe. As much as I want to make some friends, he's creepy. It's something about his thin curly hair. Also, he smells bad. He needs to take a shower. I take one every night because Mom says it's important to smell good.

"Well," he says, "maybe you can come over to my house after school today."

"I'm not allowed," I say. "I'm supposed to come right home after school."

"Maybe another day?" he asks hopefully.

"Maybe."

I don't want to hang out with Gabe any day, but I'm hoping he will just leave me alone if I say that. But he doesn't leave me alone. He talks to me the entire time we are waiting in the line for our food, and then he follows me to my table. I don't really want to sit with him, but I guess it's better than sitting alone.

# SIXTY-THREE

Nico and I ride the bus home from school together. It's not surprising that he made a bunch of new friends today, but he still sits next to me.

"How was school?" I ask him.

"Pretty good," he says. "A lot of kids like to play baseball."

I wish I was good at sports like Nico. I'm good at swimming because Dad taught me, but it's not a group activity. I don't even think there's a swim team for kids my age. The other thing I like to do is read, and that's not a group activity either.

"Some of the kids are going to the park this weekend to play baseball," he says. "Maybe Mom will let me go."

"Just be careful," I say. "Did you know that there was this kid named Braden Lundie who disappeared a few years ago? He was about your age too. Nobody even knows what happened to him."

"So?"

"So! *Something* happened to him. Maybe somebody killed him."

"Geez, Ada." Nico rolls his eyes. "You worry more than Mom."

He might be right. I don't know why I worry about things so much. I wish I could turn off my worrying.

"If you're worried," Nico says, "you can come and watch."

I might do that, but really, I would rather be spending time with kids my own age. I didn't make any friends today. Well, except for Gabe, and I really, really don't want to spend any time with him outside school. It's bad enough I have to see him *at* school.

"Did you sleep better having your own room last night?" I ask Nico.

He thinks about it for a minute and shakes his head. "No, I was scared. I missed you."

I'm glad he said that. I had so much trouble sleeping last night all alone in my room. "I miss you too."

"Maybe we can have a sleepover sometime?" he suggests. "I can bring a sleeping bag and sleep on the floor in your room."

"Or I can sleep in your room?"

"We can take turns," he says happily.

The bus arrives on Locust Street, which is the dead-end street where we live. Nico and I climb out, along with that kid Spencer who lives across the way. Spencer's mom is already waiting for him and immediately takes him home, but our mom is waiting in the house. I've got the keys to the house in my bag, and Mom says if she's not home from work yet when we get home, I'm in charge until she gets back.

As we pass the house next door to ours, I notice somebody at the window. It must be our neighbor. It's a man about the same age as Dad, and when he sees us, he waves. Nico waves back, and so do I, but I feel weird about it. I don't know why that man is standing at the window, watching the school bus arrive.

It's just a strange thing to do.

# SIXTY-FOUR

## STEP 3: LEARN TO LIVE IN YOUR NEW HOME

Nico is acting weird.

He's been going over to the Lowells' house after school because he broke their window playing baseball in the backyard so he has to work it off doing chores. Anyway, it seems like he goes there every day, and then he doesn't get home until just before Mom gets back. I asked him what kind of chores they have him doing and he said just cleaning. But then when I asked him what he was cleaning, he got quiet about it.

Whatever they're making him do, it's making him grumpy. They don't even have an animal to clean up after. Are they making him take out the garbage? Wash dishes? Are they making him push a boulder up a hill and as soon as he gets to the top, the boulder rolls back down to the bottom again?

If this were back in the old days, when we shared a room, I would have just waited until bedtime and then asked him about it. But now, Nico shuts himself in his room at night and doesn't talk to me much.

Tonight, during dinner, he was hardly eating at all. Mom made mashed potatoes with lots of butter and salt, just how he likes it, but he just kept making it into a big pile and then sculpting it into different things. So after dinner is over, I go to his room. I knock on the door, which still feels weird after sharing a room for so long.

"I'm busy!" he calls out.

"It's Ada!" I call through the door.

"Still busy!"

Then I try the doorknob, and it's locked. Why does a nine-year-old even have a lock on their door? It doesn't feel like that's safe.

Oh no, I really do sound like Mom. Great, I take after the boring parent. Just my luck.

I decide the best thing to do is ask him about it while we're walking to the bus stop the next morning. The few minutes when we walk to the stop and then later back home are the only times of the day when the two of us are alone together. But then we get to the stop and mean Mrs. Archer is standing there, glowering at the two of us—especially Nico. But lately, Nico hasn't even been waiting for me to walk to the bus stop. He just dashes out the door in the morning and barely looks at me while we wait for the bus to arrive.

So this morning, I wake up extra early to make sure he doesn't leave before I do. When I get downstairs, there's no sign of Nico. I figure I have just enough time for a quick bowl of cereal for breakfast, although when I get in the kitchen, Martha is cleaning, and I don't want to get in her way. It's so weird having a woman who comes to our house to clean. Back in the Bronx, only our rich friends had cleaning people, and I'm pretty sure we're not rich.

"Do you want breakfast?" Martha asks me.

I nod. "Can you pass me the box of corn flakes?"

Martha's eyes widen. "Corn flakes for breakfast?"

I don't understand why she looks so horrified by that. What's so wrong with having cereal for breakfast? I mean, isn't that what cereal is *for*?

But then again, Martha is strange. She hardly talks at all, she keeps her hair back in a bun so tight that it looks painful, and also, she's always staring at my mom. Like, *always*. I have no idea why.

"I can make you an omelet and sausage," she tells me. "That's a proper breakfast."

Before I can tell her no, that I don't have time, she opens the fridge and reaches for the carton of eggs. When she's reaching, the sleeve of her shirt rides up and I notice she's got a ring of dark purple bruises around her wrist. Like she was wearing a bracelet that was much too tight.

"Did you hurt yourself?" I ask her.

She freezes, the carton of eggs clutched in her hands. Her gaze drops to her wrist, and she tugs at her sleeve to cover the bruise. "I… No."

"Then why do you have bruises?" I ask, even though I know it's none of my business.

She blinks a few times. "I… I just…"

She seems so upset all of a sudden. I wonder if Martha is in some kind of trouble, and maybe I should try to help her. But what can I do? I'm only eleven years old. I can't even solve my own problems.

Speaking of my own problems, while I'm trying to figure out what to say to Martha, I hear the front door slam. Nico! Shoot, I knew I shouldn't have tried to get stupid breakfast! Now he'll be at the bus stop before we even have a second to talk.

"I have to go," I tell Martha. And she looks so relieved that I'm glad I didn't say anything else. It's not like she'd want to tell her problems to some kid anyway.

# SIXTY-FIVE

Today, Dad is picking me up at school to take me out for ice cream.

He used to do this back at our old apartment. Nico eats up a lot of attention, so Dad said we should get to hang out just the two of us. I was worried that he wouldn't want to do it anymore after we moved, especially because he's building up his business in our new town, but then yesterday he told me he was picking me up tomorrow in his truck. And now I'm waiting for him outside the school.

I've never been picked up before, only taken the school bus, so I'm not entirely sure where to wait. I end up behind the school, because there is a place for cars to pull over there. But then everybody leaves and it gets real quiet, and I can't help but start thinking about that kid, Braden Lundie. The one who disappeared.

The thought of that really scares me. Because when you disappear, what happens to you? I mean, it's not like he just vanished off the face of the earth. He didn't disintegrate. Somebody *took* him.

"Ada?"

At first, I am grateful to hear a kid's voice from behind me. Until I turn around and realize it's Gabe. Pretty much the last person I want to see.

Ever since my first day of school a few weeks ago, Gabe won't leave me alone. I found some girls to sit with during lunch, and he knows better than to try to join us, but he always gets in line behind me in the cafeteria, and then he follows me to recess. I hardly ever talk to him, so I don't understand why he keeps bugging me.

"What are you doing here?" he asks me. "I thought you take the school bus."

"I'm getting picked up," I say. "Except I don't know where my dad is."

And now that I am looking around, I realize there's no way to get onto this street from the main road. It's all blocked off. So there's no way Dad can find me here. I've got to walk around and see if I can find him. And then tell him I need a cell phone, because I really do.

"Listen, Ada," Gabe says, "I wanted to ask you a question."

I don't want him to ask me a question. "Sorry, I need to find my dad."

"Right, but I just have to ask you this." Gabe is really bad at taking no for an answer. It's annoying. "Do you think you might want to go on a date with me sometime?"

"I'm not allowed to date."

That's not an official rule, but I have a feeling that it would be if I asked. But I'm not going to ask, because I don't want to go out on a date with Gabe or anybody.

"Well, would it be okay if I held your hand?"

I don't even have a chance to say no this time before Gabe reaches out to grab my hand. His is sweaty and hot. It's pretty gross to touch. I pull away, but instead of backing off, he grabs my wrist instead.

"I don't want to hold hands," I say. Even though he's not holding my hand anymore—he's grabbing my wrist.

Gabe still isn't getting it. His long fingers encircle my wrist as he tightens his grip. "Just for, like, two minutes, Ada. Please?"

"You're *hurting* me," I say through my teeth.

"No, I'm not," he insists.

I try to wrench my hand away, but he's holding on too tightly. I start thinking about something my mom told me, about how boys are really sensitive between their legs and if you kick them there, they will leave you alone. But before I have a chance to test that out, we get interrupted by a string of angry Italian words and then my dad's voice booming out, "WHAT DO YOU THINK YOU ARE DOING TO MY DAUGHTER?"

Gabe drops my wrist instantly. Dad is running over to us, and he looks about as mad as I have ever seen him. There is a big scary vein standing out in his neck, and his right hand is a fist. He looks like he wants to pick up Gabe and break him in half. And I'm pretty sure he could if he wanted to. I mean, my dad is *really* strong.

"I… I'm sorry," Gabe sputters.

"No!" Dad waves his hand at me. "You say sorry to *her*!"

Gabe is just about to pee in his pants. "I'm sorry, Ada! I'm really sorry!"

Dad seems like he's barely keeping himself from

beating Gabe into a bloody pulp. He gets real close to him, and his dark eyes look terrifying. Mine are the same color, but they never look scary like his can sometimes.

"If you ever touch my daughter again," Dad hisses at him, "you will understand what sorry really means. You understand me?"

"Yes!" Gabe cries. "I mean, no! I mean…"

He looks between the two of us, and then without another word, he runs away as fast as he can.

Dad looks really upset. I don't know if I've ever seen him quite so angry before. At first, he's breathing hard, but then he calms down and gets this kind of sad expression on his face.

"Come on, Ada," he tells me. "We need to talk. In the truck."

Is he mad at me? I didn't do anything wrong. Did I? I didn't want to hold Gabe's hand. But maybe he couldn't tell that I was trying to get away. Except he doesn't really seem angry at me. He just seems…upset. Like, in general.

We have to walk all the way back to his truck, which he parked in the school lot. He must've parked and then walked around looking for me. He tells me to get inside, and when I start to get in the back, he tells me to get in the front.

But then when we are in the car, he doesn't start the engine. He just sits in the driver's seat, not saying anything. He's looking down at my wrist where Gabe was holding on to me. The place where his fingers were has now turned an angry shade of red. I wonder if I will have a bruise.

"Ada," he says, "that was scary."

I nod. "It's okay though. Because you were there."

"That's the scary part," he says. "I was there. But next time, I might not be there. I will not always be there."

I guess he's right, but at the same time, it seems like he *is* always there. Every time I have ever needed him, he has been there. It seems impossible that there will be a time when I need my dad and he won't be around for me. Like, Gabe was bothering me, and there he was—coming out of nowhere to scare him off and save me.

"I told my sister I would always be there," he murmurs, almost to himself, "but then..."

I am named after my dad's sister. Her name was Antonia, and she died before I was born. Dad sometimes talks about her and how much he loved her, but he's never said how she died. It must have been something bad though, because she was so young.

"If a boy is bothering you," he says, "you ask him to stop. You be firm about it. Make sure he knows."

I nod solemnly.

"But there's a chance he might not stop." Dad's dark eyebrows come together, and he gets a deep crease between them. "And if that happens..."

Dad is quiet for a second, thinking something over. Finally, he reaches into his pocket and pulls out that pocketknife he always carries around. The one that his dad gave him, which has his initials engraved on it.

"My father gave me this when I was your age," he says. "Now I give it to you."

"Dad!" I cry. "I can't carry around a knife with me! I'll get in trouble!"

"You do not get in trouble if nobody knows," he says.

I look down at the knife in his hands. Even though

I shouldn't, I'm itching to pick it up. I've always liked that knife because it reminds me of my dad. I figured he would give it to Nico someday, but instead, he's giving it to me.

"What am I supposed to do with it?" I ask him.

"Nothing," he says. "You carry it with you, but you never use it. Only if you have to."

"But..." I stare down at the knife, still in his hand. The blade is retracted, but I bet it's sharp. "You really think I could..."

"Only if you have to, Ada," he repeats. He touches an area to the right of his belly button. "You put the blade right in here. And then..." He jerks his wrist. "You *twist*."

I stare up at him. "Did you ever do that?"

"Me?" His eyebrows shoot up. "Oh, no. This is just...cautionary."

He holds the knife out to me again. This time, I take it from him.

# SIXTY-SIX

## STEP 4: START TO SUSPECT THE TERRIBLE TRUTH

It's Saturday afternoon, and I'm in the kitchen, trying to decide if I want a snack before dinner, when Nico slips in through the back door.

I haven't seen him since the morning. That's not unusual these days though. I used to spend practically every second of the weekend with my brother, but now he's either at Little League or locked in his room. I managed to catch him a few times to walk to the bus stop with him, but it didn't help. He didn't want to talk.

So it's not weird that I haven't seen him all day. But it is weird that he is sneaking in through the back. And it's even weirder that there's what looks like a pee stain all over the front of his pants.

Did Nico wet his pants?

"Nico?" I say.

He tries to hide his pants behind the kitchen table, but I already saw it. "What?"

"Are you okay?"

"I'm fine," he says. "I was at the Lowells' house, and I spilled some water I was drinking on myself."

Except I don't think he did. Because now that he's closer, he also smells like pee. He can tell that I don't believe him, and then he gets a worried look on his face.

"Don't tell anyone, okay, Ada?" he says.

"I won't," I promise. "But… I mean…how…"

How does a nine-year-old kid wet his pants? There was a time when Nico was about four years old when I remember he used to wet the bed, but that was a long time ago.

"I just held it in too long," he says.

I still don't get it. But he looks so embarrassed, it's not like I'm going to give him a hard time about it. "Okay…"

"You swear you won't tell anyone?"

"I swear."

"Because if you do, then you're a tattletale."

"I said I wouldn't!"

Finally, he looks satisfied, and then he hurries up to his room to change. But I can't stop thinking about what happened. Nico is already acting weird, and this was the most weird thing ever. I wish he would talk to me. I wish he were the way he used to be.

I wish we never moved here.

# SIXTY-SEVEN

At least my classes are going good.

I've always done well at school. Back at my old school, I always got all Es. That's basically the same as an A, but that's the weird grading system they used at my school so people wouldn't feel bad about not getting an A. E stands for Exceeds Expectations, and it's the best grade you can get. I got an E in everything except for gym. In gym, I got an M. (Meets Expectations.)

Mrs. Ratner gives a lot more homework than Ms. Marcus used to, but I don't mind doing homework. I want to be a pediatrician when I grow up, so I have a *lot* more school left to go. Good thing I like homework.

In the middle of doing my math assignment, I get thirsty and go downstairs for a glass of water. Except the weird thing is, while I am climbing down the stairs, I see Nico disappearing into the wall.

You heard me right.

I didn't know this, but apparently, our wall has a

secret door on it. Nico has it open, and he looks like he's about to go inside. Before he can close the door, I call out, "Hey!"

His face jerks up and he sees me. He doesn't look happy about it. "Oh. It's you."

I hurry down the rest of the stairs to get a closer look. "What is *that*?"

The door is partially open, so I can see inside. It's this tiny room, about the size of one of our bathrooms or maybe a little bigger. There isn't much inside—just some comic books. It's also dark. There's only one light bulb hanging from the ceiling.

"You can't tell anyone, Ada," Nico says. "This is my secret clubhouse."

Secret clubhouse? Really? "This doesn't seem safe."

"Ugh!" he cries. "You're acting just like Mom!"

He means it as an insult, but maybe it isn't such a bad insult to be compared to the one totally normal and rational person in this family. But I also hate that he is upset at me.

"Can I come inside?" I ask.

He makes a face. "It's my clubhouse, Ada. No girls allowed."

I know for a fact I'm his only friend around here because I always see him alone at the playground at school lately, so if he doesn't want to hang out with girls, he will have nobody to hang out with. He isn't allowed to play with Spencer anymore, even though our parents don't know about that.

"Please?"

Finally, he nods. I follow him inside the small square room, and he shuts the door behind us. It makes this terrible scraping noise when the door closes, and I have to cover my ears.

Once we are inside, the room feels *really* small. I could tell it was small from the outside, but when you're inside, it feels even worse. It's like being in a coffin. Or being buried alive. One of those two things.

Also, it's dirty. The floor has a layer of dirt on it so you can see his footprints from all the times he came in and out. It has cobwebs in the corners, which means there are spiders. People say spiders are the good kind of bugs, but I don't like anything creepy-crawly. But Nico likes bugs, so it doesn't bother him as much.

I can't help but think about that little boy, Braden Lundie. The one who disappeared. I imagine him finding himself locked in a little room like this with nothing but a small pile of comic books.

"You really like playing in here?" I ask. "It's so small…"

"Yes, I like it," Nico says stubbornly. "If you hate it, you can leave."

I do hate it. And I want to leave. But I haven't had a conversation with my brother in a long time, and I don't want him to think I'm some scaredy-cat that he can't play with.

"No," I say. "I want to stay."

I look at the door, hoping that it opens again when we want it to. What if it doesn't? How will we get out? Will Mom and Dad figure out that we're in here? My neck suddenly feels cold and sweaty, but I sit down next to Nico on the floor anyway. We won't get stuck in here. Dad will find a way to get us out, no matter what.

"Remember you said you wanted to have a sleepover?" I say to Nico.

"Uh-huh..."

"Maybe we could do that this weekend?"

He shakes his head. "No."

"Why not?"

"Because I don't *feel* like it."

My eyes feel watery all of a sudden. I don't understand what happened. Why is Nico being so mean to me? The worst part is Nico notices and scrunches up his face.

"You're always crying," he complains. "Is there anything that *doesn't* make you cry?"

I wipe my eyes with the back of my hand. "I'm sorry."

"If you're going to cry, then you have to leave."

I try to stop crying, but it's not that easy. I wish I could just say to myself, *Ada, stop crying*, and then it would stop. But Nico gives me some comic books, and then I feel a little better. I try to just read the comic books and not think about anything else. Even though I have a lot of homework to do.

And then Dad finds us hiding here, and he and Mom are all angry at us, so we can't go in the clubhouse anymore anyway. I'm glad, because I don't like this clubhouse at all.

# SIXTY-EIGHT

Ever since my dad yelled at Gabe, he hasn't bothered me again. He hasn't asked me out on a date. He hasn't even breathed on me.

Unfortunately, now there's Hunter.

Three times a week, we have a class called Library. It's one of my favorite classes, because you go to the school library, pick out a book, and you get to spend the whole period reading. I don't even understand why that's a class, because to me it just seems like fun. But a lot of kids in my class groan about it.

Today, I have picked a book from Louis Sachar. Aside from Lois Duncan, he is my absolute favorite. I have read everything he has written, and now I am rereading everything he has written, because sometimes it's more fun the second time. Like, you notice things you didn't notice the first time. Especially in his Wayside School series. That might be my favorite series of all time, even more than Harry Potter. The first and the second one are so good. The third one is good too, but not my favorite. The third in a series usually isn't that great, so it's not his fault.

Today I am reading *Someday Angeline*, which I love, even though it makes me cry. But a lot of books make me cry. I'm only halfway through when Hunter sits down at the table across from me.

"Hi, Ada," he says.

I don't look up from my book, but I do say hi.

"Adaaaaa," he says, "will you go out on a date with me?"

Some of his friends at the next table are listening, and they are snickering at our conversation. I don't know what is so funny about it. "No, thank you."

"How come?"

"I don't want to go out on a date."

"If you never go out on a date," he says, "then what are you going to do? Marry one of your books?"

The boys at the next table seem to find this hilarious.

Every time we have Library from then on, Hunter comes over to the table and asks me out on a date. I don't think he really wants to go out on a date—he is just making fun of me. Or maybe it's a little bit of both. Nobody at my old school ever talked about dating, but it seems to be a *thing* here.

"Can you please let me read my book?" I beg him.

"That's all you like to do," Hunter notes. "Read books. You know, if you keep reading all the time, you're not going to be able to see anymore."

"That's not true."

"It is true. If you read too many books, your eyeballs will fall out."

That is *so* not true. My mom likes to read, and her eyeballs have not fallen out. Although, to be fair, she doesn't read as much as I do—most people don't. Sometimes I think that's all I want to do with my time. And I wish Hunter would leave me alone to do it.

I think of the pocketknife that my dad gave me. It's in my backpack right now. It's all the way at the bottom, where nobody will find it. If any of the teachers knew I had it, I would be in big trouble. It would be smart to just leave it in my desk drawer at home. But Dad told me to carry it around all the time, and the truth is I like to have it.

But I'll never use it. I can't even imagine it.

Although at this moment, I would kind of like to. I bet if I took out that knife, Hunter would go away real quick.

"Ada," Hunter says, "would you marry me?"

The other boys are laughing again. I am sick of this. So I grab my bag and go to the bathroom, where I hide for the rest of the period, reading my book on the toilet.

# SIXTY-NINE

Today, we are going to the beach.

I like to swim, but I don't like the beach that much. I don't like the feeling of sand on my skin. Also, after a trip to the beach, it feels like sand is everywhere. It's between my toes, in the cracks of my elbows and knees, and even after a shower, it still sort of feels like it's there.

"I feel the same way!" Mom replies when I say this to her before we go. "But we haven't done any family trips since we moved, and I think this will be fun. Anyway, you love to swim, right?"

"I guess."

She smiles at me. "And you can bring a book."

I've got *Someday Angeline* in my backpack. The librarian let me take it home, because I don't get much reading done at school, and I want so badly to finish it. Hunter just won't leave me alone, and obviously, Dad isn't around to be scary and make him stop bothering me.

I wonder what Mom would do in a situation like that. Unlike Dad, she deals with everything in a calm and rational way. Maybe she has a solution that will help me deal with Hunter without having to take out Dad's knife, which would be ridiculous.

"Mom," I say.

She is digging through my drawer now, looking for a swimsuit that still fits me. I grew a lot this year, and I'll need all new swimsuits soon. "Mm-hmm?"

"What do you do if a boy is being mean to you?"

Mom drops the swimsuit she's holding and whips her head around. "Is there a boy being mean to you?"

Her face has turned very pink. I don't want to upset her. I heard Dad talking to her about some medical problems she has with her blood pressure. I don't want anything to happen to my mom.

"Not me," I say quickly. "A friend of mine. I'm trying to help her."

"Oh." That seems to calm her down. "A lot of bullies are just looking for attention, and if you ignore them, they go away."

"And what if ignoring them doesn't work?"

"Well, the important thing is to make it very clear that you're not going to tolerate being treated that way." She hesitates. "Using your *words*, of course."

Of course Mom is going to say to use your words, and Dad is going to hand me a big knife.

I end up going to the beach, and I do bring a book with me, although it's such a nice day and the water looks good, so maybe I won't even end up reading it much. It will be fun to play in the water with Nico, like we used to when we were little.

But when we get there, it's not as fun as I thought it would be. Mom seems like she's almost angry or something. And Nico is acting weird too.

"Hello, Nico, Ada," Mr. Lowell says to us. He's wearing a pair of swim trunks and a baseball cap. He's really white under his shirt, like my mom.

"Hi," I say, although my brother doesn't respond.

He doesn't seem to be upset that Nico didn't answer him. "Great day for the beach, huh?"

"Yes," I say politely.

Nico still doesn't answer, and I'm not sure why. He'd been going over to the Lowells' house to do chores for a while until they told him he didn't have to come anymore, so I figure he knows them better than I do. And I don't think the chores were that bad, since he usually hates chores but he hadn't complained about it at all.

"Is everything okay?" I ask Nico as we are walking to the water. The sand squishes beneath my feet, and I can feel it getting between my toes. Stupid gross sand.

"Everything is fine," he says.

"Why do you seem so angry at Mr. and Mrs. Lowell?"

"Why don't you just mind your own business, Ada?" he snaps at me.

Nico has never spoken to me that way before. I freeze in my tracks, shocked. Nico keeps running to the water, and I should go too, but I don't want to go if Nico is mad at me. Something is going on, and I don't understand what.

I look back at where we set up our chairs on the sand. Mom is sitting on a chair, and Mr. Lowell is next to her. She waves at me. I wave back.

Okay, I can't let this get me down. I'm not going to let my brother ruin the day.

I follow my family out to the water. Dad is a really good swimmer, and so am I, but he doesn't like me to go out farther than where he can reach me, just in case. I swim out as far as I feel safe, and then I swim back. On my way back, I notice Nico bobbing in the water nearby. And that's when I also notice that Mrs. Lowell is next to him and they're talking. I tread water as close as I dare, trying to hear what they're talking about, except there's water in my ears and it's hard to hear.

"Don't even think…telling anyone," Mrs. Lowell is saying to Nico. "Don't you dare… Do you know how much trouble you'll be in?"

And then Nico says in a tiny voice, "I won't. I promise."

Was she…threatening him?

I don't know what they were talking about, but I didn't like the tone of her voice. She was threatening him. I'm sure of it.

I keep thinking about it as I'm swimming, and I get madder and madder. How could she talk to my brother that way? And what were they talking about? I get so angry, I can't even think straight. And then when I'm swimming under the water, I pass by her legs.

I don't know why I do what I do next. I'm just so mad. So the next thing I know, I'm grabbing one of Mrs. Lowell's skinny legs and pulling as hard as I can, yanking her down into the water. She doesn't see it coming at all.

Right away, I'm sorry I did it. She wasn't prepared to go underwater, and it's obvious that she can't get back up. I don't know what to do. I don't know how to save her.

And I think to myself, what if she drowns because of me? I'd be in so much trouble!

But of course, Dad comes to the rescue. He grabs her and pulls her out of the water, and it turns out she's okay. So I didn't end up drowning her after all.

# SEVENTY

## STEP 5: FIND OUT THE TRUTH

I hate it here in Long Island.

I don't have any friends. I mean, not real friends. There are girls that I eat lunch with, and they are nice to me, but nothing like my old friends back home. Hunter bothers me almost every day in Library. Nico barely speaks to me, and he keeps getting in trouble at school.

I don't need a whole year to decide. I hate it already and I always will. I wonder if I have to wait the full year before asking to go back.

Oh, who am I kidding? We are never going back. We will live here forever.

I lie in the dark of my room, trying to fall asleep. There was a time in my life, like when I was a little kid, when it was easy to sleep. I don't remember lying awake when I was in kindergarten. But now it seems like every night, I can't sleep. I just stare at the ceiling every night. And the cracks in the ceiling aren't even interesting—I miss Constance.

Finally, I get out of bed and walk over to the window. One thing that's nice about living here is how clear and pretty the sky is. You can always see the moon and lots of stars. It's still not worth it though.

When I look out the window, my gaze falls on the house next door to ours. Number 12 Locust Street. The lights are out in the house, but somehow I see movement in the windows. I can't tell what room that is—the bedroom?

I can't stop thinking about what happened at the beach. There's something funny going on with the family next door. Why does Nico hate the Lowells so much? It's so weird.

I hear a noise behind me. It's a knock at the door. I run back to my bed, not wanting Mom or Dad to catch me wandering around my room in the middle of the night. I'm not sure if I should pretend to be asleep, but they probably hear me moving around, so I call out, "Come in."

Slowly, the door cracks open. I blink in the darkness, not sure if I'm seeing right.

It's Nico. And he's holding a sleeping bag.

"Can I sleep here tonight, Ada?" he asks me.

"Sure," I say. "Of course you can."

I keep the lights out, but both of our eyes have adjusted to the dark. Nico lays his sleeping bag down on the floor next to my bed. Then he crawls inside. I lie down in my own bed.

"Good night, Nico," I say.

"Good night, Ada."

But I don't close my eyes. I look over at Nico in the sleeping bag, and he is looking at me too.

And that's when I notice his eyes are wet.

"Nico?" I say.

Except he doesn't answer right away because he can't stop crying. But after a few minutes, he tells me everything.

# SEVENTY-ONE

"You can't tell anyone," Nico says to me before telling me the whole story. "Do you swear?"

"Yes."

"Swear it, Ada."

"I swear."

He looks at me, takes a deep breath, and then he starts talking.

It started soon after we moved here. When Nico broke that window and started doing chores for the Lowells. The first time he went, it was just ordinary stuff like washing dishes or mopping the floor. But then the second time, he made a freaky discovery:

The Lowells have a tiny room that is identical to ours, also hidden below their staircase.

When he was vacuuming, Nico noticed the very edge of the door on the wall, mostly hidden behind a bookcase, and—being my troublemaker brother—he decided to push aside the bookcase, open the door, and go inside. But unlike the room under our staircase, this one was not empty.

"It was filled with toys," he tells me. "Cool toys. Stuff that we could never afford. So...well, nobody was around, so I thought I could play with the toys just a little bit. But then Mr. Lowell caught me while I was playing with this really cool Transformers truck, and I dropped it and it broke."

Mr. Lowell told Nico that the toys were collectors' items, and the truck he broke had been very expensive. And now he owed the family thousands of dollars, plus the money for the stained-glass window he also broke since he had been playing instead of doing chores. Mom and Dad are always talking about how worried they are about money—I mean, they talk quietly so we can't hear, but we always hear them. So Nico was scared about them having to pay all that money.

But Mr. Lowell came up with an idea. He told Nico that he was thinking about building some toys of his own, and if Nico would help him by playing with different toys and telling him what his favorites were, then he wouldn't make our parents pay for the stuff he broke.

"So that's what I was doing when I went over there," Nico explains to me. "I wasn't doing chores. I was playing in the little room. And Mr. Lowell was watching from the camera."

Mr. Lowell explained that the door had to be closed when he was in there, because Mrs. Lowell would be mad about letting him play with the toys, so she couldn't ever find out. He recorded what was happening using a camera up on the ceiling, and he watched. But then one day, Nico needed the bathroom really badly, and he couldn't get out of the room. He was banging on the door, and nobody would let him out. He was panicking. By the time Mr. Lowell finally opened the door, Nico had wet his pants.

Mr. Lowell made fun of him for wetting his pants. He said he was going to tell all Nico's friends about it, and my brother had to beg him not to.

After that, the visits continued. Even when Mrs. Lowell found out about it, and she made Mr. Lowell tell Mom that they didn't want him coming anymore, he told Nico privately that he still needed to keep coming.

"And then I told him no," Nico whispers through the darkness of my bedroom. "I said that I couldn't come anymore. That I didn't like it, and I was bored of playing in the room. And also, I…I was scared. Except he told me that I didn't have a choice."

Mr. Lowell told Nico that if he didn't keep coming, he was going to sue our family for not just the broken toy and the broken window but also all the damage Nico had done to the other toys while playing in the room. He said that we would be homeless and that our parents would hate him. That worked for a little while, but then when Nico said that he was going to tell them anyway, Mr. Lowell used a different approach.

"He said that if I told anyone about the room," Nico says, "that he would kill my whole family. He said he would kill Dad first, then Mom, then you."

And now he's crying. I climb out of my bed and lie next to him on the sleeping bag. I put my arms around him. The weirdest thing is I am not crying. Practically everything makes me cry, but I'm not crying now.

I'm angry.

"Nico," I say, "Mr. Lowell could never hurt our dad. Our dad is a lot bigger than he is."

"He told me he could do it. He said he's done it before."

I don't think it's true. Mr. Lowell is no match for our dad. Nobody is. Mr. Lowell is just a big bully.

"We have to tell Mom and Dad about this," I say.

"No!" Nico sobs. "Ada, you promised you wouldn't tell anyone! You swore!"

"But this is really serious."

"If you tell anyone," he says, "I will never, ever trust you again for the rest of my life."

His dark eyes are shiny in the moonlight. He looks like he means it. But Nico is only nine years old. Even if I tell, someday he's going to realize I did the right thing.

Right?

"You promised you wouldn't tell!" he reminds me. "You better not break that promise, Ada."

"Okay," I finally say. "I won't tell them. I won't tell anyone."

Nico lets me wrap my arms around him, and eventually, he stops crying and then his breathing evens out. He's asleep. But I'm still wide awake.

I'm going to keep my promise to my brother. I won't tell anyone about the secret he told me.

Except Mr. Lowell needs to know that Nico is never going over to his house ever again.

# SEVENTY-TWO

## STEP 6: STAND UP FOR YOUR LITTLE BROTHER

I haven't been over to the Lowells' house since that dinner we had with them when we first moved here. Their house is a lot bigger and nicer than ours, although I honestly feel like ours is too big. I wait to go over until Mr. Lowell's Mercedes arrives and disappears into their garage, so I know he's home.

I don't know what I'm going to say. But he needs to know I am aware of what he is doing to my brother and that if it ever happens again, I will be telling our parents. And I am not scared of him.

Once he hears what I have to say, he won't bother Nico ever again, and I'll never have to tell Mom and Dad. Except just as I'm leaving the house, I decide at the last minute to grab the pocketknife that Dad gave me. It's not like I'm going to use it, but I just feel more comfortable when I have it. I put it in the pocket of my jeans, and then I cover it with my T-shirt so it's not visible.

Now I feel better.

I take the shortcut, cutting across our backyard to theirs. Dad is in their backyard, doing some work on their bushes. He's got some of his equipment going, and it's really loud. And when I say loud, I mean that I have to cover my ears. It sounds exactly like a saw going through metal, even though that's not what's happening. It's so loud that he doesn't even hear me walking to the back door. I almost wave to get his attention, but then I realize if he sees me, he'll ask me what I'm doing, so it's actually better he doesn't know I'm here.

I knock on the back door, but it's so loud back here that he can't hear me. I think about going around the front, but then I try the back door and it's not even locked. So I let myself inside.

I definitely saw Mr. Lowell's car go into the garage, but the house is weirdly silent. I don't hear any footsteps or noises coming from upstairs. It sounds like nobody is even home. "Hello?" I call out.

No answer.

I don't know where he went, but it doesn't seem like anyone is here. Maybe he left again while I was putting on my sneakers. Or maybe he's in the shower or something. I guess I'll leave and come back later.

But then as I'm walking through the house, I pass by the stairwell. There is a bookcase leaning against the wall, exactly where the door to the secret room is in our house. It's just how Nico described it. If I move this bookcase, will I find the secret room?

Now that the idea is in my head, I have to see this room.

The bookcase isn't that heavy, because it doesn't have many books in it. I lean all my weight against it, pushing as hard as I can. Once it starts moving, I can push it the rest of the way easily. And sure enough, behind it is the outline of a narrow door.

This one was concealed by the bookcase instead of having been covered with wallpaper. Like the one in our own house, it looks like it pushes open, although there is a hole for a key. That keyhole makes me nervous. I remember the way Nico talked about trying to get out of the room, but he couldn't because the door wouldn't open.

It hits me that if Mr. Lowell had locked him in the room and covered it with the bookcase, nobody would have known he was there. After all, Mom and Dad thought he stopped coming here to do chores. Only Nico and Mr. Lowell knew the truth.

I stare at the outline of the door. I'm not a curious sort of person. I don't need to know what's behind every door. That's more Nico's style. The room exists—that's all I need to know. Right?

But then again, what is the harm in one little peek?

Slowly, I push open the door to the room.

# SEVENTY-THREE

It's not what I expected.

The room under our staircase was just an empty space. But this one is filled with…with *stuff*.

I can see why Nico was attracted to it. It's like every toy he has ever played with or wanted in his life is in this room. Transformers, trucks, model cars, action figures. Most of them look like they have been played with recently. And the room is brighter than the one below our stairwell, lit with actual lights that require a light switch. Nico mentioned Mr. Lowell kept a camera mounted on the ceiling, but I scan the corners up above and don't see one. Maybe he took it down. But the strangest part of the room is what is in the far corner.

It's a bed.

A small bed, meant for a child maybe even a little younger than Nico, but about that age. It has a white bed frame and a thin mattress with no box spring. It's more like a cot. It's covered with a quilt, and each of the patches on the quilt has a different kind of insect sewn into the fabric.

Even though I know I shouldn't, I walk over to the bed. I run my fingers along the quilt, which feels stiff, like it hasn't been used in a long time. I guess when Nico was here, he played on the floor. I pull back the quilt and...

Oh my God.

There's a dark brown stain all over the white sheets. It's darkest right in the center, but there are splatters of it all over the sheets. I don't know if Nico ever pulled back these sheets and saw what I am seeing. If he did, maybe that's why he took Mr. Lowell's threat so seriously.

"Ada?"

I whip my head around in the direction of the voice behind me. I thought no one was home because it was so quiet. That was really stupid. I saw the car pull into the garage. I should have realized Mr. Lowell was here. He was probably upstairs or something. Or maybe he was hiding. Waiting. Watching.

And now he is *here*. In the room, with me.

He is wearing a pair of tan slacks and a dress shirt that is unbuttoned at the collar as well as a tie hanging loose around his neck. He has a layer of moisture on his forehead, which glistens in the overhead lights. He has thinning hair on top of his head, and each of those strands seems wet from his sweat.

I open my mouth to squeak out a reply, but nothing comes. I had intended to tell Mr. Lowell that he needed to leave my brother alone. I had intended to tell him in no uncertain terms that Nico would never be back here. I had intended to keep my brother out of trouble.

But now I could be the one in trouble.

"What are you doing here, Ada?" Mr. Lowell doesn't seem mad exactly. He almost looks like he finds it interesting that I am in here. "Did you move the bookcase?"

"I just..." I squeak out. "I'm sorry. I thought..."

Why am I apologizing? Ugh, I sound like my mom. She's always apologizing for things she didn't even do wrong, and now *I'm* doing it. I mean, I guess I am in his house without permission. But *he's* the one who has been locking my brother in this room. And what are these stains all over the sheets that look suspiciously like dried blood?

"You were snooping," he notes.

I don't say anything to that.

"Did you tell your parents that you were coming over here?" he asks me.

"Yes," I say.

His lips twitch. "You're lying, Ada."

"I'm not!"

"I can always tell when children are lying. You are all so obvious."

I want to run out of the room, but Mr. Lowell is blocking the exit. Not only that, but he has closed the door. Still, he couldn't have locked it. Because he's in here with me, so there's no way.

Right?

"I think," he says, taking a step closer to me. Which is too close, because this room is really, really small. "I think that you didn't tell anyone at all that you came here."

I take a step back, hitting the wall behind me. Mr. Lowell's gaze briefly flickers down to the mattress. At the bloodstains on the sheets.

"Oh, Ada," he says, "I really wish you hadn't pulled back those covers."

My breath catches in my throat. "I'd like to leave now," I manage.

He cocks his head to the side. "Would you?"

"Yes."

"The thing is," he says, "I'm not sure I can trust you. Your brother is very good at keeping secrets, but I get the feeling you're not."

I remember how Nico came home with pee all over his pants. And right now, I'm scared the same thing is going to happen to me. I don't know if I've ever been this frightened in my whole life.

"I can keep a secret," I squeak out.

Unlike me and my brother and my dad, Mr. Lowell has light eyes. So I can see when the black part in the middle grows larger. "I don't think you can," he says. "Which means…"

He's close enough now that I can smell his sour breath. I squirm, wondering if I can get past him. I need to get out. The whole room is so small, and the door is so close. If only…

"I can't let you leave, Ada," he says.

I remember when Gabe told me about that missing boy, Braden Lundie. I had imagined him being trapped in a room just like this. The thought terrified me, yet here I am. And just like Braden, nobody might see me ever again.

Except I have one thing that Braden didn't have.

I reach into my pocket, and my fingers close around my dad's pocketknife. After he gave it to me, I practiced in my room. I practiced opening and retracting the blade quickly, the way I have seen Dad do it. Mr. Lowell is staring at my face, so he doesn't see me slide the knife out of my pocket and extend the blade. He doesn't see the glimmer of the knife in the overhead lights until I have jammed it right into his belly, exactly where my dad told me to put it.

And then I twist it.

Mr. Lowell howls. I got him right where it hurts. Well, like Mom says, it hurts more between the legs, but I didn't really want to go for that area. This did the job anyway. Mr. Lowell sinks to his knees, clutching his belly.

"You bitch," he gasps.

I don't have time to think. I race past him, prying the door open, and then before he can get back up again, I shove it closed again.

The keyhole on the door is calling out to me, but I don't have a key. I can't lock it. So I do the only thing I can do, which is run out of the house as fast as I can.

When I came in, Dad was working in the backyard. But he's gone. I don't know where he went. Maybe back in our garage to get some more equipment? I don't know. I want to look for him, but I also really want to go home.

When I get inside, I run up the stairs. I run to my parents' bedroom, looking for either one of them, but the bedroom is empty. And then, while I'm standing in the doorway, I hear the footsteps behind me. Growing louder.

Oh no.

It's Mr. Lowell. I should have figured out a way to block off that door. Or stabbed him again, just to make sure I finished the job. But I stupidly left him there. And now he's followed me back into my house.

He's ready to finish me off.

But then I turn around, and my shoulders sag. It's not Mr. Lowell. It's Nico, standing in the hallway, his mouth hanging open.

"Ada?" He has a horrified expression on his face. "What happened to you?"

For the first time, I look down at my clothing. I have a few small bloodstains on my shirt, but my right hand is wet with it. Also, the knife has a lot of blood on it. I didn't even notice.

"Ada?" Nico says again.

"Where… Where's Dad?" I stammer.

"In the garage getting some equipment, I think." Nico frowns at my bloody hand, still clutching the knife. "Ada, what happened?"

"I…"

I can't tell him. How can I tell anyone what I've done?

"Ada?"

"I… I think I might have killed Mr. Lowell." The words come out in a jumbled rush. "I think he might be dead."

"*What?*"

I wipe tears from my eyes, smearing blood on my face. I'm only making this worse. "I didn't tell anyone what you told me—I swear. But I wanted to talk to him. I wanted to tell him to leave you alone."

"Ada…"

"He wouldn't let me out of the little room." My voice breaks. "So I had to…"

We both look down at the knife, glistening with Mr. Lowell's blood. He's definitely dead. I stabbed him with the knife right where Dad told me to—and I twisted it. I watched the color drain out of his face as he sank to the floor.

Oh God.

"I need to talk to Dad," I blurt out.

Nico's eyes widen with panic. "You can't tell Dad. You can't tell any grown-ups. You will be in such big trouble."

"Dad won't let anything bad happen to me…"

"It's not up to him. You know what happens to kids who do bad things, right?" He chews on his lower lip. "They take you away from your parents. You have to go to this kid jail called juvenile tension. My friend said his brother had to go after he stole something. And that's just for stealing. You *killed* someone."

I start to cry. He's right. I can't just tell people I killed Mr. Lowell and expect not to get punished at all, even if he was the one doing something wrong.

"So what should I do?" I ask.

"Did anyone see you there?"

I shake my head no.

"Then nobody will know it was you, right?"

I look down at the knife in my hand and realize that he's right. I can wash the blood off the knife and stuff it in the back of a drawer. I can wash the blood off the shirt and hide it in my closet. Nobody will know.

Nothing bad will happen.

# PART IV

# SEVENTY-FOUR

## MILLIE

My daughter killed a man.

My eleven-year-old daughter stabbed a man, and now he's dead. And after I hear the whole story, I wish she hadn't killed him, so I could do it with my bare hands.

Because I would have really made him suffer.

"I'm sorry, Mom." She's crying so hard, it's difficult for her to talk. "I didn't want to do it. I just had to get out of that room."

I'm not angry at her. She doesn't owe me any apology. I feel *sick* at the thought of what was happening right under my nose. I was the one who sent Nico over there to do chores. In my defense, it seemed harmless at the time—a good way for him to take responsibility for breaking their window. I could never have imagined…

"This is not your fault, Ada." I wrap my arms around her skinny body. "You did what you had to do. I…I would've done the same."

That is an understatement.

"Where's the shirt you were wearing?" I ask her. "The one with the blood on it?"

She wipes her eyes and crosses the room to get to her pink dresser. She rifles around for a moment until she pulls out the navy-blue shirt she'd been wearing that day and hands it over to me. If I squint, I can just barely see the stain, but I can see how the police would have missed it. They weren't expecting to find anything incriminating in a little girl's drawer of shirts.

"I washed it really well in the sink," she says, although if the police had found it, they would have easily identified Jonathan's blood.

I clutch the shirt in my hand, not sure what to do with it. Could I really turn my own daughter in for murder?

"I don't want to go to jail," she sniffles. "But I don't want Dad to get in trouble when I was the one who did it."

Enzo knew. He figured out Ada must have been the one who stabbed Jonathan after he discovered that the knife he gave her was the murder weapon. That's why he was so quick to take the blame. I hate him for doing that. But also, I love him more than I have ever loved him before.

"You are not going to jail," I assure her. "I promise you. We are going to call Dad's lawyer, and she is going to straighten everything out. I swear."

I've got to call Cecelia. I've got to tell her everything before Enzo does anything else stupid like confessing to murder to protect his daughter.

I don't want Ada to hear this call, but I also don't

want to leave her alone when she is so fragile. As much as I have reassured her that she didn't do anything wrong, she is still inconsolable. I need to keep a close eye on her, so I step right outside her bedroom door, keeping the door cracked open so I can see her as I click on Cecelia's number.

Thankfully, she answers right away. "Millie? Everything okay? I just got to the police station."

"Yeah," I breathe, "but I heard some extremely interesting information."

I tell her everything as quickly as I can. She is mostly silent for the entire story, although a few times, I hear her quick intake of air. It's hard to repeat the details Ada shared with me. Honestly, it makes me sick to my stomach. I'm relieved when I've told her what I need to and I can stop talking.

"Jesus," Cecelia breathes, "that's…"

"I know."

"Damn it, Enzo," she mutters to herself. "He better not have said anything to the police without me. I've got to get in there as quickly as I can and set things straight."

"He needs to hear everything," I say. "If he thinks there's a chance Ada might get punished for this, he is going to want to take the fall. He has to know that it was self-defense. She didn't do anything wrong."

"And she's *eleven*," Cecelia reminds me. "No court would prosecute a child that age as an adult. Enzo is throwing himself on his sword for nothing."

"Please, Cecelia, don't let him do anything stupid."

"Don't worry, Millie," Cecelia says. "I'm incredibly convincing."

I let her go so she can do her thing, and then I am

left alone with my children. And I have a pretty big job to do to make things right again.

I don't know exactly what was going on inside that room at the Lowells' house. If Jonathan laid a finger on my son, I will… Well, I guess I can't kill him anymore, but I will set fire to his grave or… I'll travel to the after-life and wreak vengeance upon him. I can't *believe* Nico was going to that house for months because he was so scared of us having to pay for some broken toys. It breaks my heart.

After all this is over, the whole family is going to need therapy. That man did a terrible thing to us, and I am determined to get my husband out of jail so we can help the kids start healing again.

# SEVENTY-FIVE

Enzo is currently at the police station in a holding cell. He has been booked and fingerprinted and had mug shots taken, according to Cecelia. There will be a bail hearing tomorrow, but there's no way we can afford any amount of bail.

I'm desperate to know how he's doing, but all I can get are updates from Cecelia. I keep the kids home from school—I have taken so many personal days now that my coworkers must be furious with me—and I spend a lot of time talking to them about everything that happened. I knew something was going on with Nico, but somehow this went under my radar. I thought there was something wrong with his brain and that it was all because of my faulty genes, but in reality, it was all Jonathan Lowell's fault.

"Will Dad come home soon?" Nico asks me hopefully as we eat dinner together. I've made macaroni with butter on it. I didn't even have the bandwidth to add cheese.

"I hope so" is my honest answer.

"But he didn't do anything wrong," Ada says in a tiny voice. "Why does he have to be in jail?"

"Because you can't just tell the police you didn't do it and they let you go," I explain to them. "But don't worry, because he has an amazing lawyer. He'll be home soon."

If I tell myself that enough times, maybe it will come true.

After dinner, I pop some popcorn in the microwave. Miraculously, I manage not to burn it like last time, and I get the kids set up on the sofa watching cartoons and eating microwaved popcorn. Right after I turn on a movie, my phone rings.

The number comes from the local police station.

I jump off the couch and jam my thumb into the green button to take the call. I make it into the kitchen when that familiar Italian accent comes on the other line: "Millie?"

I almost burst into tears. "Enzo! Oh my God… I can't believe they let you call…"

"I have five minutes. That is all."

Five minutes isn't nearly long enough to say everything I have to say, but it's a start. "You idiot. Why did you confess?"

"For Ada," he says in a quiet voice, like he's worried they might be listening. "I would do anything for her and Nico. Wouldn't you?"

"Yes," I admit. "I would."

"For you too, Millie."

That's all it takes. My eyes are welling up. "We need you back here though. Please. She's not going to get in trouble for this. She's only eleven."

"Millie, she slit his throat with a pocketknife. This is trouble for her."

That's the part of it that tugs at me. Jonathan Lowell had two stab wounds. Ada stabbed him in the belly to get him out of the way, but there's no way she is tall enough to effectively cut a grown man's throat while he was standing in front of her. She didn't tell me every detail—only that she stabbed him to get him out of the way—and I didn't want to push her because she was already so upset.

So I can only imagine what must have really happened. I found Jonathan in the living room rather than in the hidden room, so the knife in his belly must not have immediately taken him down. He must have tried to follow her, then collapsed soon after. And then she turned around and sliced his throat while he was lying on the floor. Just to make absolutely sure he was dead.

That's cold. Even for me. Yet if she truly believed he hurt Nico, and he was coming after her, she did what she had to do.

It's still hard to argue something like that could be self-defense.

"It doesn't matter," I say. "Enzo, we need you home. We're lost without you. Please, tell the truth, and let Cecelia handle it."

"I will not turn my daughter in. No. Never."

I hate how stubborn he is. But given the opportunity, I would do the same.

"Did you confess to the police?" I ask him.

"Not yet," he says. "Cecelia would not allow me. But tomorrow..."

"Please don't do this," I beg him. "I know you think

you're helping Ada, but she's not going to be better off with her father in prison. That will wreck her life. Don't you realize that? You need to come home, and then we will figure out a way to deal with this."

A voice is shouting at him in the background. He has used up his five minutes.

"Millie," he says urgently. "Please tell the kids that I love them. No matter what happens."

"We love you too," I start to say, but I'm pretty sure I get cut off after the first word. The line is dead.

Tonight, Enzo will spend the night in a cold, uncomfortable holding cell. Actually, it's the summer, so it will be a hot, uncomfortable holding cell. Maybe after a night of that, he'll realize he does not want to do this for the rest of his life.

At least that's what I have to hope for.

# SEVENTY-SIX

I barely sleep that night.

Enzo might be the one spending the night in a cell, but I'm the one tossing and turning. I keep thinking back to when I was in prison. I was surrounded by people, but I felt so lonely all the time. I always felt like I didn't belong there. I don't think anybody feels they belong there.

I wish Enzo understood how awful it is. He might not be so quick to give up his life.

I decide to send the kids off to school the next morning, just to maintain some semblance of normalcy. I walk them to the bus stop, and I'm not surprised to see Janice there with Spencer on his usual leash.

Janice sniffs. "I'm surprised to see *you* here."

"I live right over there," I point out. "Why wouldn't I be here?"

Janice doesn't find me even the tiniest bit amusing. "I mean, after the terrible thing your husband did. Aren't you ashamed to show your face?"

I can't believe she said that right in front of my

children. I have been taking a lot of her crap since I moved here, just to keep the peace, but I am done with that. After all, I'm fairly sure that no matter what, we're not going to be living here much longer.

"My husband didn't do anything, Janice," I say. "You got it all wrong."

She snorts. "I don't think so. A man who looks like that is always going to be trouble."

She thinks my husband is a murderer because he's too handsome? "Enzo is a good man," I say firmly. "And I don't need some busybody neighbor to tell me otherwise. So why don't you mind your own damn business from now on, Janice?"

Janice's mouth falls open, like she's not quite used to being spoken to that way. I look over at the kids, and for the first time since their father was arrested, I detect the tiniest hint of smiles on their faces.

Once my kids are safely on the bus, I return to my house. I reach the front lawn just as that familiar black Dodge Charger pulls up to the curb. The driver-side window rolls down, and Detective Benito Ramirez sticks his head out.

"Millie," he says. "Get in the car."

I trust Ramirez more than I trust any other cop in the world, but I am still not excited to get in a cop car without any explanation. "I have to get to Enzo's bail hearing in less than two hours."

"We need to talk," he says in a grave voice.

"What about?"

"Millie, will you get in the car? Pretty please? Come on. You want to get back in time for the bail hearing, right?"

Oh, what the hell.

# SEVENTY-SEVEN

"You know about Ada, I assume," I say to Ramirez as we sit together in the front seats of his Dodge.

"I do," he says. "Cecelia told me everything."

"She killed Jonathan Lowell," I say, even though part of me still can't believe it. How could my little girl have slit a man's throat?

"Sounds like that pervert deserved it."

"Still."

He shrugs. "Like mother, like daughter."

I flinch. Ada does not know anything about my history. Maybe she would feel better if I told her…

No, I can't tell her. I don't want her to lose respect for me.

"So what did you want to talk to me about?" I ask.

Ramirez levels his gaze at me. His eyes are just as dark and serious as my husband's can be. "It's about Suzette Lowell. There's something I need to tell you about her, and you can't tell another soul."

"Okay…"

"I mean it, Millie. I'll lose my job."

Now my interest is piqued. "I won't tell anyone. You have my word."

"They checked out that room below the stairs," he says. "And guess what they found."

If he says there was a child's skeleton in there… "I'm not sure I want to know."

"Millie, they found Suzette Lowell's fingerprints."

It takes me several moments to process what he's saying to me. If Suzette's fingerprints were in that room…

She knew about the room. She knew everything about that room. *That's* why she didn't want Nico at her house. It wasn't because she was worried about him breaking something or making a mess. She didn't want him over because she knew that her husband was a pervert.

And she let him come over anyway. How dare she? What if Jonathan hurt Nico or Ada? What if…

"I'll kill her," I gasp.

"What's about to happen to her," he says, "is going to be far worse than that. They found something else in that room."

And then he tells me something so horrifying, I want to throw up all over the upholstery of this car.

"She's staying at a hotel," he tells me. "The police are planning to bring her in for questioning. I wanted to tell you first."

My head is spinning with the revelations Ramirez has dropped on me. Suzette knew. She *knew*. And now she's going to be charged as an accomplice to the terrible things her husband did. If that's not justice, I don't know what is.

Except it won't change the fact that Ada is the one who killed Jonathan. It won't change the fact that Enzo refuses to turn our daughter in and will spend the rest of his life in prison to protect her.

And then it hits me. There might be a way to fix this.

"Benny," I say urgently. "Do we have time to talk to Suzette before the police pick her up?"

His thick eyebrows shoot up. "You're joking, right?"

"I need to talk to her."

"I can't bring you with me on police business. I'll get *fired*."

"Fine." I tap my fingers on the knee of my blue jeans. "Then drive me to the hotel, and let me talk to her myself."

"No way. I'm not leaving you alone with that woman. The kids don't need their mother locked up for murder too."

"Please," I say. "You owe me one, Benny."

"Actually, I owe you at least ten." He scratches the stubble on his jaw. "What do you want to talk to her about anyway?"

I nod at the steering wheel. "I'll explain everything to you on the way over."

# SEVENTY-EIGHT

Ramirez drives us to a swanky hotel on the outskirts of town. It looks like the sort of hotel that has a spa in every room and linen that gets replaced every hour on the hour. In other words, it's a hotel that I could never afford in my wildest dreams.

A valet takes his keys to park the car, and we walk together into the hotel and up to the concierge desk. Ramirez reaches into his pocket and pulls out his badge, sliding it across the table. "My name is Detective Ramirez of the NYPD. I'm looking for a guest of the hotel named Suzette Lowell."

The concierge picks up the phone and calls Suzette's room. When he reports that a member of the NYPD is here to see her, we are immediately granted access to the room. "Up to the tenth floor and all the way down the hallway," the concierge tells us.

I walk purposefully in the direction of the elevator, and Ramirez hurries to keep pace with me. The elevator walls are entirely mirrors, which makes me feel a little sick to my stomach. Or maybe I'm sick to my stomach because I'm visiting the wife of a man who threatened both my children and she just let it happen. God knows what he would have done to Nico if Ada hadn't intervened.

"I don't know about all this, Millie," Ramirez says. "I'd rather do this by the book when she's at the station."

"Please give me a chance to talk to her," I say to him. "This is our best shot at getting my family off the hook. We have to try."

He just shakes his head.

The elevator dings as we reach the tenth floor. I dismount the elevator and stride in the direction of Suzette's room—Ramirez has to jog to keep up with me. I don't stop until I have reached her door. I lift my fist to knock while Ramirez sighs and shakes his head.

"Just a moment!" a voice calls out from behind the door.

A second later, the door to the hotel swings open. Suzette is standing there, wearing a white fleece bathrobe with the name of the hotel printed on the lapel. She had managed a pleasant smile on her painted lips, but that vanishes when she sees me standing at the open doorway.

"What are *you* doing here?" Suzette hisses.

"Mrs. Accardi is with me, Mrs. Lowell," Ramirez says.

She looks between the two of us, and for a moment, I'm certain she's going to slam the door in our faces. And that would be her right. "Are you really with the NYPD?" she asks him.

"I assure you, I am," he says. "And if you'll allow me and Mrs. Accardi to come inside, I'd like to make you an offer that can save us all a great deal of grief moving forward."

She puts her hand on her hip. "Show me your ID."

Ramirez obligingly reaches into his pocket again to pull out his badge. He shows it to her, and she takes a moment to examine it, as if she could possibly tell the difference between a fake ID and a real one. But if that makes her feel better, she can knock herself out.

"Fine," she says stiffly. "You can come in for a minute, but I was about to take a shower."

"I bet they have nice showers here," Ramirez says as he strolls into her hotel room. Suzette has a chance to slam the door in my face, but she doesn't take it, and I manage to slip inside with him. "Not as nice as the ones in your house though."

"Thank you," Suzette says stiffly. "I can't go in there right now, for obvious reasons."

"Oh, I know." He stops when he gets to the giant, king-size bed. "You want to take a seat, Mrs. Lowell?"

"I don't think we need to get too comfortable."

One side of his lips quirks up. "Fair enough."

"So what did you want to talk to me about, Detective?"

"Well, actually," he says, "it's about your house. The police were in there, you know."

She rolls her eyes. "That's how it works with a crime scene, I assume."

"And they saw every part of it."

Her eyes narrow, and I detect a tiny flicker of fear. "What is that supposed to mean?"

"I mean," Ramirez says, "they saw the room below your stairwell."

If I hadn't been staring at Suzette's face, I would've missed the way she blanched. I swear to God, if Ramirez weren't standing next to me right now, I would scratch that woman's eyes out. I would rip her heart right out of her chest.

"I...I don't know what you're talking about," Suzette sputters.

"No?" Ramirez arches one of his dark eyebrows. "So you didn't know there was a room below the staircase on the first floor of your house concealed behind a bookcase?"

She shakes her head slowly. "I think I saw some sort of storage room when we first moved in, but we never ended up using it."

"That's so strange," he muses.

"Not really," she says. "Jonathan already owned the house when I moved in, so I never went through the floor plans."

"Even though you're a real estate agent, you never looked at the floor plans of your own house?"

She shrugs. "We already owned it and weren't considering selling. Why should I have? Is that a *crime*, Detective?"

"Here's the thing though." Ramirez levels his eyes at her. "Your fingerprints are all over that room. So if you didn't know about it, how did that happen exactly?"

When he first came in, she had declined the offer to sit. But now she sinks onto the mattress, her face ashen. It's gratifying to see how terrified she looks. She deserves it.

"You know what else the police found in that room?" Ramirez asks her.

She can only mutely shake her head.

"We found blood and DNA belonging to a kid named Braden Lundie," he says. "A kid who disappeared three years ago. The police are digging up your backyard as we speak. Any idea what they're going to find?"

Suzette seems to be having trouble breathing. She looks like she is at a complete loss for words, much as I was when Ramirez told me that piece of information when we were in his car. Unfortunately for her, I am no longer at a loss for words.

"You're the accessory to the murder of a little boy, Suzette," I hiss at her. "You're going to jail for the rest of your life. And you deserve it." A lump forms in my throat. "You knew that your husband murdered a child, and you didn't tell a soul. You let your husband walk free. You still let my kid into your home! How could you? What is wrong with you?"

Suzette buries her face in her hands for a moment. She still hasn't said a word.

"Mrs. Lowell?" Ramirez says.

When Suzette lifts her face from her hands, her cheeks are streaked with tears. "I didn't know about Braden until after. I swear. If I had known…"

"But you *did* know," Ramirez says in a low growl. "You knew what he did, and you didn't call the police. You didn't tell anyone."

"What would have been the point? It was too late!"

I'm sick to my stomach. Janice mentioned that kid who went missing years ago, but I thought she was being dramatic, especially after Suzette claimed the boy had been found. It turns out Janice was the one who had it right. The fact that Suzette said it's too late means there will not be a happy ending for that family.

"I hated him too, you know." She wipes the tears from her eyes with the back of her hand. "I couldn't even stand to be in the same house with that man. But I stayed with him to keep an eye on him and make sure he didn't do anything…you know, like *that* ever again. I kept any other children from getting hurt."

I glare at her. "Wow, you're a saint."

"Millie," she murmurs, "if I called the police, do you *know* what that would have done to my life? I would have been the wife of a child murderer. Do you know what that would have been like?"

I shake my head. "You're despicable, Suzette."

At least she has the good grace to hang her head.

"Detective Ramirez came here to bring you to the police station," I say. "But I talked him out of it. Instead, we're going to give you another choice."

Suzette looks up at me in surprise. I glance at Ramirez, who nods at me, and then I continue. "You need to confess to your husband's murder. Say you killed him because you found out what he was doing in that room, and that's why your fingerprints are all over the room. You can call it self-defense."

"You want me to lie?" she gasps.

"You got another choice," Ramirez speaks up. "Second choice, you let Enzo Accardi go down for a murder he didn't do, and then we prosecute *you* for conspiring to kill that little kid. And believe me, we will go after you *hard*."

Suzette stares at us, shaking her head. "But I didn't kill Jonathan."

"But if you did, nobody would blame you, right? You get a good lawyer—which you can afford—and you might not go to jail at all. But if they nail you for that kid…or even if people *think* you were involved, which we both know they will…"

She sucks in a breath. We have given her two terrible options. For a split second, I almost feel sorry for her. Then I remember what she did.

"What about the blood on Enzo's knife?" she asks. "The police told me about that."

"Enzo left his knife behind in your house." Ramirez shrugs. "You used it to kill your husband, then tried to get rid of the evidence by returning it to him."

Suzette drops her eyes, looking down at the palms of her hands. No matter what she decides, her entire life is about to change forever. "Can I think about it?" she asks in a small voice.

Ramirez looks at his watch. "You can think about it, but I'm telling you now that Detective Willard is on his way. He'll be here any minute."

She takes a ragged breath. "Would you mind leaving my room so I can get dressed?"

Ramirez agrees to leave the room—we've got to get out of here before Detective Willard catches us and discovers what we've been up to. As the door slams shut behind us, I stare daggers into the door to the hotel room. I never liked Suzette Lowell, but I had no idea about the depths of her depravity. I had no idea that she would cover up such horrible crimes just for the sake of her own reputation. When I look over at Ramirez, I can tell he's thinking the same thing.

"Only for you and Enzo, Millie," he says. "I'll pull

every string I've got to make this come together and get him off the hook."

"So we're even then," I say.

"No, I think I still owe you a few more."

I bring my ear close to the door to the hotel room, listening for sounds coming from within. "What if she tries to kill herself in there?"

"She won't do that. She's a fighter. You can just tell."

"What do you think she'll decide?"

He smiles sadly. "She's going to confess to killing her husband—I'm sure of it. She doesn't want that other charge. And she knows they have her."

I hope he's right. I need my husband back. And I need this nightmare to be over.

Although I have a feeling it's not going to be over for a very long time.

# SEVENTY-NINE

It's been almost two weeks since Suzette Lowell confessed to the murder of her husband, Jonathan Lowell.

The four of us are having breakfast in our kitchen, something that didn't seem like it would ever be possible again only two weeks earlier. But now Enzo is home again. After Suzette confessed, all the charges against him were dropped.

Ada's part in the murder is only known to us.

"I love chocolate chip pancakes," Nico says as he happily digs into the plate of pancakes I made.

Enzo flashes me a smile from across the table. He still looks tired from the events of the last few weeks, but he's here, and that's what's important. And our family is healing. Nico especially is going to need a lot of therapy after everything that happened, but that's okay. We are going to bounce back from this.

We are not going to let what the Lowells did destroy us.

"One more week of school," Enzo reminds the kids,

"then you get summer vacation. We take trip somewhere, yes?"

"Where?" Ada asks.

"Yes, where?" I ask, because this is the first time I'm hearing about this alleged trip.

"We will decide," he says. "I think we need to get away."

He's right. We do need to get away. This summer, we are selling this house. After everything that happened, I can't imagine living here anymore. We need to find a place that is cheaper so we are not stressing over every single bill. Maybe we need to relocate somewhere entirely different. A fresh start would be nice.

"I want to go to Disneyland," Nico pipes up.

"Me too!" Ada says.

"Florida is very hot in the summer," I remind them.

"That's Disney *World*, Mom," Ada corrects me. "Disney*land* is in California."

California? Is she serious? I was thinking more along the lines of a trip to the Jersey Shore. I look over at Enzo, who shrugs. I don't think we're going to California this summer—four round-trip tickets across the country isn't in our budget. But I don't have the heart to shut down their Disneyland dreams right now.

The school bus is coming soon, so we usher both the kids out the door for them to make the bus with seconds to spare. Just as the bus drives away, that black Dodge Charger pulls up into our cul-de-sac. While I'm always happy to see my friend, I can't say I don't get a flash of anxiety when I see a police officer parking in front of my lawn.

But Enzo doesn't seem the slightest bit concerned.

He waves at Ramirez as he gets out of his car. "*Buongiorno*, Benny!"

Ramirez waves back, then he sees my face and quickly says, "This is just a social visit, Millie. Everything is fine."

Thank God.

"Would you like to come in?" I ask him.

"Can't," he says. "Busy morning. But I just wanted to check in on the two of you while I was in the neighborhood. Everything going okay?"

"We are good," Enzo says. "Thank you for everything."

"And the kids?" Ramirez asks. "They are handling everything okay?"

"Yes," I reply, but with hesitation.

"Millie is worried about Ada," Enzo speaks up.

He's right. I hate to admit it, but I have become obsessed with what my daughter did. I recognize that Jonathan Lowell was a horrible person, and he deserved to die, but I just keep seeing him lying on the floor with his throat gaping open.

My daughter did that.

"Ada will be fine," Ramirez assures me. "Look, she did what she had to do, Millie. You can understand that, can't you?"

"I guess so."

"It was my fault," Enzo says. "I gave her the knife. My dad gave it to me at the same age, and I thought this is no problem. I just want her to be safe. But we live in a different world now."

I can't blame Enzo though. The knife is what saved her life. If she hadn't been carrying that pocketknife, God knows what would have happened to her.

I am just troubled by what she did with it. We've still never spoken about how she slit Jonathan's throat.

"Anyway," Enzo says, "if you are too busy to come in for coffee now, come by for dinner tonight, yes?"

"Actually..." Ramirez tugs on his tie. "I got a date tonight."

For a moment, I am pulled from my worries about Ada, and a smile spreads across my lips. "A date? *Really?*"

Ramirez returns a smile that is an endearing combination of excited and nervous. "Believe it or not, Cecelia set me up with her mother. This is only our second date, but we've been talking a lot on the phone, and... I know it's early, but I like that woman a lot. She's really something."

I almost burst out laughing at what is most certainly the understatement of the century. "She really is," I agree.

"Maybe you retire now," Enzo teases him.

"Never," Ramirez says.

But if anybody could convince that man to finally retire, it would be Nina Winchester.

"Anyway," he says, "I gotta head out. But anything you need, give me a yell."

Ramirez gets back in his car, and we watch him drive away. I've got to get to work as well, but lately, it's been hard to focus. I'm happy that my husband has been released from jail, but I feel consumed by my worries about my children. Especially Ada.

"Millie," Enzo says. "You need to let go of your worries." He adds, "Is bad for your blood pressure."

"My blood pressure is fine now, thank you very much."

It actually is. I've been checking it every day, and for the last week, the numbers have been perfect.

"So we keep it that way." He kisses me on the cheek. "Ada will be fine. Her mama was fine, and she will be fine."

He's right. I just have to keep telling myself that. Ada did not do anything wrong. She is a hero, as far as I'm concerned.

But I am her mother. It is my job to worry. So I will keep watching her and worrying.

# EIGHTY

## ADA

Library period is halfway over.

I'm sitting at one of the tables by the windows, reading this great book called *Rebecca* by Daphne du Maurier. It's old, but it's so haunting. When I read it, I get chills. There's only a week left of school, and I hope I can finish it in time.

But if I can't, it's because of that kid Hunter.

He laid off me for a little while, but today he is back with a vengeance. He sits down across from me at the beginning of the period, and the first thing he says to me is, "Will you go out with me on Friday night, Ada?"

"No, thank you," I reply stiffly.

"What about Saturday night?"

"No."

"Sunday? Monday?"

I stick my nose back in my book. I'm just going to ignore him. That's what you're supposed to do with kids like him. If you don't give them any attention, they go away. At least that's what Mom says.

"Ada," he says in a singsong voice. "Has anyone ever written a song about you?"

I don't look up. I don't respond.

"I'm going to write a song about you right now," he says. And then he starts singing: "Adaaaa. I went and I got her a potataaa. Then she went with me on a date-aaa."

The librarian hears Hunter singing, and she gives the two of us a sharp look. "Ada, Hunter, please quiet down!"

If the librarian thinks we are fooling around, she will take away our books and make us sit in the corner. I really want to finish this book.

"Please stop," I say. "You're going to get us in trouble. I just want to read my book."

"No, you don't!" he says too loudly. "You're just pretending to like the book and being hard to get. That's what my dad told me."

"Your dad is wrong."

"My dad is never wrong. And at least he didn't go to jail for killing someone."

It makes me angry that he said that. Dad didn't kill Mr. Lowell. But after he came home, he told me if he knew what Mr. Lowell was doing to Nico, he would have done the exact same thing I did.

The police still have Dad's pocketknife—the one I used to stab Mr. Lowell. I wish I still had it. I'll probably never get it back, which is sad because I loved that knife.

Then again, I don't need a pocketknife.

I put down my copy of *Rebecca*. I get out of my seat

and then take the one next to Hunter. He didn't expect this, and his eyebrows shoot up.

"Hunter," I say. "I need you to know something."

He grins at me. "Yes? Are you finally coming around?"

"No." I look him straight in the eyes, holding his gaze. "If you don't leave me alone—right now—then tonight I am going to sneak into your bedroom while you're sleeping." I wait a beat, watching his reaction. "And then when you wake up in the morning, you are going to pull back the blankets and you will find your bloody balls lying on the sheets next to you."

He laughs. "What?"

"You heard me. If you bother me—or any other girls—ever again, I will castrate you in your sleep." "Castrate" is a word I learned recently from a book I was reading. I think I'm using it correctly here. It means to cut off somebody's testicles.

I like the way all the color drains out of his face. I watch him trying to recover. "You…you couldn't do that," he stutters.

"Hmm, maybe not," I say. "But actually, I think I could. Would you like to find out?"

From the look on his face, I don't think he would like to find out. He jumps out of his seat, backing away from me. "You're a psychopath," he says.

I just shrug and smile at him.

He stumbles away from the table, practically tripping over his own feet in his eagerness to get away from me. I don't think he's going to be bothering me again. I'd like to think he isn't going to be bothering *any* other girls again.

I pick up my book to continue reading, but before I do, I glance out the window next to me. It's gloomy enough outside that I can almost see my reflection in the glass. It's funny, because I always thought I was practically identical to my dad with my dark hair and eyes. But now that I'm looking at myself in that blurry window, I realize as I've gotten older, my facial features have become a lot more similar to my mom's. I never noticed it until this very moment.

I look just like her. How funny.

# EPILOGUE

## MARTHA

I am staying at a motel far away from Long Island.

Jed hasn't come looking for me since I left, so I am starting to finally feel safe. He told me that if I ever tried to leave him, he would hunt me down and rip off my scalp, but he hasn't found me yet. I have that gun Enzo gave me though, in case he does show up. It makes me feel secure.

I worry about money though. Jed took all my paychecks, so all I've got left is what I managed to stash away, plus a small amount Enzo was able to give me. I can try to work under the table, although it's hard to find jobs like that in a new place without word-of-mouth referrals. It will take time, but I'm a hard worker and willing to prove myself. I've been waiting a long time for my freedom from that monster.

And I knew that when the Accardis moved in next door, it would be my ticket out.

Many years ago, back when I was young and full

of hope about my life, I worked for a wealthy family. They had a teenage son who was the sort of boy who believed anything he wanted should be his. I disliked him intensely, especially after I saw a girl dashing out of his bedroom in tears. He laughed about it later, when I was changing the sheets on his bed that were spotted with her blood.

Three months after that, he was dead.

The first time I heard about Wilhelmina Calloway, the girl who would become Millie Accardi, was when she was being charged with the murder of the son of my employers. I had no doubt that he deserved the justice Millie doled out, but the jury didn't see it that way. She went to prison for his murder.

I recognized Millie when she came to look at the house at 14 Locust Street with her handsome husband. She was much older, of course, yet I knew her instantly. There was something about her that was hard to forget. Something in her eyes. A quick internet search proved she was who I thought she was.

At that moment, I knew Millie would be the only one who could help me escape from Jed. I just needed her to move into that house.

But the houses in this neighborhood always went for ridiculous amounts of money. It was clear the Accardis wouldn't be able to afford a bidding war. So I helped them. I made conversation with prospective buyers, mentioning the leaky roof or the mold in the attic. One by one, they dropped out, and the Accardis bought the house for a bargain, just as I had hoped they would.

I wanted so badly to tell Millie everything the moment she moved in. I was always looking out the window, watching her house, waiting for a time when I could get her alone and spill my guts. I was sure she would help me. But when I started working for her, I could never find the right time. I froze whenever I tried.

After all that, it wasn't Millie who ended up helping me. It was her husband, Enzo. He was so kind to me. He offered me more than he could afford, and he wouldn't allow me to say no.

Even so, I feared my stash of money wouldn't be enough once I was on the run, which is why right before I left the hotel where I was staying and started on the next leg of my journey, I went to Suzette Lowell's house one last time. I parked in the back, so that nosy neighbor of hers wouldn't tell Suzette that I had been there. She had a ton of jewelry and other stuff that I could hock.

I feel guilty saying that. I'm not a thief. I have always lived my life with honesty and integrity. My husband has turned me into this. I hope I never see him ever again.

I planned to spend fifteen minutes going through Suzette's jewelry. I knew which pieces she wore a lot and which ones she would never miss. She has so much jewelry, and all of it is so expensive. Three or four pieces would have been enough to tide me over.

But as it turned out, when I went to the Lowells' house, Mr. Lowell was already home. I hadn't expected him to be there during the day, so it surprised me when I descended the stairs after taking three of Suzette's necklaces and found him standing in the living room, breathing hard as he leaned against a bookcase positioned against the wall by the stairway like he was trying to shift it with his body weight. He grunted loudly, then hunched over as he gripped his belly. I wondered why he was trying to move that bookcase. It was clear that he hurt himself doing it, because when he took a step, he winced.

"Where is she?" he mumbled under his breath. "Where'd that little bitch go?"

Before I could figure out what on earth he was talking about, he raised his eyes, and that was when he saw me. He knew I was not scheduled to be here today, and immediately, his face clouded with suspicion.

"You," he growled. "What are you doing here?"

"I...I'm cleaning," I stammered. Even though I clearly had no cleaning supplies with me.

It might not have been so bad if I hadn't been holding those necklaces in my left hand. Everything would have been different if I had brought my purse into the house and could have stashed those necklaces out of sight.

"You've been stealing from us!" he cried. "I knew it! I *told* Suzette that's where her jewelry was going! I *told* her she should fire you!"

"No," I said frantically. "I didn't..."

But Mr. Lowell was furious. He kept raving and ranting about how I was a dirty thief. He said all these terrible things about how he was going to call the police now, and they were going to take me to jail. The whole time, he was clutching his stomach. But all I could think about was what Jed would do to me if I got arrested for stealing.

He would probably kill me with his bare hands.

I don't know at what point I noticed the letter opener lying on the coffee table next to us. It all happened so fast, honestly. I grabbed it, and really, I just wanted him to stop talking. I just wanted him to stop saying that he was going to call the police. But the next thing I knew, he was lying on the floor, and there was blood gushing from his throat, pooling around his dead body.

I had to run. There was certainly no time to clean it up. Especially when I heard Millie knocking on the door.

When I went out the back door, Enzo was in the yard next door. I was afraid he would see me, but it looked like he had just cut his hand pretty badly on something, and he was trying to stop the bleeding with his shirt. He was distracted. He didn't see me dash back into the clearing to where I parked my car.

Later, I saw on the news that Enzo had been arrested. I felt so terrible about that, especially after everything he did for me. Money was tight for him, but he still helped me out. He is such a good man, and he didn't deserve to go to prison for what I did. I was seconds away from calling the police to tell them that I was the one who killed Jonathan Lowell. But before I could do it, a story came on the news that shocked me.

Suzette confessed to killing her husband.

I didn't quite understand it, but I didn't feel nearly as bad about Suzette Lowell being sent to prison. She's really quite a horrible person.

For the last two weeks, I have been certain the truth would be discovered. I have been certain that the police would come knocking on my motel door, ready with an arrest warrant for the murder of Jonathan Lowell. But it hasn't happened. They haven't arrested me. They haven't even questioned me.

I suppose nobody ever suspects the housemaid.

# ACKNOWLEDGMENTS

Wow, it has been such an incredible journey since the original Housemaid was published in April 2022. I can hardly believe that my little book made it onto the *New York Times* bestseller list and that millions of people have now read it. After that amazing response, it was only natural that I would want to continue Millie's story in *The Housemaid's Secret*, and now once again in *The Housemaid Is Watching*.

I want to thank Bookouture for being the ones to bring the Housemaid series to life, and especially Ellen Gleeson for her incredible amazing insights into both my writing and Millie as a character. A big thank you to my literary agent, Christina Hogrebe, as well as the entire team at Jane Rotrosen Agency, who always believed in me and supported me. Thank you to the team at Sourcebooks for your tireless work in getting *The Housemaid Is Watching* into the "wild" and into the hands of more readers. It is much appreciated!

And thank you to all the people who laid eyes on the manuscript while in the editing process: my mother, Pam, Kate, and Val. I'm sure it gets tiresome for me to keep handing you a manuscript and saying, "Sorry, this probably needs work," so I just want you to know how grateful I am.

And finally, thank you a million times to my incredibly supportive readers! This is all because of you! You asked for a third Housemaid book? Well, here it is!

# ABOUT THE AUTHOR

#1 *New York Times*, *USA Today*, *Washington Post*, *Publishers Weekly*, and *Sunday Times* internationally bestselling author Freida McFadden is a physician specializing in brain injury. Freida is the winner of both the International Thriller Writers Award for Best Paperback Original and the Goodreads Choice Award for Best Thriller. Her novels have been translated into more than forty languages. Freida lives with her family and gray cat in a centuries-old three-story home overlooking the ocean.